Advance Praise fo .... g *Forever*

"An insightful novel that depicts the difficulties a relationship can experience in spite of the love that's clearly present. *Finding Forever* doesn't pretend that love makes everything easy, and through the narrator's relationship with his newfound lover, it will show how all loving relationships are—at one time or another—confronted with the question: what is love worth? A truly profound question posed to us readers by a remarkably young writer."

—Miles Fisher, Editor of *Italian America*

"You would be hard pressed to find an intelligent, well-written romantic novel today. It's been several decades since *The Notebook* was a huge success. Along with that the genre of Romantic Comedy has all but vanished in Hollywood. Anthony Sciarratta with his *Finding Forever* successfully bucks the trend. In his stream-lined novel people do meet, they do fall in love and their partners not only bring them satisfaction, they also bring them stability. Set in an authentic working-class world, with flourishes of humor and modern angst, *Finding Forever* is a comforting and thoughtful read about romantic love."

—Playwright, author, TV writer, screenwriter, and actor, Richard Vetere

Coming Soon by Anthony Sciarratta

The Letter

Faith in the Unknown

ANTHONY SCIARRATTA

FINDING FOREVER

A 1970s LOVE STORY

POST HILL
PRESS

A POST HILL PRESS BOOK
ISBN: 978-1-64293-420-5
ISBN (eBook): 978-1-64293-421-2

Finding Forever:
A 1970s Love Story
© 2019 by Anthony Sciarratta
All Rights Reserved

Cover design by Cody Corcoran

This book is a work of fiction. People, places, events, and situations are the product of the author's imagination. Any resemblance to actual persons, living or dead, or historical events, is purely coincidental.

Post Hill Press
New York • Nashville
posthillpress.com

Published in the United States of America

For my Elvira Vaughn

1

CHAPTER

The year was 1978. A time when music had soul, hairiness was sexy, and cars were made to last. Farrah Fawcett was the end all be all, of every man's dreams. Families sat together in the living room huddled around one television to watch *The Carol Burnett Show*. *Saturday Night Fever* was the bestselling movie soundtrack of all time. Crime was rising, and New York was a dangerous place to be. Queens was little escape from all the chaos. This love story takes place in a small area, outside Manhattan, called Astoria.

Michael Coniglio waited on line at the coffee shop. The coffee shop was a local hub for all of Astoria's coffee lovers. It served quality coffee from across the world. Michael mainly spent his time there drinking the Italian roasts. The coffee shop was always crowded. It was essential to stop there at least once a day.

Michael was a naturally troubled man. There was never a day in Michael's life where he didn't worry. He always had more going for him than he thought. This anxiety he constantly felt was unnoticeable to others. He carried himself in a way that was confident. He was handsome and had a smile that could make any woman weak. Not a single person would have guessed that this man was troubled. The smell of coffee in the air calmed him down. There was nothing greater than a whiff of fresh brewing espresso to an Italian.

Michael approached the cashier. "Can I have a small coffee please," he asked. "Just milk, no sugar."

The cashier handed Michael his coffee. He sat at a table facing the entrance to the store. He glanced quickly at his watch and again at the door. A few moments later a woman walked in. Michael's demeanor instantly changed. The nervousness on his face was suddenly visible. This wasn't nervous fear, but anger.

"Fucking bitch," he mumbled.

Michael took a sip of his coffee. Angela Marcella sat down across from him. She had long flowing black hair that stretched down to her waist. Her hair and makeup were done perfectly. She wore tight clothing that showed her voluptuous body. It was hard for any man not to glance at her walking down the street.

"You're late," Michael said.

Angela was not fazed by his snarky comment. She clearly didn't care that she was late for their date.

"I got home at three last night. I overslept," Angela said.

Michael gripped the side of his chair and shook his leg under the table. Angela noticed that Michael didn't wait to order coffee for her. Small things like this always bothered her. Normally, Michael would have waited.

"You ordered a coffee without me?" Angela asked. "Go and get me a coffee light and sweet."

Angela took a mirror out of her purse and checked her makeup. Michael crossed his arms and leaned back in his chair.

Michael interrogated Angela. "Who the hell were you with last night? I'm gunna give you one chance to tell me the truth."

Angela abruptly put away her mirror. She stood up in defense and got the attention of everyone in the coffee shop. It was always like her to make a scene. The attention was never enough for Angela. She never missed a chance to make a fool of Michael.

"You want the truth? I'm screwing someone else Michael! I was with him last night."

The customers around them stared. Some even snickered at how Angela brutally violated Michael's manhood. Michael let out a large scream, "You whore!"

Before Michael could even get up out of his seat, Angela took his piping hot coffee and spilled it all over him. Michael screamed in pain from the burns.

"You'll never amount to anything," Angela said. "You're nothing more than a wannabe big shot. Even your own family doesn't respect you."

The onlookers stared in disbelief as Angela marched out of the shop. An employee quickly brought Michael ice and a rag. He smacked the ice out of the employee's hand.

Michael lived on his own for a while now. He moved out of his parents' home when he was only twenty years old. His father, Angelo Coniglio, was a blue-collar worker. There wasn't a day in his life that Angelo didn't go to work. To him, work was everything. He truly had the old school Italian mentality. Angelo was a large man who required a lot of maintenance. Carmela Coniglio waited on him hand and foot, she was a saint. She had her moments of crazy rage, but what Italian women didn't? Carmela was always the loudest person in the room. When she walked in, everyone knew it was going to be a party. Michael was very close to his mother, as most good Italian boys are.

Unfortunately, Michael's old school upbringing worked against him. His father was never satisfied with any of his work in school. Michael wasn't cut from the same cloth as his parents. He was much more creative and loved the arts. Writing and singing were a few of his many passions. The difference in values caused a rift between Michael and his father. Angelo would never be content unless he took up a real profession, which he considered to be a lawyer or doctor.

Michael's apartment didn't appear as if he did well for himself. It was dusty, messy, and looked as if a pack of wild animals ran amuck. There were countless amounts of empty beer bottles inside his kitchen sink. Michael was limping from the burns on his leg. He dragged himself over to the freezer where he kept a half empty bottle of vodka. Sitting on his couch, Michael tried to drink himself to sleep.

As he finally began to numb the pain, the phone rang. Michael could barely get a word out without slurring it, "Who is it?"

The voice on the other side of the phone was piercing and strong. It could have been no one else but his mother.

"Michael," she said. "You're drunk, aren't you? You're a borderline alcoholic."

Michael let out a large laugh and finished the bottle of vodka. "Borderline? I think I'm a full-blown alcoholic at this point," he said.

Carmela screamed so loud that Michael was forced to take the phone away from his ear. He held his ear in pain.

"It's that bitch Angela, isn't it?" she asked. "I told you she was no good! You never listen to your mother."

Michael slammed the phone on the receiver and hung up. Everyone always told him how bad Angela was, but he never listened.

Michael cried. "God, why me? What have I done to deserve this pain?"

The next morning Carmela banged on Michael's apartment door. She held a hot coffee in her hand with a fresh loaf of bread.

"Michael," Carmela said, loudly. "Open up the door, it's your mother!"

Carmela heard a large thump followed by a crash. Michael quickly got off his couch and opened the door. "Ma, I love you but it's nine o'clock in the morning. I had a long night."

Without even asking, Carmela barreled her way past Michael into the apartment. She immediately started to clean. "You live like a pig. That no good *puttana* made you like this. You were always a clean boy."

Michael sat down on the couch. He put his head in his hands and cried. "She cheated on me ma. We're through. You won't have to worry about her anymore."

Carmela stopped her cleaning spree and sat down next to her son. She gently rubbed his back. "You'll find a nice girl Michael. God is going to help you. You've been a good person your whole life. He's going to protect you."

Michael shook his head. His lack of faith based on his reaction was clear. "God isn't helping me, it doesn't work that way," Michael said.

Carmela smacked the back of Michael's head. She said dryly, "Don't say such a thing. He hears all that you say."

Michael rubbed the back of his head. He glanced at the clock in the room. Michael jumped out of his seat. "I'm late for work! My boss already hates me." He gently escorted his mother out of his apartment and kissed her on the cheek. "I gotta go ma."

The lack of encouragement and scolding from his father led Michael to take a typical nine-to-five desk job. He worked at an accounting firm in Manhattan. Although the job paid well, Michael was slowly losing his soul at age twenty-seven. His passions lied elsewhere and no amount of money in the world could fix that. Michael lost his drive as his life plunged further down an emotionless trail. His borderline alcoholic tendencies were more than enough proof of that.

The office was gloomy and depressing. There were rows of cubicles. The walls were painted a dull white and grey. Not a single person in the room looked happy to be at work.

The atmosphere reeked of depression. Michael entered his cubicle and acted as if he was already at work for some time. He spilled a pile of papers over his desk and rapidly looked through them. The entire time Michael attempted to put on this elaborate charade, Derek Coleman, was quietly watching him. Derek was the boss of the entire accounting firm. He was bald and had a mustache that was so thick he probably had to spend extra time combing it every morning. His large round glasses were so clean that the light in the room glistened off them.

Derek had it out for Michael since he started working at the firm. He approached Michael's desk and leaned over the wall of his cubicle. "Listen Mike," he said sternly, "What do you think you're doing? I thought I told you we should be on top of the new account that was booked last week. Did you look at it yet? I don't see any of the papers on your desk."

Derek had no reason for not liking Michael; he just made it his mission to make his life miserable. Michael always had that problem throughout his life. People didn't like him because they realized how talented he really was. Envy and jealously could sometimes be worse than a knife. "I'll get right on it," Michael said. "I got caught up with some other work this morning I was behind on."

Michael grabbed a group of papers out of his desk drawer. He turned his back to Derek and continued to work. Derek turned Michael's chair around to face him. He snarled at Michael. "You were late for the third time this month," Derek said. "I've been waiting to do this for a really long time."

Michael smiled at Derek. He tapped Derek's face with his hand a few times and grabbed his cheek. It was Michael's way of letting him know he wasn't going to be intimidated. "Let me guess! I'm fired? C'mon say it with me now," Michael yelled.

Derek's face turned red. He was filled with fury and anger. "Get the hell out of my firm! You're fired. I'm going to make sure you never get a job in this business again. Consider yourself blackballed from the accounting world."

Michael sat in silence. He grabbed his sports coat off the back of his chair and walked towards the door. Before he left, Michael stopped at the water cooler. He slowly drank a glass of water and stared at Derek for a few more moments.

"I never liked this shithole anyway," he said calmly. Michael screamed out, "I'm finally free of this place!"

* * *

Carmela and Angelo lived in Forest Hills. Their home was small, but it was clear they made a decent living for themselves. Their house was two floors high. The first floor had a living room, dining room, and kitchen that were all connected. The floors were covered with granite and the countertops with marble. Angelo sat lazily on a couch in his underwear. Whenever he wasn't at work, he was in that one spot watching television. Carmela was cooking dinner while she waited for Michael to arrive. She really enjoyed it when Michael visited. He hardly came around just to avoid seeing his father. Carmela made sure to make his favorite dish, Baked Ziti, as an incentive for him to stay around the house a little longer. Carmela stood directly in front of Angelo's view of the television.

Carmela yelled, "I swear to God if you start with Mike we're through. I'll file for divorce!"

Angelo nudged her out of the way with one foot. "You'll file for nothing. See what happens if you do that," Angelo said.

She responded to his threat by pulling the plug from the television. This forced Angelo to get up out of his chair, something he hated doing. He grunted, "I married the world's biggest bitch."

Carmela marched over to the door to let Michael in. She kissed and hugged him. Despite their differences, Michael immediately went to go pay his respects to his father. Angelo acknowledged his presence with a brief welcome. "Hey son, how's work going?"

Carmela nodded in approval of Angelo's greeting from across the room. Michael stuttered. It was his intuition telling him a fight was about to brew.

"It's going well, Michael said. "My boss isn't too fond of me. I'm afraid he might fire me soon." Angelo looked at Michael with disdain.

Carmela saw what was happening and tried to defuse the situation with food. She shouted, "Dinner's ready!"

Michael and Angelo sat at the dining room table together. Carmela filled their plates with food. She was the last one to sit down. Michael started eating his pasta and Carmela quickly smacked his hand. "I raised you better than that," she said. "We have to say Grace first."

They said a prayer in unison before eating their home-made meal. The dinner was quiet. Not one of them spoke. Carmela tried to improve the conversation casually but failed. Michael and Angelo were the first to finish dinner. One trait Michael got from his father was fast eating.

"I never liked lying to you guys. I might as well say it," Michael said.

Carmela and Angelo had completely different reactions to Michael's statement. While Carmela looked concerned, Angelo looked like a tiger ready to pounce on its prey. He was waiting for Michael to slip up. He wanted Michael to say he was right. Michael stood up out of his seat.

"I lost my job today. My boss fired me for tardiness," Michael said. "Believe it or not I think this is a good thing. I've been miserable working this job for a long time. The money was good, but my happiness means more. I think I'm going to pursue my passion instead. I think I have more than enough to live off my savings for a while. I haven't touched the account in years."

Angelo folded his hands and stared at Carmela. "This is the son that you raised," Angelo said. "I don't know who he is anymore. This is all because I let you baby and spoil him."

Carmela shook her head in disbelief. She threw a plate on the floor and cried. "Maybe if you weren't out philandering you could have helped me raise our son," she screeched.

Angelo snapped after seeing the plate break. He pulled the table cloth onto the floor, sending all the food and sil-verware with it. Michael grabbed his father and pinned him against the wall. As a child, Michael had seen too many of these fits. When Angelo got angry, every item in the house was his weapon. He threw things all over the floor and against the wall. Even after a few minutes in submission, Angelo still didn't calm down.

He continued to scold Michael. "What are you gunna do with your life now? You really think you're going to be a fucking singer or a fucking writer? You can barely hold down a desk job!"

Michael let go of his father. Angelo pointed his finger in Michael's face. "You'll always be nothing but a bum."

Michael punched a hole in the wall next to Angelo's head. His father flinched. Angelo knew he may have gone too far this time. His son's reaction took him completely by surprise. Michael was always a fighter, but he was obedient when it came to his family. Angelo walked into the living room and turned on the television as if nothing happened. This was all a regular day in the Coniglio home. Carmela had already stopped crying and started to clean up. Michael helped her clean the mess.

On his way home, Michael stopped at the coffee shop. He had to have at least three coffees a day.

Coffee had the opposite effect and used it to calm down his nerves. He walked into the shop only to see Angela sitting with another man. This man was large and had a dominating presence. His hands looked so large. They could pop a basketball with a small squeeze. Most people would hesitate to start an argument with this man, but not Michael. He was fearless when it came to those he loved and those who have hurt him. Angela spotted Michael and pointed him out to her new lover. Michael didn't hesitate to walk over and let his presence be known. He made a sarcastic thinking face.

Michael asked, "This is the guy you've been banging?"

He tapped Angela's lover on the shoulder to get his attention. Michael's voice was deep and powerful. "Let's think about this for a moment. Hey buddy, I don't know who you are or what your name is. I just want you to know that this *puttana* was banging the both of us at the same time."

Angela's lover stood up out of his seat and towered over Michael. "I don't wanna see you get hurt," Angela said. "You better quit while you can still walk out of here."

Michael laughed. There was not a trace of fear in his eyes. "You think I'm scared of this meat head? I thought you knew me better than that."

Without a warning, her lover punched Michael in the face. The blow from the punch was so hard that it knocked Michael on top of a table and onto the floor. The bystanders gasped.

Angela hugged her lover. "Baby let's go," she said.

They left the coffee shop without even bothering to see how injured Michael was. A woman offered to help Michael off the floor. She cradled his head in her lap to check if he had any injuries. He was completely stunned by the sight of her. For a few moments, Michael froze in time. He was numb from all the pain in his skull. Michael analyzed her. She was unlike any woman he had ever seen before. Her body resembled a runway model. It was impossible to tell whether her eyes were blue or green. They would change color depending on the lighting in the room. She stood almost taller than Michael himself. Her hair was short and blonde. Her voice was soft spoken. To Michael, she was completely exotic. Even her name, Elvira Vaughn, sounded foreign to him. Michael suddenly came to. He found his place back in the present time. Elvira helped him off the ground and onto his feet. They locked eyes for a few moments.

Elvira blushed. "Are you ok?" she asked. "You took some punch. I think you should go see a doctor."

Elvira checked his face. "I think I'm ok," Michael said.

He attempted to walk away. After Michael took a few steps, he stumbled. There was a constant ringing in his ear. The entire right side of his head was swollen. Elvira quickly came to his aide again. She held his arm, so he could stand up properly.

She asked, "Since you won't see a doctor, will you at least let me help you?"

Michael was completely taken off guard by her comment. He paused and thought of a response to her kindness. Michael wasn't used to being treated kindly by women.

Michael tried to hold back a smile. "Now, why would you want to help me? I'm a stranger. You don't know anything about me."

Elvira said confidently, "Because you seem like a nice guy." She rubbed his shoulder. "My apartment isn't too far from here. I can take you there and patch you up. What do you say?"

Michael's cheeks turned a rosy color. "I guess that would be ok. By the way, my name is Michael Coniglio."

They walked towards the door interlocking arms. She replied, "I'm Elvira Vaughn."

Elvira's apartment was well decorated. Her furniture was rustic and antique. It was easy to tell that Elvira was disorganized; there were papers all over her apartment. A large bookcase towered over the entire room. It was practically touching the ceiling of her apartment. The bookcase was filled with classic literature including various plays. Placed next to the bookcase stood a cabinet that had a record player in it. The record player was twenty years old. The cabinet was filled with albums from artists like George Gershwin, Tony Bennett, and Elton John. Michael was lying on the couch holding his head. A crucifix rested on the wall above the couch. Elvira brought over a large bag of ice for him.

"Press that down on your face," Elvira said. "It will bring down the swelling."

Michael sat up and pressed the bag of ice to his face. He examined Elvira's apartment. Michael was particularly drawn to her bookcase. She quietly watched him comb through her books. One stuck out from all the rest. It was labeled, *The Passions of the Mind*, written by Irving Stone. Michael didn't know much about Freud aside from the fact that Italians hated him. Italians thought people who went to therapy belonged in a mental ward.

"I can tell you like to read often," Michael said.

Elvira smiled. "I could sit here and read books all day. I love classic novels. When I read, I feel like I'm escaping from this crazy world we live in."

Michael sighed. "I wish I had an outlet like that. Something to help me zone out and get away from it all. I was never much of a reader. I always enjoyed writing more."

Elvira was excited by the idea that Michael enjoyed writing. She wasn't easily impressed. Elvira loved the idea of a man indulging in the arts.

She said enthusiastically, "What kind of writing? Do you like to write for fun or would you like to be a novelist?"

Michael paused. He thought about his response for a moment. "I would really love to write a novel. I've written about many events in my life before. Maybe I could put it all together somehow."

The energy that Elvira gave off was pleasant. She acted like she didn't have a worry in the world. It almost seemed as if she had life figured out. She was the polar opposite of Michael in this one way. Her easygoing attitude complimented Michael's anxiousness.

"Maybe you could show me your writing sometime? I would love to read it. You could consider it an outside opinion," Elvira said.

Not a single person had ever offered to read Michael's writing. He never had the nerve to show his parents because his father looked down upon it. Angela, like many of Michael's previous girlfriends, never bothered to take an interest in anything he loved. They didn't care enough. This simple gesture from Elvira dumbfounded Michael.

Michael became uneasy and turned his back to Elvira. He pointed to his swollen face. "I don't know if I would be able to do that. I've never showed anyone my writing before. How could I show a stranger my most personal thoughts and feelings? In case you haven't noticed, I've had a little too much trouble in my life lately."

Slowly, Elvira became interested in finding out more about Michael. Her intuition told her that he was different from other men. His body language showed he was closed off, like he was sheltering himself from the rest of the world. He looked like a lost soul, waiting for the right person to come along. Michael had hopeless romantic written all over him and Elvira picked up on it.

Elvira replied jokingly, "These troubles you refer to are they girlfriend troubles or ex-girlfriend troubles? I really hope that bitch in the coffee shop isn't your girlfriend after today."

Michael laughed. "Ex-girlfriend troubles."

From the corner of his eye, Michael spotted Elvira's record collection. He looked through the record cabinet. He was taken by surprise when he saw Tony Bennett's I *Wanna Be Around* record. Michael was filled with excitement. He asked, "You like Tony Bennett? "This is my favorite record of all time! I can't believe you have it."

Elvira nodded, "I love Tony. His songs got me through some tough times. I always viewed him as a father figure in some weird way."

Elvira had Michael's full attention. Michael had a series of questions he always asked women he was interested in. He truly believed in the idea of having a deep connection with the person you love, being able to share passion on more than just a physical level. The answers to his self-made test were meant to determine how well he would get along with a woman. Not one of his girlfriends passed the first question to the test. Michael decided to give it another shot. After all, he literally fell into Elvira's lap by chance.

Michael pulled a Frank Sinatra record out of the cabinet. He brought the Sinatra and Bennett records over to Elvira. He placed them in front of her. He asked, "Tony Bennett or Frank Sinatra?"

"Is that even a question?" she said sarcastically. "Tony Bennett blows Sinatra out of the water. He's a better singer by far."

Michael was astonished by Elvira's answer. Finding a woman to even listen to these records was hard enough. Now he met one by accident who loves Tony Bennett just as much as he did.

"Now let me ask you a question Michael. Did that girl at the coffee shop like Tony Bennett?"

Michael shook his head. "She hated when I played his records. We would get into fights about it all the time."

Elvira got up out of her seat and placed Bennett's record on the turntable then turned the volume up as loud as it could possibly go. She screamed out, "Then screw her!"

Elvira danced along with the music as Michael watched her have a good time all by herself. In only an hour of knowing her, he already felt smitten. Michael wanted to pull her in for a dance, but every instinct in his body told him not to. Michael was fearful of yet another heartbreak. He was already hanging on to his sanity by a thread. The anxiousness and negative thoughts stirred in his mind. His anxiety worked him up into a panic. He abruptly walked towards the door.

Michael said coldly, "I have to go."

Elvira turned off the music. "But you just got here! You didn't even let the swelling in your face go down."

Michael didn't know how to respond. He tried to come up with a valid excuse for leaving. He blurted out the first thing that came to his mind. "I have to go water my plants. I'll see you around."

He ran out of her apartment so quickly he forgot to close the door. Elvira watched him walk down the apartment building hallway. It all happened so quickly that Elvira was left in a whirlwind of confusion. She said to herself, "Water plants? What sense does that make?"

2
CHAPTER

Elvira Vaughn worked as a receptionist in an oncologist's office. The office was in the Upper West Side of Manhattan. She enjoyed her job to a degree. Working in an oncologist's office could get depressing for some, but Elvira found it inspiring. She went out of her way to make the patients feel good. A warm smile and attitude went a long way for the terminal ones.

Like Michael, Elvira left her home at a young age. She was born in Pennsylvania and lived in an area that was rural for most of her adolescence. Elvira didn't fit in with the rest of the small-town girls. She had the mind of a city dweller. As a teenager, she spent her summer's working at the local movie theater. All the money she earned was placed in a little envelope. She didn't spend a dime of it on herself. Elvira was determined to leave her life behind and move to new beginnings. She left for New York City when she was only seventeen years old.

This burning motivation to leave was fueled by her life at home. No person decides to leave their family overnight.

Her father, William Vaughn, wasn't around for much of her childhood. William was a talented man and was often on the road pursing his own career in the music industry. When he did come around, he was tough on Elvira. Her father held her to a high standard. William served as Elvira's singing coach. The time they spent together practicing strained their relationship even further. She clearly had inherited many of her father's great talents. However, Elvira could never stack up to William's insanely high expectations. The worst part was that her voice was better than just fine, it was beautiful. She had soul behind her singing, which was a rare trait. When she sang, an entire room of people would come alive.

Elvira sat in her office's break room eating lunch. She was accompanied by her longtime friend, Allison Williams. Allison was an attractive woman. She had long and curly brunette hair. Her body was slender. Her eyes were dark opposed to Elvira's light eyes. Elvira and Allison had been friends since she came here to New York. They saw each other through many years of rough times. It bothered Elvira that Michael left suddenly. She blamed herself. She sought the council of her good friend.

"I met this guy the other day at the coffee shop," Elvira said. "It happened in the most unusual way. His ex-girlfriend's new boyfriend knocked him out in the middle of the place."

Allison couldn't help but laugh. The situation was a little comical. "This guy sounds like trouble," Allison said. "Who gets into a fight at a coffee shop?"

Elvira was too embarrassed to say what she was truly thinking. The short time Elvira had spent with Michael felt right. It was a feeling she couldn't put her finger on exactly. There were lingering thoughts in her brain that wouldn't rest. How could she possibly explain to her friend she might have fallen for a man she hardly knew? The same kind of love people see in movies and write about in novels.

Elvira shook her head. "This guy definitely isn't trouble. He seems like such a sweetheart. I got that feeling from him almost immediately. I took him back to my apartment to patch him up. We had such a great conversation about Tony Bennett. Then he just got up and left."

Allison was always overly protective of Elvira. Elvira had a rough and complicated past. New York City was a dangerous place for a full-grown adult and Elvira had to make her way in this dreaded city when she was barely twenty. Without her father's help, she decided to pursue a career on Broadway. Ever since she was a little girl, she enjoyed Broadway plays. The music was enticing and creative. The actors and actresses had unbelievable amounts of talent. It was Elvira's dream to become a Broadway star and join this talented group of individuals. Elvira had a few stints here and there, but nothing would stick. She was constantly told she wasn't good enough. Allison didn't want Elvira to face another major let down.

"Babe, you're my best friend and I love you," Allison said. "But don't you think this is crazy? He literally fell in your lap and you took him back to your apartment. Do you know how dangerous that is? Is he even handsome?"

Elvira's face was blank. She continued her story and ignored her friend's opinion. "Oh, so now you want the good details?" Elvira said humorously. "He has this really nice smile. His frame is large, and he has a more defined shape to him. He looks like a real man. At the same time, I think he's sensitive. That's a double win in my book."

Allison replied, "What does he do for a living?"

"He never exactly said what. All I know is that he loves Tony Bennett and writing."

Allison rolled her eyes. "A writer? You gotta be kidding me."

Now thirty years old, Elvira had her share of tumultuous relationships. One of her past lovers especially treated her awfully. This man abused her both physically and mentally. He took advantage of a young girl who was already broken in many ways. Elvira stayed with this man for years, until she finally gained the courage to get herself out of that relationship. The aftermath left her self-worth in pieces. She constantly battled the idea that she wasn't good enough for anyone. The idea of a man enjoying her quirky personality didn't register. Elvira considered the things that made her who she was, annoying to others. She never thought there would be a man who would love her exactly the way God made her.

Allison picked at Elvira's lunch while she continued pleading her case. "Before he ran out, he mentioned not watering his plants," Elvira said. She shrugged her shoulders. "I don't even wanna try and figure out that one."

Elvira pushed Allison's hand away from her food. Allison rubbed Elvira's back. Her tone of voice suddenly became comforting. Allison could see that this was clearly taking a toll on her friend.

"If it's meant to be you will find each other," Allison said reassuringly. "No person can escape their fate. It's in God's hands now. Besides, maybe he really did have to water his plants."

* * *

Michael was watching a football game in Billy Benfatto's apartment. Billy was from the north end of Queens near Little Neck. He lived in a condominium that was quite large. Billy was a childhood friend of Michael's. They met in kindergarten and have been best friends since. Billy was loud and obnoxious. His whisper was a normal person's way of talking. His body resembled a pear. Michael often viewed Billy as his brother. They fought probably just as often as brothers do. Billy wasn't the best at giving advice, but Michael didn't have anyone else to turn to. Elvira was on the forefront of his mind since they met.

"Billy, I gotta talk to you about this girl I met last week."

Billy ignored Michael. He was too into the football game to pay attention. Michael punched him in the arm.

"Yeah Mike, I'm listening," Billy mumbled. "I'm just glad you're finally moving on from Angela. Go out and get laid. I've been telling you that for weeks."

Billy's comment annoyed Michael. Michael didn't like the idea of using women for meaningless sex. He gave into temptations when a situation presented itself, but he always felt horrible after. Michael wasn't looking for casual sex. That part of his life was long behind him. He wanted a woman he could truly connect with on an emotional and physical level.

"It's not like that," Michael replied hastily. "I met this girl right after Angela's boyfriend hit me. She made sure I was ok. I ended up back at her apartment. She patched me up."

Billy was suddenly interested in his story. He ignored the football game for a few moments. "Tell me you made a move Mike," Billy said hopefully.

Michael threw his hands up in the air. He always thought Billy's mind was in the gutter. "She's not the typical whore you pick up at the bars. I could tell within a few minutes of meeting her that she was genuine."

Michael always dated controlling women. He felt completely disregarded by his past lovers. He was never allowed to play his classic records that were outdated. There was always a complaint. Women had a hard time understanding his corny sense of humor. Whether it was the clothes he wore or the music he played, they always tried to change the person Michael was. It was never possible for his girlfriends to take an interest in anything that he loved. What Michael enjoyed the most in this world was the movies. Film is what inspired him to take an interest in writing and singing. It played such a significant role in shaping his life. Yet, his girlfriends would never bother to watch films like *Casablanca* with him. They simply weren't interested enough.

Billy walked over to the refrigerator to get beers. He opened two cans and placed them in front of Michael. "I got a feeling it's gunna be one of those days," Billy said. "Tell me how you fell in love again for the tenth time? That's why I brought you two beers. The drinking might as well start now."

Michael pushed away the beers. He wanted to make it clear he was being serious. "I don't know much about her," Michael said. "You're gunna think I'm crazy, but I felt this connection. I felt like I knew her my whole life. She passed the first question of the test, Billy. Do you know what this means?"

Billy laughed. "You and that fucking test. How on earth do you base a potential relationship off a test you came up with in fifth grade? No girl you have ever known has even passed the first question. How many questions do you even have on that stupid test?"

Michael pulled a piece of paper out of his wallet. The paper had a list of five questions. He handed it to Billy. It was crumpled and barely legible. "Take a look at it for yourself," Michael said. "She was the only girl to pass the first question."

This test that Michael made had more meaning than Billy could ever imagine. Even in his early youth, Michael always had a hard time connecting with women of his generation. He was ten years old when he wrote it. The beauty of all this is that a child's mind is pure. They see life more simply and clearly than adults do. Michael came up with that test to find the woman of his dreams. He narrowed it down to five things that would mean the most to him.

Billy quickly glanced at the piece of paper. He couldn't believe what he was reading. The questions were insanely specific. Michael was really looking for a woman who was his match, but he couldn't understand why he chose such silly things. If Billy made a list, it would have been much different and probably raunchy. He handed it back to Michael. He wasn't the kind of guy who believed in what he considered to be romantic garbage but decided to play along. "You want my advice? Ask her out and see where it goes. You got her telephone number, right?"

Michael took a sip of the beer. He knew Billy was going to scold him. "No, I didn't," Michael said woefully. "I chickened out. We were having such a great conversation. I started to have all these feelings. I couldn't figure out what they were. It freaked me out so badly that I left. I practically had an anxiety attack."

Billy could never understand Michael's anxiety. Billy never overthought anything. He never thought anything through at all. Billy swore nothing bad could happen to him. That's why he always got himself and Michael into trouble. Wherever they went, Billy would get Michael caught up in a mess out of stupidity. At the end of the day, it was harmless, and they always ended up having fun. It took extra patience for Billy to handle Michael when he got like this.

"Of course, you did that," Billy said. "You always do that kind of stuff to yourself. Go back to her apartment, you remember where it was right?"

"I can't just show up at her house," Michael said. "I have to make it seem more natural than that."

Billy rolled his eyes. "Then hang around the coffee shop until she shows up. Fucking *stunad*."

Michael continued to doubt himself. He paced back and forth. "You really think I should? I think it might be too soon."

Billy grabbed Michael by the shoulders. He shook him around a little. "We've been friends for more than twenty years and I've never seen your face light up that way when you talk about a girl," Billy said. "Find her. Ask the questions on your stupid test. Then worry about everything later."

Later that week, Michael returned to the coffee shop. He made sure that he looked presentable. Michael always knew how to dress sharply, but he started to let himself go after Angela left him. He sat down at a table with a newspaper. Michael was so determined to see Elvira; he waited in the coffee shop for a whole five hours. He read the newspaper from cover to cover about six times. Every time the door opened, he would glance up to see if it was her. As time winded down, the more upset he became. Michael knew he missed his chance. Michael stayed until the employees asked him to leave for closing time.

It was raining, there was not a single person on the sidewalk or a car in sight. Michael began the long walk back to his apartment. He was soaking wet in only a matter of minutes, but it didn't bother him. His thoughts were swarming. Michael was convinced there had to be something he could do to find Elvira. The entire street was foggy and dimly lit. He could barely see a few feet in front of his face. Only one store on the street was still open. Michael went inside to wait out the storm.

Michael wandered into a bookstore. It had to be more than thirty years old. The smell of musty paper filled the air. The bookshelves looked run down. There weren't more than a few people browsing around. Michael saw the irony in the situation. He spent the whole day waiting for Elvira in a coffee shop and ended up in a bookstore. He remembered how much Elvira said she loved to read. He decided to pick up a book on Sigmund Freud while he was there. Michael was curious to know more about this man and why Elvira seemed to take an interest in him. Michael made his way to the biography section of the store. Elvira sat in the corner of the section, Indian style. She seemed to be in a relaxed and tranquil state. Michael couldn't believe what he was seeing. For once, he thought lady luck was finally on his side. Michael tried to contain his excitement. He tapped her on the shoulder.

"Do you know where they are hiding the classic literature around here?"

The last person Elvira expected to see in a bookstore was Michael. She came here to unwind and escape from the rest of the world. It was her second home. She wasn't wearing any makeup and looked plain. She didn't think it was necessary to dress up for a trip to the bookstore. Now that Michael showed up, she felt a little self-conscious. Elvira got up from the floor and dusted herself off.

"Hey Michael! How are your plants doing?"

Michael's face turned red. He couldn't believe she remembered the stupid excuse he gave. Michael was never good at lying or thinking on his feet, but he had to play along. "The plants ended up doing ok. They didn't die or anything," Michael said nervously.

Elvira was always a prankster. To her family, she was known as the mischievous imp. It was a childhood name that her grandmother gave her. Elvira knew Michael was excited to see her and now she wanted him to sweat it out. She wasn't the kind of girl that ever made it easy to pick her up.

Elvira always wanted a man to work a little for her attention. It was all fun and games to her.

"What are you doing in a bookstore?" Elvira said curiously. "I remember you saying that you weren't much of a reader?"

At this point, Michael knew that Elvira was messing around with him. One of the many gifts God gave Michael was his ability to be intuitive. He could sense what a woman was thinking without even trying. Michael leaned against the bookcase standing next to her. He puffed out his chest.

"I needed inspiration for the novel I'm trying to write. I really thought about what you said the other day. I figured, why not give it a shot?"

Elvira gently moved Michael's face from side to side. Michael blushed when she came so close to him.

"You didn't bruise too badly. I guess that ice treatment I gave you worked."

Michael knew that Elvira gave him an opening. This was his chance to ask her out on a date. She was flirting with him openly.

"I never had the chance to thank you for everything," Michael said. "I was thinking that maybe I could make it up to you with dinner?"

While Elvira was excited Michael had finally asked her out, she still didn't want to give in. She wanted to make him suffer a little longer for running out of her apartment. It was her way of checking how high his interest level really was. She turned her back to him.

"I'm not sure if I want to have dinner with you Michael," Elvira said firmly.

Elvira smiled while her back was turned to him. She could feel the change in his demeanor without even seeing it. Michael gently grabbed her hand and turned her back in front of him.

"Now why is that?"

Elvira laughed and smiled. She pointed at him. "Because you might run away from me again," she said.

Michael took a few moments to respond. He knew that he had to come up with an answer that was witty.

"I promise this time I won't forget to water my plants," Michael said jokingly.

They both laughed together. The connection they felt for one another was present and strong. It almost was as if the universe was coming together to ensure they would go out on a date.

"Pick me up at eight tomorrow," Elvira said confidently. "You remember where I live right?"

Michael was horrible when it came to directions. He got lost going around the block. Elvira could see the confusion on his face. She searched her purse for a pen then grabbed Michael's hand and wrote down her address.

Elvira gave Michael a kiss on the cheek goodbye and placed the book she was reading into his hand. Michael watched her leave the bookstore with a goofy smile on his face. The book she placed in his hand was *Mere Christianity* written by C.S. Lewis. He sat down on the floor and read the book. It was probably the first time he's read a book since high school.

3

CHAPTER

Michael took Elvira to a steakhouse on their first date. This was yet another one of Michael's tests. Food is such an important part of Italian culture. To Italians, enjoying what you eat is one of the simple pleasures of life. Making a good meal for a person is equivalent to saying, *I love you*. Michael didn't want a woman he was dating to order a typical house salad for dinner. It was important that she loved to eat. More importantly, that she loved to eat with Michael.

Gallagher's Steakhouse on West Fifty-second Street was the perfect choice. It was an old styled restaurant, everything looked a little outdated. The music playing was usually jazz or crooner era style. He knew Elvira would appreciate the ambiance. Gallagher's was unusually packed the night of their date. Michael was lucky to have booked a reservation with only a day's notice. The hostess led Michael and Elvira to a table that was in the middle of the entire restaurant. Michael instantly noticed that Elvira had suddenly become uncomfortable.

"Is there something wrong Elvira?"

Elvira shook her head. "No, I'm fine," she said. "I just have this weird quirk that's all."

The two sat down together. A waiter handed them menus. The uncomfortable look on Elvira's face still didn't go away. Michael was determined to find out what was wrong.

"What kind of weird quirk are we talking about here? God please don't tell me you're a vegetarian?"

Elvira laughed. She was nervous to tell Michael what was wrong. "I'm definitely not a vegetarian," she said. "When I go out to eat I like to sit in a certain place. I just have this thing about sitting in the middle of a restaurant. It makes me feel uncomfortable."

Elvira put her head down in embarrassment. She didn't want Michael thinking she was a difficult person. Michael did think this was odd. A girl had never brought that up to him on a date before. At the same time, he found it amusing and adorable. She seemed so self-conscious about something that wasn't a big deal. He would have been more than happy to accommodate her.

Michael said, "It's really not a big deal at all. Where would you like to sit?"

Elvira pointed to a table in the far corner of the room facing the entrance. "That table over there looks nice."

Right after she pointed out a table, the hostess sat another couple down there. Michael called the hostess over. He explained the situation and was denied his request. Michael pleaded with the hostess. The hostess refused to ask the couple to switch, citing that it would reflect poorly on the restaurant. Elvira felt more embarrassed as the situation progressed. She saw how hard Michael was going out of his way to switch tables. Elvira tried to reassure him that the table they were sitting at was okay.

"Michael, I really have no problem sitting here. It's just a tiny thing that bothers me sometimes. That's all."

"Hold on, I have one more idea," he said.

Michael walked over to the couple sitting at Elvira's preferred table. He explained the situation to them. Elvira watched from afar as they both shook their heads in denial. Michael reached into his pocket and handed the couple money. The couple took the money and left the table without further issue. Michael waved at Elvira to come over. She was completely taken back.

"How'd you manage to make them switch?" she asked.

Michael held out Elvira's seat for her. "I gave them one hundred bucks to switch. Money is no object with me. You can't put a price on going out with a beautiful woman like you."

Elvira giggled. "Oh, you're good."

Michael ordered a bottle of Opus One for the table. There was not one moment of silence during the entire dinner. Michael and Elvira shared stories about their lives and passions. The two even laughed so hard at one moment, they almost cried. The wine was going to both their heads quickly. The bottle was polished off before their steaks even came. Elvira answered the second of Michael's five questions by ordering a porterhouse steak. When the steaks arrived at the table, Elvira took a plastic jar of steak seasoning from her purse.

"Did you just pull steak seasoning out of your purse?" Michael asked.

"Yes, I did! It's called Buck Seasoning. I carry it around with me whenever I go out to eat. A friend of mine gets it for me every time she goes upstate. It's homemade from a farm."

Elvira smothered the seasoning all over her steak. Michael watched in awe. He burst out into laughter.

"I've never been on a date where a girl pulled her own personal steak seasoning from her purse. You really are full of surprises, aren't you? You know what, pass that over here."

Michael sprinkled the seasoning on his steak. The waiter watched them and gasped. The waiter couldn't believe how they were ruining the steak the kitchen just prepared. Michael noticed the waiter's reaction and scolded him.

"What are you looking at? You got a problem with my special seasoning?" Michael said.

Michael and Elvira laughed together. The waiter walked away.

"It's awesome, isn't it?" Elvira asked. "The best part is that you can use it on anything. I even put in on my fish."

Michael took a bite of his steak. "I can't believe how good this is!"

Elvira never felt more comfortable around anyone before. Her past lovers couldn't stand that they constantly had to switch tables or carry around a plastic jar of steak seasoning. They found these quirks to be quite annoying. Michael on the other hand, adored them. He got such a kick out of her. He enjoyed that she was unique. Vibrant feelings ignited between them, like fireflies lighting up the night sky. The relationship was beginning and the two of them just clicked.

The New York City subways could make anyone cringe. The stations smelled of a horrible odor, homeless people wandered around, and crime was rampant. Elvira had every reason to feel threatened taking the subway home during the evening time, but she had never felt safer with Michael there. As they entered the train, the passengers stared at them. Elvira clung to Michael's arm as they quietly waited for their stop.

Ditmars Boulevard was dimly lit. It was chilly outside. There was a slight breeze in the air. The wine kept Michael and Elvira warm for their walk home. Michael suddenly stopped. He stared into the window of an antique store. A beautiful acoustic guitar was the centerpiece of the window display. The guitar had a cherry wood finish with a brown pick guard.

"That's a beautiful guitar," Elvira said.

Michael placed his hand on the window. He looked deep in thought. "I used to play you know," Michael said.

They continued to walk down Ditmars. Michael held out his arm for Elvira to lean on. They interlocked arms as she leaned her body on Michael's shoulder.

"What kind of music did you play?" she asked.

"A little bit of this, a little bit of that."

Elvira noticed Michael had a hard time talking about his life. He was a great conversationalist, but there were certain questions he always danced around. It was clear he didn't enjoy talking about his career or future. She decided to ask Michael about it.

"You're really bad at opening up, aren't you?" Elvira asked. "We need to fix that. Sigmund Freud would have said you have intimacy issues."

Michael remembered Elvira's book on Freud. He had a feeling she must have studied to be a psychologist. Italians didn't like anything about psychology or Freud's theories, it was a stigma in their culture. Michael could only imagine telling his parents he wanted to date a future shrink.

"I bet you could diagnose me with all that psychology reading you do," Michael said.

"I've always found the concept of therapy fascinating," Elvira said. "I want to go to school to become a therapist one day."

Michael and Elvira stopped walking. They stood in front of her apartment building. There was a large stone staircase leading up to the door of the building. Michael sat down on the staircase.

"Maybe I could be your first client?" he asked.

"As tempting as it sounds, that would be a conflict of interest," Elvira said sternly.

He gently grabbed Elvira's hand and guided her to sit next to him. They sat knee to knee.

"It would only be a conflict of interest if we became intimate in some way," Michael said.

Elvira replied sarcastically, "I never planned on that happening anytime soon."

They gazed into each other's eyes. He ran his fingertips along her face, admiring her beauty. He kissed the far end of her cheek. Then kissed her again, slowly moving closer to her tender lips. She trembled as she felt the touch of his lips get closer to hers. Michael gently put his warm hands on the back of Elvira's neck. His mouth parted her lips. They clung to each other. Shivers went down both their spines. Their bodies reached a point of pure ecstasy. He pulled away.

"I think you have the most beautiful eyes I've ever seen," Michael said. "From the first day I met you, I couldn't tell whether they were blue or green. The color changes every time I see you. I think it's the most amazing thing."

"Do you really mean that?" Elvira said softly.

"I've never been more serious," Michael replied.

Elvira jumped off the staircase. She raced up to the top of the steps. She shouted down to Michael with a smile on her face. "I have to go water my plants now. Call me sometime!"

Michael followed her up the steps. He knew Elvira was going to make him work for her affection, and he wanted to prove he was up for the challenge. "But, I don't have your number!" Michael yelled.

Elvira believed that God had a set plan for every single person. Everyone had a destiny. She decided to leave her relationship with Michael up to fate. "If we are meant to be together, you'll find my number," Elvira said.

Elvira walked into her apartment building and shut the door behind her. Michael walked down the steps. Not a single person had seen a smile that bright on Michael's face for years. Maybe not ever in his life, for a few moments, he felt at peace with the world. His anxiety quelled.

* * *

La Cue a pool bar, was the hangout of Michael and Billy's choice. They would spend hours drinking beers and playing pool. The two of them spent every Saturday night there. Billy ordered a round of beers from the waitress.

"Can I have two beers honey?" Billy shouted.

The waitress acknowledged his request. Billy pointed at Michael.

"Mike, you want something?"

"You know what, I actually don't," Michael said confidently.

Michael tried to cut back on his drinking. It was rare he refused an ice old beer on a Saturday night. He normally drank to get a little loose and take the edge off his mood. For once, he felt naturally loose.

Billy screamed out, "Michael Coniglio? Refusing a beer? What the fuck, is the world about to end?"

Michael chalked his pool cue. He aimed a shot and broke the pool balls across the table. "I'm trying to cut back Billy," Michael said coldly.

Normally, Michael would feel anxious about his date. Debating in his mind how Elvira felt about him. He felt oddly confident and it showed. Billy shot a pool ball and knocked it off the table. "Seriously, what's going on?" Billy asked. "Is this about that chick Elvira?"

Michael picked the pool ball up off the floor. He sat down in a chair with a goofy smile on his face. The waitress handed Billy his round of beers. "She's different. She's unlike any girl I ever met before," Michael said.

Billy patted Michael on the shoulder. He discreetly knocked a pool ball into a pocket with his hand. Billy tried to hand Michael a beer, but Michael pushed it away.

"You need a nice girl in your life," Billy said enthusiastically. "When's the last time you met a nice girl?"

Michael laughed loudly. He pointed to the ball Billy knocked in the pocket. Michael wanted Billy to be aware that he couldn't cheat him.

"Never. I never met a nice girl before," Michael said softly. "I feel like I'm not good enough for a girl like Elvira. She seems so well put together. I mean look at me, I'm an emotional wreck."

Billy shook his head. He placed the beer in front of Michael once again. "That's only in your head buddy. Don't get all flighty with this one. She seems alright. Now shut up about this girl and have a beer. I hate drinking alone."

Michael took the beer Billy kept forcing on him and offered it to a girl standing nearby. The girl accepted the drink. Michael pointed to Billy and acted like it came from him.

* * *

Elvira and Allison were drinking at a rooftop lounge in Manhattan. The lounge looked upscale and modern. The décor was brightly colored. A jukebox was playing music in the corner of the room. The bartender poured them two glasses of red wine. Allison was excited to hear about Elvira's date with Michael.

"How did the big date go," Allison asked curiously. "I want details! Be specific."

Elvira took a sip of wine. Her eyes lit up as she began to tell the story. She talked fast from all her excitement. "It was one of the best dates I've ever been on," Elvira said. "I've never been treated like such a lady in my entire life. Michael ordered a bottle of Opus One for us. He held out the seat for me before I sat down. He even paid a random couple to switch tables with us because of that quirk I have."

Allison was expecting to hear that this guy had issues. She was never sold on Elvira's initial feeling about him. Allison gave Elvira a seductive glance. "How did the wine influence the end of the night?"

"He walked me home," Elvira said. "Then kissed me on my stoop. He told me I had the most beautiful greenish-blue eyes." She folded her hands on the bar and batted her eyes. They laughed together. Allison continued to search for the raunchy details of the date.

"How was it when you kissed him?" Allison asked. "Was he a sloppy kisser? I hate sloppy kissers."

Elvira's face turned a bright red color. She moved around in her seat nervously. "He's alright."

Allison pushed Elvira's arm and laughed. Allison knew Elvira long enough to figure out what made her tick. Her body language instantly gave away that she was attracted to Michael. "You should have seen the face you just made. You totally have the hots for him. This guy is good, isn't he?"

Elvira sipped her glass of wine. Allison kept pressuring Elvira to give her more details. "I really don't know how to describe it," Elvira said. "It felt natural. Like the whole world came together for the few moments we were kissing. I've never experienced anything like it in my life. It's almost scary."

Allison's jaw dropped. "Does he have a brother?" she asked. It was hard for her to find the words to respond. Allison was happy for her friend, but at the same time felt a tiny hint of jealousy. What woman wouldn't want to have those feelings?

* * *

Michael paced throughout his apartment. He held the telephone in his hand. The cord stretched across the room with him. After a few moments of pacing, Michael finally sat down. He placed the telephone on the table. He opened a phone book and searched for Elvira's name. There was a listing for three numbers. The first phone number he dialed was disconnected. Michael was nervous. He didn't want Elvira to think he wasn't interested. Michael dialed the second phone number. A woman answered. She claimed not to know who Michael was. At this point, Michael was getting anxious. He walked into his bedroom and pulled a crucifix from the bottom of his dresser.

"Jesus, I know I haven't talked to you in a while. I'm sorry for that. If you can hear me, now would be a really good time for you to perform a miracle." Michael placed the crucifix on his wall for the first time in ten years. He had thrown it in his drawer and forgotten about it long ago.

Michael walked back to the table and dialed the last number. As the phone rang, his heart skipped a beat. Elvira finally answered the phone. "Elvira?" Michael asked nervously.

Elvira recognized Michael's voice right away, as his accent was distinct and strong. He talked like a typical New Yorker. She twirled the phone cord between her fingers. "Ah! You managed to find my number after all," she said jokingly.

"It took a little investigating, but that kiss was enough motivation," Michael said smoothly.

Elvira was impressed with Michael's determination to find her phone number. She knew there were multiple phone listings in the area and that Michael would have to call each one. That still didn't mean she was going to make it any easier on him. Michael still had a while to go before he proved himself.

"I'll remember to make it harder on you next time," Elvira said.

Michael planned to take Elvira ice skating in Central Park. If there's one thing Michael had a knack for, it was choosing fun dates. There wasn't anything dull about him. His ideas were always out of the box and interesting.

"So, there's going to be a next time?"

Elvira liked that she could joke around with Michael. She could tell he was enjoying the chase.

"That part is up to you," she said.

"How about we go ice skating this Friday?" Michael asked. "I was thinking we could go over to Wollman Rink in Central Park. If you're not sick of me falling all over the place maybe we'll get a drink after."

Elvira said curtly, "Under one condition, you have to tell me more about you. No more closed off, macho man nonsense."

Elvira was determined to crack Michael's shell. She could tell he was a little closed off. Elvira had the chance to see the happy and loose person he could be on their date. Her goal was to help him have that all the time.

Michael laughed. "Deal, I'll see you Friday then."

The weather was perfect for a night in Manhattan. The cold wasn't unbearable, but comfy. A light sweater or jacket would be good enough to get through the night. Wollman Rink was packed with families and couples. The lights from the buildings around Central Park lit up the rink. The beginning of Christmas season was only around the corner. There was music playing in the background.

Michael and Elvira sat on a bench. The two of them put on their ice skates. Michael didn't know that Elvira was an experienced skater. She used to roller blade throughout the city in her twenties. Michael on the other hand, had never picked up skates in his entire life. Elvira skated right onto the rink with little effort. Michael slipped and held the side barrier for support.

"Have you ever been skating before," Elvira asked.

Michael laughed. "I couldn't skate if my life depended on it. Try not to laugh at me too much."

Elvira skated about fifteen feet away from Michael. She shouted, "Skate out to me!"

Michael tried to move away from the barrier. He slipped and fell on his back. Elvira tried not to laugh. He pulled himself back up onto his feet. Elvira moved a little closer to him.

Michael breathed heavily, "I don't know if I can."

"Try it one more time, but this time push off the barrier," Elvira said. "Don't worry I'll catch you if you fall."

Michael finally caught his breathe again. "Can I trust you?" Michael asked.

Elvira pointed to Michael. "Trust is a two-way street."

Michael pushed himself off the barrier and skated out to Elvira. He waved his arms in the air to try and keep his balance. Elvira held her arms out to catch Michael as he propelled into her. Michael held onto her arm to keep his balance on the ice.

"Now was that so bad?" Elvira asked.

"That was actually kind of fun."

Michael attempted to skate off on his own and slipped again. Elvira grabbed his hand to pull him back up.

Elvira smiled. "I'll guide you around the rink."

Michael and Elvira skated around the rink together. They moved slowly, the other skaters passed by them quickly. Michael wasn't any better at skating than the little children who were there with their parents. The skaters in the rink came alive when the Bee Gees' top single record started playing over the speakers. Everyone danced on the ice and moved along with the rhythm of the music.

"We should be dancing," Michael said excitedly.

"You can barely skate and you want to dance on the ice?" she asked.

Michael let go of Elvira's hand. He stood on his own confidently. "I can't skate, but I still got moves."

Michael danced in one place and almost fell again. Elvira
was skeptical of what Michael was up to. She still decided to
play along.

"I'll tell you what," she said. "Dance right here on the ice.
If I like your moves, there might be a kiss in it for you. What
do you say?"

The funny part about all of this is that Michael could
dance well. He just had to overcome his fear of the ice. The
bet Elvira made with him was more than enough motivation.
He was determined to get that kiss. More than that, he wanted
to impress her. Michael snapped his fingers and skated from
side to side. He tried to move along to the rhythm of the
music playing. Elvira loved the way that Michael danced. She
thought he was cute skating around in one small circle.

"You're not so bad," Elvira said.

Elvira followed Michael's lead and danced along. Michael
spun Elvira around and pulled her into his body. He held
Elvira tightly and gazed into her eyes. "Maybe I downplayed
the bad skating a little bit."

Elvira bit her lip and smiled. "I think you hustled me for
that kiss."

Elvira tripped while dancing and began to fall. Michael
reacted quickly and caught her before she hit the ice. Michael
lost his balance while holding her. They fell on top of each
other. The two of them laughed so much their faces turned
a light purple color. Elvira and Michael looked at each other

for a few moments. She kissed Michael slowly while they lay on the cold ice together.

"Even in my most goofy moments I could be romantic," Michael said jokingly.

"I don't think you're goofy at all. I love your sense of humor. You probably think I'm the weird one."

Elvira looked away from Michael. Elvira felt Michael did think she was weird. As Michael got to know Elvira better, he would get to see how odd she really was. She was nervous he would get sick of it. Elvira had no clue she kept answering the questions to Michael's self-made test. To him, it was important that a woman was unique. Michael motioned for Elvira to look at him.

"I think you're a little out there, but I've always liked girls who were original. I don't think weird is the right word. I think you're, you're quirky! And I love it."

"Well since you love it, I have a request," Elvira asked. "Can we go get chicken thighs? I'm craving roasted chicken thighs. I even brought my Buck Seasoning."

"Chicken thighs huh? I think I know a place we can go."

By the time Michael and Elvira got to a supermarket, it was almost closed. Michael had to convince an employee that he desperately needed to purchase one item. He filled a shopping cart with chicken thighs and raced towards the register with Elvira by his side. It all happened so fast that Elvira didn't have a clue what was going on.

"I hope you know I meant cooked chicken thighs, right?" Elvira asked curiously.

"Of course, I did. I figured instead of going to Kentucky Fried Chicken, we might as well cook them ourselves."

Elvira shook her head. "I hate to break it to you, I'm not the best cook in the world."

Michael handed the cashier money. He placed the chicken thighs in a large brown paper bag. "Who said you were going to cook?"

Elvira couldn't believe what she was hearing. A man had never offered to cook for her before. That would be a shocking thing for most women of her era to hear. Men usually let their wives or girlfriends do the cooking. Michael was different because of his Italian ancestry. It wasn't a big deal if a man decided to pick up a pan and cook. In Italy, both men and women knew how to cook. They passed those talents onto the children and grandchildren.

Michael brought Elvira back to his apartment to cook the chicken thighs. Elvira watched him vigorously clean his apartment. Michael grabbed a garbage bag from under his kitchen sink cabinet. He started to throw away any garbage lying around. Michael didn't think twice about what he grabbed. The bag quickly filled to the top in a matter of minutes. He placed the bag in a large trash bin. Michael washed his hands at the sink.

"I forgot to mention, I'm kind of a chef," Michael said jokingly.

You're really a chef?" Elvira asked.

Michael went into a cabinet and pulled out a variety of chicken seasonings. "No, I'm just Italian."

Elvira put away the seasonings Michael took out. She waved her finger at him. "Not so fast buddy don't forget the Buck Seasoning."

Michael scratched his head. "How could I forget that?"

Elvira handed Michael the Buck Seasoning. She washed her hands and put on an apron that was hanging on the stove.

"I want you to teach me how to cook," Elvira said. "We can cook this meal together. Who knows, if you teach me well enough maybe one day I'll surprise you with a home cooked meal."

Michael's jaw dropped. His eyes opened wide. If there was one thing Michael loved more than women, it was food. Food was the way to Michael's heart. To Michael, that gesture was one of the most meaningful things Elvira could have ever said.

"Those words are music to my ears. I couldn't get a girl to cook for me if my life depended on it," Michael said.

"I'm thirty years old and a man has never offered to cook me anything," Elvira said sadly.

Michael got the notion that Elvira may have not been treated well in the past. He couldn't help but wonder why the kindness he showed her seemed strange. For a man to have such disrespect for a woman was crazy in his eyes.

Michael raised his eyebrows. He said reassuringly, "Clearly you've never dated an Italian man before."

Elvira knew Michael had let those words slip. They never agreed on formally dating, but it was clear that was on the forefront of Michael's mind. Michael tried to pretend like he never said anything and continued preparing the chicken thighs.

Elvira stepped in front of Michael. She smiled at him seductively. She gently nudged his arm. "Hmmm, dating, now are we?" she asked.

Michael dropped a few chicken thighs onto the floor. His cover was blown. To Michael, this was a miniature version of hell. Michael truly thought his chances with a great girl flew out the window with those few words. Michael said nervously, "That's something I would like. I mean, if you're interested that is."

Elvira hugged Michael and kissed him before he could say another word. She said softly, "That's definitely something I would be interested in."

Michael's mistake was that he automatically grouped Elvira with his past girlfriends. He was used to getting mocked or turned away from. It made him emotionally closed off. Michael failed to see that Elvira had no problem dating him. In fact, she was overjoyed that he was even thinking about it.

Are you Italian by any chance?" Michael asked. "I think you'd make a great Italian."

Elvira laughed. "I'm definitely not Italian."

Michael and Elvira finished marinating the chicken thighs then placed them in the oven. They sat on the couch together and waited for their meal to cook. Michael put his arm around Elvira. She moved his arm and rested her head on his chest. Her hand stroked his abdomen.

"I normally don't do this you know," Michael said.

"Cook chicken thighs with girls you meet at coffee shops?" Elvira said playfully.

Michael ran his fingers through her hair. "Very funny, but no. I'm going to keep my promise and tell you more about me. Actually, I'm going to tell you something no one knows about me."

Elvira was happy Michael finally decided to confide in her. She could tell that it was extremely difficult for him.

"Growing up, I had two passions. For a while, I wanted to be a singer. Then I realized my voice wasn't all that great. I took up writing and I fell in love with it ever since. I have a journal filled with experiences in my life that I would love to make into a novel. I want to be able to leave my mark on this earth before I move on."

Elvira was amazed by Michael's passion. It could be seen through his eyes how badly he wanted to have an impact on others. Michael's outlook on life was impressive and inspiring to her. They had the same burning determination and similar goals.

Elvira danced her fingers along Michael's arm. "You know," she said. "I'm a singer. I've been a singer my whole life. I moved here when I was only seventeen years old from Pennsylvania. I spent a year in college studying Psychology, then I dropped out. I decided I wanted to be a Broadway star. It was a dream of mine since I was a little girl. I was doing well for a while, but then things ended up not working out. I guess it just wasn't in the cards for me."

Even though their relationship was new, it was already special. The two of them were drawn to one another. They had this gift of being able to see through each other. Michael and Elvira had the ability to read each other's feelings. It was a deep connection of the heart, mind, and soul.

"That's bold," Michael said. "It must have been tough to be on your own at such a young age. I'd never be able to do something like that."

Elvira turned her head away from Michael. She started to get emotional. Michael felt a slight tremor of fear throughout her body. Her eyes resembled clear reflective pools of water.

"I needed to get away from it all," Elvira said emotionally. "I wasn't completely alone when I came to New York. I met a guy. He eventually became my boyfriend for a few years. It didn't work out too well, but I still ended up making a life for myself here I guess."

With only a quick glance, Michael saw all the pain in Elvira's eyes. It radiated off her skin. Her story was written on the wall for Michael to read. Michael gently moved her body to face his. "Elvira... What happened?"

Elvira cried in Michael's arms. Michael used all the power in his body to stay strong for her. On the inside, seeing her like this killed him. His heart hurt just as much as hers. Michael felt her pain, and it was a pain unlike any other before. Their bond was strong enough that when one hurt, they both did. Their feelings were the same down to the degree.

Elvira held back her tears, so she could speak. "His name was John. I met him a few months after I came here. I was lonely. I didn't really have anyone else. He seemed to be a guy that was nice enough. We eventually moved in together. John made me feel like I was some worthless whore he picked up off the street. He abused me daily both mentally and physically. The worst part of it all is that I bought into it all. I felt like I deserved everything I was getting, and that maybe John was right."

Michael finally broke down. He cried with Elvira. Hearing her story killed him. Growing up, Michael learned to be a protector. He lived in an abusive household. Protecting his mother from the constant abuse his father brought all of them. Because of his past experiences, Michael learned to lay his life on the line for the people he loved. His mind was programmed this way. It didn't process in Michael's brain that someone could hurt her like this. He only knew Elvira as sweet and innocent. Michael saw how passionate she was about everything that she did. It took every ounce of Michael's being not to fall in love with her the first day they met. To Michael, she was perfect. The idea of anyone trying to make her great qualities bad, killed him. Michael was deeply sad, but at the same time filled with rage towards John. He hugged her tightly. He held her face between his smooth hands and wiped away all the tears.

"Elvira, you can't possibly believe any of that is true. Can't you see how amazing you are? I've only known you for a few weeks and you already have a huge impact on my life. I've suffered from severe anxiety since I was a child. I also grew up with a stutter that still plagues me until this day. When I'm with you, I don't feel any anxiety. I feel normal. You're like a breath of fresh air into my body. When I'm with you, I don't stutter no matter how much I talk. Ask any of my friends how often they see me dancing on ice skates. This is all because of you. Knowing you has made me a better person and makes me continue wanting to keep at it. You allow me to be Michael Coniglio."

Elvira stopped crying. It was hard for her to process the compliments Michael was giving her. Elvira had a hard time believing she had these great qualities. She had a hard time believing Michael cared for her this much. She wondered if she really made such an impact on his life. The kindness, the cooking, the intimacy, and most importantly, the connection was all new to her. She had a hard time trusting any man, but she knew Michael was different. It was a scary feeling.

Elvira said, "Michael."

Michael kissed her. He pointed at her and then smiled. "Don't let anyone ever tell you that you're worthless. Worthless is the last word that describes you. I've never met a more interesting person in my life. All I want to do is talk to you, day and night."

"That may be the most beautiful thing anyone has ever said to me," Elvira said passionately.

The oven bell rang loudly. Michael ran over to the oven and opened it to check on the chicken thighs. He smelled the fresh chicken in the air. With excitement he took the chicken out of the oven and placed it on the counter. He made a plate for the two of them. When he turned around, he saw Elvira asleep. Michael placed the plates back down on the counter. He filled a cup with water and placed it next to Elvira. Then, Michael covered her with a blanket. He sat in a chair across from her, crossed his arms, and fell asleep.

The next morning, Michael woke up before Elvira. He thought she looked beautiful, even while she was sleeping.

He opened a can of fresh espresso and smelled it. The aroma alone could wire even the most tired human being. Michael placed the coffee in a *maginet pot*, which was slang for an espresso maker. He put on an Italian flag apron wearing only boxers and a tank top. This sight would be humorous to anyone. He was determined to surprise Elvira with breakfast before she woke up. He decided to cook pancakes for the two of them. While he cooked, he sang "Love Is Here to Stay." Between the singing and the strong smell of coffee brewing, Elvira slowly awoke from her deep sleep.

Elvira found herself wrapped in a blanket and with a tall glass of ice-cold water next to her.

She tried to remember if she covered herself before she fell asleep. It took a few minutes for her to process Michael did all of this. She drank her water, then peered over the couch and watched Michael sing. She adored his voice, he sounded just like a crooner. Still wrapped in the blanket, Elvira pulled herself off the couch. She hummed along with Michael. He turned around, and in that moment a thunderbolt struck his heart. He couldn't get over the way Elvira looked. Her hair was messy, she was wrapped in a blanket from head to toe, and her eyes were glowing. She looked beautiful the way she was. It was a natural kind of beauty. If she never wore makeup again, it would never bother him.

"Is that breakfast I smell?" Elvira asked excitedly.

Michael flipped the pancakes from the pan and into the air. He smiled at her. "Yes, it is. I hope you like pancakes."

The strong smell of coffee filled the air as the *maginet pot* brewed. Michael poured the two of them coffee and placed the mugs on the table. He brought over two plates filled with stacks of pancakes. Elvira sat down at the kitchen table.

"We need to talk about last night," Elvira said coldly.

Michael sat down. He didn't touch a stitch of food yet. Her tone of voice made him uneasy. "Ok," he said.

Elvira crossed her arms. She pouted. "If we are going to start dating, you need to keep wearing boxers and aprons. I think it's sexy."

They both laughed together. Elvira was an incredibly good actress. She used that to her advantage when she pulled pranks like this. Michael couldn't get enough of it—he loved to be teased by her. Michael got up out of his seat and picked Elvira up, playfully. She squirmed around and laughed as he carried her over to the couch and dropped her. They wrestled around playfully pushing and kicking each other.

4

CHAPTER

Allison was waiting outside a movie theater for Elvira to arrive. On this particular night, the movie theater was showing a special screening of *Casablanca*. This was one of Elvira's favorite films. To her, the film portrayed an era of class. The way the characters dressed was tasteful. Men donned suits and top hats while women wore long elegant dresses. Elvira felt people lived life differently then as opposed to now. She wished she could have lived her youth during such a time. Elvira also had an affinity for Ingrid Bergman. She was a stunning woman and actress, carrying herself with a quality of originality. She never sold out to Hollywood when they kept pressuring her to change. The beauty of *Casablanca* is that it pulls on the strings of one's heart. It tells the story of a forbidden love, a love between soulmates. It shows the monumental sacrifice a man is willing to make for the woman he loves.

Allison scolded Elvira for being late. She only came to the movies as a favor. Elvira didn't know anyone else who would enjoy watching such an old film. The difference in the demeanor of the two women was astounding. Elvira watched *Casablanca* on the edge of her seat as if it was the first time she's ever seen it. Allison couldn't keep pace with the story. She thought it was too confusing. Elvira and Allison exited the movie theater with two different mindsets.

"What did you think Allison?" Elvira asked. "It's probably one of your favorite movies now."

Allison shrugged her shoulders. "To be honest, I really didn't get it. Why did he leave her at the end? If he really loved her, he should have ran away with her. She wanted to be with him, not the other guy."

Elvira grabbed Allison's hand. "Don't you understand!" Elvira said enthusiastically. "He made the ultimate sacrifice for her to be happy. He thought life would be better for the woman he loved. If she stayed in Casablanca, she would have gotten hurt. He was thinking for the both of them."

Allison shook her head. "Eh, I just don't get it. Maybe it's just me."

Elvira put her head down. "No one really does get it. At least not anyone I know."

Allison and Elvira walked over to a diner across the street. The diner was raggedy. It had a 1950s element to it. The booths and stools were a plush red color. The tables were shining silver. Elvira enjoyed the ambiance of the diner. Allison thought it was just creepy and old. While Elvira and Allison had a strong friendship Allison never wanted to go to these kinds of places with Elvira. Elvira didn't have anyone to share her love of the classics, often feeling alone in this new modern world.

"I mean this in the nicest way possible. Next time, please take someone else. I don't know if I can sit through another old movie like that," Allison said.

Elvira looked out the window of the diner. She stared at the theater back across the street. "I wonder if Michael gets it."

* * *

Billy aggressively drove down the street towards Michael's apartment building. He pulled on the sidewalk and parked on the curb. Billy was never a good driver. Michael always felt like Billy should make people sign waivers before driving with him. Michael entered Billy's car.

"I need you to take me to Radio City Music Hall," Michael said. "Just double park somewhere I'll be in and out."

Billy was disgruntled. He thought Michael wanted to hang out and go for a few drinks. Michael was smart enough to know Billy would have never agreed to drive him unless there was a promise of going out after.

"C'mon Mike," Billy whined. "I thought we were gunna go out for beers? You always have to do this. Can't you just have a drink with your best friend? Why the hell do you need to go to Radio City anyway?"

Michael couldn't help but laugh. Billy sounded exactly like a whiny girlfriend sometimes. "We'll go out for drinks after. I need to pick up tickets for a concert I wanna take Elvira. I'm going to surprise her with tickets to see Tony Bennett."

Billy pulled out of his parking spot and onto the street. He blew a red light and raced down Astoria's small streets.

"What the hell are you taking her to a Tony Bennett concert for? Are you trying to put her to sleep? Good luck getting laid after that, I'm sure she'll be really pumped."

Michael looked at Billy with disgust. "You really are a classless piece of shit," Michael said. "How the fuck do you not like Tony Bennett? Sometimes it's hard for me to believe you're even Italian."

Billy made a sharp turn. The car swerved towards the entrance of the Queensboro Bridge. He yelled at Michael. "When are you gunna stop being such an old man? You take a girl out to see the Stones, not Tony Bennett. Next thing I know you're gunna make her sit through that old movie you're always ranting about. What was it called, Casa-something? Don't cry to me when she runs away."

Michael sighed. "I wonder if she gets it."

5

CHAPTER

Michael exited his apartment building. He took a minute to soak in the sights around him. Lately, the world
looked differently to him. The colors of the skies popped a
clear crystal blue and the clouds, a snowy white. Those colors were always there, but the new vibrant life is what struck
Michael. He now saw the world through a different lens. The
air was suddenly sweet to breathe. Michael walked a few
blocks over to Elvira's apartment. There was an odd skip in
his step. He was for once a happy man.

Michael waited promptly outside Elvira's apartment at
the time they agreed to meet. He stared at the stoop for a
few moments. The moment Michael and Elvira first came
together happened right at this very spot. He couldn't help
but smile at the thought of it. That stoop was a symbol of
something more than he could have even imagined. Without
Michael knowing, Elvira was standing at the top of the steps.
She watched him gaze at the stoop.

Elvira giggled. "I know what you're thinking about," she
said. "That's our stoop."

Michael was lost in his own mind. He jumped when he heard Elvira's voice. Michael was surprised by her sudden appearance. He collected his thoughts. "I like the sound of that," he said. "Our stoop."

Elvira slowly walked down the steps. Michael grabbed her hand and guided Elvira down the final few steps. They greeted each other with a passionate kiss. Michael and Elvira made plans to explore Manhattan tonight. The two of them were spontaneous. Random, thrown together plans like this were always fun for them.

There are few sights in the world better than walking through Manhattan at night. Even though the streets were dirty and there were homeless people everywhere, the views made up for it all. Michael and Elvira walked down Fifth Avenue side by side. As their arms brushed together, Elvira nonchalantly took Michael's hand. She interlocked her fingers between his. Elvira's hand was cold to the touch, sensitive to the weather, his hand warmed hers.

They passed by one of New York City's famous street food stands. This vendor happened to be selling roasted nuts. Elvira stopped to buy a bag of cashews. He studied her as she ate the bag of roasted cashews. Most people would place a few cashews in their hands and throw them in their mouth. This would be the causal way to eat cashews. Elvira on the other hand ate her cashews differently. She took one cashew out of the bag at a time and put the cashew in between her teeth. Almost as if she was savoring every last one of them.

"Has anyone ever told you they love the way you eat cashews?" Michael asked.

Elvira looked completely confused by Michael's statement. "No, I don't believe anyone has ever said that to me."

These were the traits that Michael grew to adore. What he loved about Elvira the most was her originality. Michael knew it would be rare to find another woman that ate cashews that same way. When a person falls in love, they begin to adore the little things about their partner. The way they do or say certain things, it becomes a staple of their personality. This was the day Michael realized that he was starting to fall in love with Elvira.

"I've never seen someone eat cashews like that," Michael said. "It's the most adorable thing. You take them one by one and put them in between your teeth."

"I really eat cashews like that?" Elvira asked curiously.

"Yes!" Michael said.

Michael took a cashew out of the bag. He mimicked the way Elvira ate cashews to show her. They laughed together.

"If you never would have noticed that, I would have never realized I ate cashews that way."

Elvira loved the way Michael noticed things about her. He noticed traits Elvira didn't even know she had. Elvira never realized she ate cashews in this peculiar way. There was one word to describe the way Michael made Elvira feel. That perfect word would be special. Michael made her feel like she was the only woman in the world for him. All the men in Elvira's life happened to let her down. They made her feel like she was disposable. Michael was a different breed of man. He made Elvira feel irreplaceable. At this same moment, Elvira knew she was falling in love with Michael.

They continued to walk down Fifth Avenue. A man was singing on the corner of the street. He left a hat on the floor for people to throw money in. Elvira hummed along to the man's singing. Michael threw a few dollars into the man's hat. The man nodded his head in appreciation.

"Why do you always hum?" Michael asked. "I've never heard you sing before, only hum."

Elvira put her head down. She let out a large sigh. "It's because I was always told I wasn't good enough. By my father, judges, directors, and my boyfriends. I hardly let anyone hear me sing."

Michael stayed silent for a few moments. "Do you trust me?" he asked.

Elvira nodded. "I trust you Michael," she said.

"If you don't mind, I would love to hear you sing."

Elvira paused. She thought about Michael's request for a few moments. She yelled with excitement. "Come with me!"

Elvira grabbed his hand and pulled him in the direction of a department store nearby. They entered the store and passed through all the customers beginning their Christmas shopping.

"Where are you taking me?" he asked.

"You'll see" she said.

Elvira marched towards the back of the store. She kept looking for signs pointing to the nearest restroom. She put her hand up to Michael as she walked into the ladies' room. Michael stood still outside for a few moments. He was extremely confused. Elvira walked in first to make sure it was empty. She came back out of the bathroom and dragged

Michael inside. She looked in all the stalls and found the cleanest one. She shoved Michael into the stall and closed the door behind her. Elvira pushed Michael's shoulders and motioned him to sit down on the toilet seat.

"Wait a minute. Where is this going?" Michael said jokingly.

Elvira punched him in the arm gently. "You're going to hear me sing."

"In a public bathroom?"

"You wouldn't think it, but it's the perfect place. The echo in the bathroom carries my voice well. Now, close your eyes."

Michael closed his eyes. He took a deep breath and prepared to listen. Before she even sang Michael knew she had the voice of an angel. Elvira sang the song, "I've Got a Crush on You." It was an old Gershwin classic covered by many of the greatest singers in history. Elvira carried her voice perfectly. She hit high notes with ease and added a tiny hint of rasp to the chorus. He was completely blown away by the soul behind the words she was singing. You could tell it came from the fire in her belly, the same fire that fueled her passions. As she sang, Michael slowly opened one eye to peek at her. She was moving her body along with the groove of her voice. Her voice was more eloquent than words. The way Elvira sounded was exactly how she was feeling. The first thought that came to Michael's mind when he heard her voice was sexy. He thought her voice was simply astounding. Michael couldn't believe anyone had ever told her she wasn't good enough.

"Holy shit," Michael mumbled.

"What?" Elvira asked nervously.

"You have the voice of an angel," he said softly.

Michael got off the toilet seat. Elvira kissed him. Her body pressed against the back of the stall door. There was a large bang in the bathroom. Michael and Elvira both jumped. Elvira peered outside the stall door and saw a group of women listening to their conversation. They all looked at Elvira and Michael with eyes that resembled a puppy's. They felt the love in the air, despite being in a public bathroom. The group of women nodded at them and left. The two of them quietly exited the bathroom.

The department store was filled with Christmas decorations even though it was too early. Candy canes, Santa hats, and rows of red ribbon were hung from the ceiling at every single section of the store. The vibe was cheerful and pleasant. Michael and Elvira explored the store from top to bottom. They rode the escalators up and down like playful children. Elvira suddenly stopped in the women's department of the store. A row of elegant dresses caught her eye. There had to be hundreds to choose from. Michael followed her. He watched as she combed through a rack of dresses.

"Why don't you try one on?" Michael asked.

"I shouldn't," Elvira said. "I'd be keeping you here all day. I'm very picky."

"What size dress are you?"

"I'm a size four." She paused. "I'd love a dress that's sexy, yet elegant. It should be more along the lines of an evening gown. Nothing too short." She paused. "Oh! And I love any dresses that have an open back."

As Elvira rambled on about the kind of dress she wanted. Michael tore apart the rack of dresses. He looked at each dress quickly, throwing dresses onto the floor and over his shoulder. Michael stopped at one. As Elvira finished her description, Michael laid out the dress he chose in front of her.

"Something like this?" he said.

Elvira gasped. Michael happened to choose the exact type of dress she described. He was listening to her the entire time she described her idea of a nice dress. Elvira looked at a mirror nearby. She placed the dress over her body to get an idea of how it looked on her. Michael came from behind her and kissed her on the cheek.

"Michael how did you know? It's like you read my mind."

"I think you should try it on," Michael said. "See how it fits. It's silk so it should feel nice on your soft skin."

Elvira ran towards the dressing room. She was excited to see herself in the dress. She was even more excited for Michael to see her in the dress he picked out. While Elvira was changing, Michael explored a row of women's hats near the dressing room. One hat stuck out in particular. It looked like more of a summer hat. He wondered for a moment what a summer hat was doing in the store during a winter season. It was beige and had a salmon colored ribbon around it. The ribbon was about a foot long and stretched down the back of the hat. He examined the hat for a few moments.

Michael vividly pictured Elvira wearing this hat. It was exactly her kind of style. The hat was different; the brim was large and would protect her face from the sun. Michael remembered her saying she wasn't fond of staying in the sun for very long. He imagined her wearing this hat on a tropical island. Michael walked back over to the dressing room to wait for Elvira. He placed the hat on top of his head.

Elvira exited the dressing room. His hat was the first thing she noticed. She couldn't help but giggle. "You look adorable Michael," she said.

Michael was silent. All he could concentrate on was the way Elvira looked. She was stunning. The dress fit her perfectly. The dark color brought out the lightness in her eyes. There was a small cut near the bottom of the dress that revealed one leg. The cleavage wasn't too revealing. Her shoulders were bare aside from one small strap. The dress was classy, but at the same time had a sexual element to it.

She spun around slowly. "What do you think?" Elvira asked.

Michael grabbed her hand. He danced with her. "I think you're the most beautiful woman I've ever laid eyes on," he said softly. "Any man on this planet would be lucky to have you."

Elvira's heart felt like it was melting. Her feelings for Michael were growing stronger every moment they spent together. No man had ever paid her such beautiful compliments. She knew Michael was truly one of a kind. Michael made her forget all the problems she had. The pain of her past that viciously haunted her was starting to disappear. She could only concentrate on her feelings for Michael. Elvira wanted Michael to know she wasn't going anywhere. "You must feel pretty lucky, don't you?" she replied.

Michael spun Elvira around. "You need this dress."

Elvira checked the price tag. "I think I might need this dress a year from now because that's how long it would take me to pay it off."

Michael checked the tag. He sighed. "Woah. You weren't kidding." He pointed to the hat he was still wearing. "What about this hat?"

Michael placed the hat on Elvira's head. She looked in the mirror. "I love it!" she said cheerfully. "You're two for two so far. That's impressive."

"I think I know you pretty well," he said confidently. "I'd like to buy you this hat."

"You don't have to do that," she said. "It's really ok, I'll come back another time and get it."

Michael shook his head. "I insist," he said firmly. "I feel bad that you can't get the dress."

Elvira smiled. "Well if you put it that way."

Throughout her life, Elvira was never given presents. Her past boyfriends weren't the kind of men who cared enough. It eventually took a toll on her after a while. Having birthdays and holidays pass without a thoughtful gift was hard. Elvira saw it as a reflection of herself. This form of rejection made her think that maybe she wasn't good enough for a gift.

Elvira walked back in the dressing room to change. Michael scrambled around the dress wrack looking for the exact same dress Elvira had tried on. When Michael found it, he raced over to the register. He asked the cashier to put the dress on hold for him. The cashier informed him that he would have to come back the next day to pick it up. Elvira exited the dressing room. Michael threw the dress behind the cash register abruptly. The cashier gave him an outlandish look. Michael placed the hat on the counter before Elvira came over.

He handed the cashier money. "I'd like to by this hat please," he said nervously.

Michael placed the hat on Elvira's head. She thanked him with a long hug and a kiss. While she changed in the dressing room, Elvira came up with the perfect idea. An idea that would surely help bring Michael out of his shell. She was determined to break down the gigantic wall he built in his mind and heart, a wall that shut out everyone and everything including Elvira.

Although Michael was starting to fall in love with her, emotionally he still had a long road to travel down. In the back of Michael's head, he still had the paralyzing fear of losing Elvira, a fear of getting hurt and all this meaning nothing. Some would say that's a part of life, but to Michael the constant fear was real. It hindered his quality of life in many ways.

Elvira said, "Now it's your turn."

"What?" Michael said. "Me? No, I can't sing. I especially can't sing in front of crowds."

"I heard you at breakfast the other day," Elvira said. "You sound just like Sinatra. Don't be a stick in the mud. I know the perfect place we can go."

The Crooner Club had an ongoing theme. It's what would soon be popularized as one of the first flashback bars. Everything in this bar was authentic to the 1940s. A dark stage with a red curtain stood in the far center of the room. Behind the red curtain was a full band. Sitting on the stage was one seat and a microphone. A large handmade oak bar was filled with patrons drinking in the far corner of the room. Antique tables and chairs surrounded the stage. A sign stood by the stage that read, "Open Mic Night."

Michael and Elvira sat at a table near the front of the stage. A waiter came over to take their orders. "Gimme a Manhattan Special please," Michael said. The waiter acknowledged his request.

The waiter turned to Elvira. "Do you have Asahi Honnama by any chance?" she asked. The waiter shook his head no.

"What's an Asahi Honnama?" Michael asked.

"It's a Japanese style beer I love," Elvira said. "Not many places sell it though. What's a Manhattan Special?"

"It's espresso coffee soda. I figured I could use a nice pick me up."

Elvira turned to the waiter. "That sounds interesting. I'll have a Manhattan Special, also."

Michael loved the atmosphere of the bar. He really felt at home. Michael often lived in a different world for most of his life. You could tell that simply by the kind of drink that he ordered. A Manhattan Special was a very specific drink. It was never heavily advertised and not many people knew what it was. Michael enjoyed living in this older styled world, but the one problem was that it got lonely. When you don't have anyone to share these values and feelings with, it could end up taking a toll on the mind. Luckily for Michael, Elvira happened to live in that same world.

"I'm surprised," Michael said. "I thought I was the only one who drank Manhattan Specials."

"I've never had one before," Elvira said. "But that doesn't mean I'm not willing to try something new. It sounds good. Is it an Italian drink?"

"No, I don't think so," Michael said. "I would know if it was Italian."

Elvira had a feeling Michael was wrong. She shook her head. "I think you're wrong about this one, but I'll let you have your moment."

Michael loved the way that Elvira fired back at him. Some women tended to be robots and go along with whatever a man says. Elvira was the opposite, she held her own opinion. Her opinion was strong, and it was hers. She kept Michael on his toes, always. You never knew what you were going to get with Elvira.

Michael was nervous. Like Elvira, he didn't let anyone hear him sing. However, his fear was different from hers. Michael never sang to anyone in his entire life. He only sang when he was alone driving in a car or taking a shower. There was never a crowd or even a person around. Elvira was the first to ever hear him. "I can't ever imagine performing in front of all these people," Michael said.

Elvira knew Michael was going to try and find a way out of singing. She wanted to put him on the spot and force him out of his comfort zone.

"I'm going to go to the ladies' room quickly," Elvira said.

Elvira got out of her seat and walked towards the bathroom. She approached a man who appeared to be the manager of the bar. Elvira tapped him on the shoulder. "See that guy sitting over there at that table?" she asked. She pointed

Michael out of the large crowd. "He wants a slot in open mic night."

The bar manager acknowledged her request. He said, "You're in luck, he's got the first slot of the night. What's his act going to be?"

Elvira shrugged her shoulders. "He likes to be spontaneous. Expect a song by Sinatra or Tony Bennett. His name is Michael Coniglio.

Elvira walked back over to her table. She smiled and giggled. Elvira had to use all her willpower to conceal her plan. Michael noticed her laughing. "Did I miss the joke?"

The bar manager walked onto the stage. He got the crowd riled up for the first contestant in open mic night. He spoke loudly into a microphone. "Our first contestant of the night is going to be Michael Congilio! Give him a round of applause."

A large spotlight shined on Michael's table. He turned pale. All the color drained from his face. The crowd cheered and whistled for him. Michael turned to Elvira who was smiling and clapping. She leaned over the table and motioned for him to come close to her. Elvira grabbed the sides of his face with her hands and gave him a long kiss. She whispered in his ear. "I know you can do it."

Michael walked onto the stage. He placed his hands in his pockets. His shoulders were down. The red curtain pulled away and the band was revealed. This was probably at the top of Michael's worst nightmares. The talent manager handed him a clip-on bow tie and a neat whiskey. He downed the whiskey with one large swig to help take the edge off his nerves. Michael's face twisted from the bitterness of the drink. The crowd got a real kick out of that. He clipped the bow tie around his neck and grabbed the microphone. The whiskey hit him almost instantly. His demeanor became smooth. He felt the warmth of the alcohol in his blood.

Michael pointed to the crowd, "How's everyone doing tonight?"

The crowd had mixed reactions. They were still feeling him out. Elvira cheered the loudest. She screamed out, "Sing!" The crowd cheered along with her request. They started shouting out "Sing" multiple times.

Michael put his hand up to the crowd. The room got eerily quiet. "Alright. Alright, I'll sing Sinatra." The crowd cheered. Michael coughed into the microphone a few times to clear his voice. "I would like to dedicate this song to a woman I recently met. We met by chance. It was a total stroke of luck. Something you'd see in a Hollywood movie. A few weeks ago, we were nothing more than strangers passing by each other. Now, my whole world changed. It turned upside down, and I couldn't be happier." The crowd stared at Elvira.

Michael sang, "Strangers in the Night." When Michael uttered the first words to the song, Elvira's heart fluttered. He sang with charisma and charm. The full band complimented his voice tremendously. The women in the room screamed as he hit the high notes. Michael ignored all the screams. He walked off the stage and knelt beside Elvira. He sang his heart away right at her feet. Michael wanted Elvira to know all the women in the world could be yearning for him, but he only had eyes for her. Before he went back to the stage, he kissed her hand. The crowd went absolutely wild for the two of them.

Michael chose to sing "Strangers in the Night" for a reason. He felt that it perfectly described the way they met. Two people who came together by chance and found love. Michael knew Elvira sang her heart out earlier that night. The song she chose was intimate. There was meaning and feeling behind it. It described the way she was starting to feel about Michael. He picked up on all of it and wanted to reciprocate with a song of his own. It was a way for two people who were closed off to communicate how they were feeling without saying the words.

Michael walked off the stage. Elvira greeted him with a Margarita, Michael graciously accepted the drink. He took a large swig.

"Can I buy the man of the hour a drink?" Elvira asked.

"You're going to have to wait in line like the rest of the girls," Michael joked.

Elvira pulled his bow tie. She stood nose to nose with Michael. Her lips were almost touching his. "What are the chances I can take you home tonight?" Elvira chuckled.

Michael raised his eyebrows. He knew she was kidding around, but he played along. "Very high."

Elvira got even closer to Michael. Her lips grazed his. "Try again next time," she whispered. She playfully pulled away from Michael and trotted towards the door and exited the club.

The heat of the moment was intense, even though it was all in good fun. Elvira made Michael sweat. He mumbled to himself, "My God." Michael followed her out the door.

Michael hailed a cab outside the Crooner Club. Elvira waited beside him for the cab to pull over. The cab driver aggressively drove onto the curb and hits a massive puddle. The water missed Elvira by a few inches and splashed over Michael. He was completely soaked by dirty street water. Michael's initial reaction was to scream at the cabbie, but instead his anger dissipated. He never wanted Elvira to see the old Michael, who had a short fuse and punched holes through walls. Elvira's presence alone helped him remain calm. Since meeting her, all the anger he had built up in his heart was slowly leaving. She was changing the core of his being by undoing all the negativity and evil Michael had endured in his life.

"We need to get you cleaned up," Elvira said.

"My place or yours?" Michael joked.

Elvira smirked and rolled her eyes. They entered the cab. Elvira instructed the driver to take them back to her apartment in Astoria.

"This cab really smells funky," Elvira said.

Michael looked down at his clothes. He pulled his wet and dirt filled shirt up to his nose. His shirt smelled like mold.

"I think that's me," Michael said.

Elvira looked at Michael and tried not to laugh. There was dirt all over his face and shirt. She couldn't help but think about how cute Michael looked when he was dirty. He looked like he just came back from a hard day working construction. Elvira thought it was sexy.

When the two of them got back to Elvira's apartment, Michael was still soaking wet. Elvira opened a closet door and handed him a few towels that were inside.

"You can take a shower if you want," Elvira said. "The bathroom is the first door on the right."

Michael suddenly became shy. He started to ruminate. Would she truly feel comfortable with him taking a shower in her apartment? What other clothes would he wear? He clearly couldn't put these clothes back on. Michael didn't want Elvira to think he was trying to take advantage of her in any way. Could he really be misreading a clear sign? Michael walked towards the bathroom.

"What should I do with these dirty clothes?" Michael asked innocently.

"Take them off in the bathroom then hand them to me," she said. "I might have a big T-shirt lying around here some-where. I'll try to dry the pants."

"Maybe I should just go home," Michael said. "It's only a few blocks."

Elvira had a feeling Michael was acting a little off. "Are you embarrassed to take a shower in my apartment?"

Michael became defensive. He didn't mind taking a shower in her apartment. The last thing Michael wanted was for Elvira to assume he was just another jerk.

"No, it's not that...I don't know. I just didn't want you to get the wrong idea or anything." Michael walked into the bathroom and closed the door behind him. He sat on the toilet and put his head in his hands. Michael thought he looked weak. He was embarrassed. This was his inner self critic talking.

Elvira happened to understand exactly what he was trying to say. Most men would have probably stripped naked right there in front of her, not having any regard for her feelings. Not having any respect for her as a woman. Michael on the other hand, stopped to think about it. That's because he truly cared. Elvira was happy that Michael decided to be such a gentleman about something so small. It spoke volumes about his character.

Elvira knocked on the bathroom door. "Can I have your pants?" she asked.

Michael handed her the pants through the crack of the door. He closed the door quickly. She knocked on the door again.

"Michael," she said softly.

Michael pressed his forehead against the door. "Yes," he sighed.

Elvira pressed her forehead against the door. "I know what you did there. I know exactly what you were trying to tell me. I want to thank you for being careful with me."

Michael smiled. His anxious thinking stopped. "I never want you to think I'm like the people who hurt you. I'm different. I'll never let you down."

Elvira placed her hand on the door. She was silent for a few moments. She could hear the sincerity in his voice. Elvira knew Michael meant everything he said. There was never any exaggeration or lying.

"In the past, I've made mistakes. I met bad people. I've had a lot of heartache. I guess you could say I'm a little reckless sometimes. Not one person stopped to care about it all. They kept taking advantage of me. But you. That didn't even cross your mind. Respect from men is a really big thing for me. You have done nothing but give me respect. This takes a lot for me to say, but I trust you."

It bothered Michael that Elvira had a hard life. Michael wanted to do anything in his power to take her suffering away. He couldn't picture Elvira doing anything terrible. To him, she was fragile and gentle. She was this amazing woman who created a life for herself in one of the world's biggest cities. She was inspiring and talented. She had so much to offer the world. No matter the terrible deed, he would never judge her. When Michael loved, it was true and unconditional.

"I see someone completely different from what you're describing," Michael said. "I see a beautiful, independent woman who learned from her past mistakes. A woman who is going to have me here to take care of her from now on."

The more Michael spoke, the more alive Elvira felt. His words meant the world to her. The beautiful words that rolled off his tongue were intimate. She walked away from the door. Elvira sat on the couch with a hair dryer attempting to dry Michael's pants. There was a smile on her face that wouldn't fade away.

Michael finally stepped into the shower. The warm water falling on his body relaxed his tense muscles. He leaned against the tile wall and soaked in the warmth of the water. The steam of the shower filled the air in the bathroom. The dirt came pouring off his body. Michael dried himself with a towel. He looked in the mirror. He flexed his chest and arm muscles a few times to make sure they popped.

Michael opened the door to the bathroom. The steam poured out into the rest of the apartment. Michael entered the living room with just a towel around his waist. Elvira tried not to look at Michael, but it was difficult. There was water still lightly dripping from his body. His chest was sculpted and hairy. His biceps weren't defined, but large. He smelled like fresh soap. There was an essence of manliness about him. A sexual tension between the two of them filled the room. Elvira unknowingly bit her lip. She tried to center herself.

"Your pants are almost dry," Elvira said softly. She looked down at the pants trying to avoid eye contact with Michael.

"Thanks for letting me take a shower here," Michael said. "It feels good to get all that dirt off me. Did you find that shirt by any chance?"

Elvira got up off the couch. She walked a full circle around Michael into the bedroom. It was clear she avoided standing too close to him. Michael finally started to pick up on what was going on. He was flattered. Michael grabbed his pants off the couch. While he walked back to the bathroom, he checked them for any stains from the dirt. Elvira walked back towards the living room. She was trying to determine whether the shirt would be able to fit Michael or not. The two of them bumped into one another. Elvira slammed into Michael's bare chest. Michael's instant reaction was to grab his towel and stop it from falling off his waist.

Michael and Elvira stood and did nothing. They both felt this animalistic yearning to jump on one another. Neither of them made a move. They basked in the moment, the feeling of sexual euphoria. Michael tied the towel around his waist tighter, so it wouldn't fall. Elvira continued to breathe into his chest. She was so close that she could hear Michael's heart beating. With one finger, Michael moved Elvira's chin slightly to the left. He kissed her neck. His lips were soft and felt warm on her skin. She beamed with pleasure. Elvira placed her hands on his chest. She filled her hands with Michael's skin, feeling the hair from his chest between her fingers. Michael moved further down her neck and kissed her collar bone. She let out a light moan. Elvira lifted Michael's head to face hers and feverishly kissed him.

Michael and Elvira slammed against the wall. His towel was still hanging on by a thread. Michael picked up her legs with his hands and pressed her body against the wall. His towel finally fell to the floor. Elvira's hands clawed into Michael's back. Even though she was still fully clothed, Elvira could feel the sensation of Michael's naked skin touching her body. Filled with passion, each breath grew heavier as the moments passed. Michael's hands moved down Elvira's body until he reached her breasts.

Elvira whispered. "Michael," she moaned quietly.

"Yes," Michael said.

"I don't think I'm ready yet," Elvira said softly.

Michael and Elvira looked at each other. Without saying another word, Michael complied. He gently released Elvira. She looked down at Michael's naked body and raised her eyebrows. She pointed down with one finger. "I think you forgot to put your towel back on."

Michael looked down at himself. He awkwardly smiled and abruptly tied the towel around his waist again. Michael picked his pants up off the floor. He went back into the bathroom to change.

Elvira collected her thoughts. She placed her hands on her chest and let out a large sigh of pleasure. "Jesus Christ."

Michael's head popped out of the bathroom. "What was that?" he asked.

"Jesus Christ!" she said quickly. "We need to talk more about Jesus. I've been meaning to talk about your faith."

Michael awkwardly smiled. "Ok, we can talk about Jesus. Just not with my clothes off." They both laughed together.

6

CHAPTER

Michael and Billy raced through a crowd of people at the department store. He was in search of the dress he put on hold for Elvira. The store was still filled with angry Christmas shoppers. Shopping in New York during the holidays could become a stressful experience. Billy was annoyed that Michael once again dragged him on another adventure he thought was meaningless.

"Why did you drag me here Mike?" Billy asked.

"Because I need you to back me up in case I get into a fight with an angry Christmas shopper," Michael joked.

Michael approached the cashier who kept Elvira's dress on hold. The cashier wasn't tending to the needs of customers, sitting behind the register filing her nails, ignoring any questions the customers asked. Michael nicely waved his hand to get her attention.

"Hello, remember me?" Michael asked. "I was here yesterday and asked you to put a dress on hold for me."

The cashier grunted. She glanced under the register at an empty box that read, "holds." "There's nothing here," the cashier replied. "Sorry." The cashier turned her back to Michael and went back to filing her nails.

Michael felt sick. He saw the way Elvira looked at that dress. Her reaction reminded him of a child opening presents from Santa Claus on Christmas morning. Throughout her life, Elvira never got presents. Years of birthdays and holidays passed without her ever receiving a thoughtful gift from a man. She eventually thought it was because she didn't deserve one. The saddest part of it all was that Elvira would have been fine with a simple card with a thoughtful note. This gesture would have meant more than an expensive gift.

Michael tapped the cashier's shoulder. "You're joking right? I was here yesterday. You looked right at me when I threw the dress behind the counter. I asked to put it on hold."

The cashier sighed. She crossed her arms and pouted. "Look sir!" she yelled. "I can't keep track of the hundreds of customers that come in here a day. If it's not here, then someone probably bought it. Christmas is coming, what more do you expect?"

Michael was getting angry. Billy tried to pull Michael away from the cashier before he said something stupid. Michael marched back over to the women's section of the store. He vigorously looked through a rack of dresses. Billy stood next to him in awe.

"You can't be serious," Billy complained.

Michael ignored him. "Hold this for me."

Michael piled the dresses in Billy's arms. He was completely tearing apart the rack. The stack of dresses eventually got so high that Billy could barely see in front of him.

"Mike, the people in the store are gunna think we're gay."

"Well, that wouldn't be a surprise, I always thought you were gay," Michael snickered.

Billy dropped the pile of dresses on the floor. He crossed his arms. Billy was never the kind of man who could take a joke lightly. Michael held one dress in his hand. The dress he originally chose for Elvira was gone, but this one may have been even more beautiful. He walked over to the mirror and held the dress in the air.

"Next thing I know you're gunna try it on," Billy said.

Michael examined the dress. "What do you think?" he asked.

Billy rolled his eyes. "It's fine Mike, can we get out of here?"

Michael was deep in thought. He tried to visually picture her in this dress. He let the material of the dress run through his fingers. It didn't feel like silk. Michael threw the dress on the floor. He shook his head. "There goes my plan. You should have seen her face Billy. She wanted that dress in the worst way. All I want to do is make her happy. It would have been such a nice surprise. I bet she loves surprises."

Billy put his hand on Michael's shoulders. "You know what would make you feel better? A nice cold drink." Billy guided Michael towards the exit before he changed his mind. On the way towards the exit, Michael noticed a female mannequin. It stood tall in the window of the store. Michael walked away from Billy and came closer to it. Michael's face lit up. He got Billy's attention and raced over to the window. The mannequin happened to be wearing Elvira's dress.

"Gimme a hand!" Michael yelled.

Billy's jaw dropped. "Are you fucking kidding me? You're really gunna strip that mannequin down from the display window in front of all those people on Fifth Avenue?"

Michael shrugged his shoulders. "The things I'd do for love."

Billy fired back, "The things you do because you're a sap."

Michael and Billy dragged the mannequin out of the display window and onto the floor. Michael took apart the arms and legs of the mannequin and removed the dress. Michael proudly carried the dress all the way back to the women's department to the nasty cashier who lost it in the first place. He placed the dress on the register.

"I'd like to buy this dress please. You know the dress you said that wasn't here?"

The cashier once again was not fazed. She rang up the dress and placed it in a large cardboard box that bore the name of the store. "You don't have any gift wrap?" Michael asked. The cashier pointed to a small room in the corner where they wrapped the gift boxes.

Billy interceded in the conversation. "Can we please fucking go now!" he yelled.

"Five minutes," Michael said shortly.

He walked into the gift wrapping room. There were at least fifty samples of gift wrap on the wall to choose from. Billy's eyes were popping out of his head with anger. He continued to scream, "What the hell is wrong with you? Enough is enough."

Michael examined every single kind of wrapping paper on the wall. "You wouldn't understand," Michael said. "I have to do this the right way."

Most of the wrapping paper had odd mixtures of colors. It almost looked like the kind of wrapping for a child's toy. Michael chose one style of wrapping paper that stuck out. It was plain white, but had small designs carved into the paper itself. Instead of being flimsy, this paper had a smooth feel to it. It felt more like plastic than actual paper. A woman behind the counter wrapped the box at Michael's request.

"That's some beautiful dress," the woman said. "Your lady is a lucky one."

Michael smiled and nodded. "Give me the biggest, most elaborate bow you have to wrap around the box."

The bow was a bright blue color and had a white stripe going across it. The woman behind the counter tied it in such a fashion where the bow popped. Michael smiled and the thought of Elvira seeing the big bow. He knew how excited she would be to tear the gift wrapping apart.

Billy hissed, "Take the dumb smile of your face."

Michael patted Billy on the back. "You'll understand one day," Michael said calmly. "When you find the woman of your dreams, you'd want to do anything for her to. She'd be one of a kind. A woman God made just for you."

Billy rolled his eyes. "Since when did you become so holy?" he asked. "What's all this God talk about now? You haven't gone to church in years."

Michael put his head down. "For a while, I lost faith. My life took a bad turn, and I had no one to blame but God. I was always a good person, I began to ask why me? You wanna know what Billy? Now I understand why. Everything led me to this very moment. Let's say I found the inspiration to get me back on the right side of the afterlife."

* * *

Uncle Giuseppe's, an Italian import store was truly one of a kind. They sold everything from coffee and fresh pasta, to cookies and Italian soda. The owner of the store was an old Italian woman named Signora Bianchi. Signora Bianchi was around five feet tall. She wore very thick glasses and a flower printed dress. Her hair was completely white and pinned back in a bun.

Uncle Giuseppe's was filled with old Italian men and women speaking their native language. It was sparkling clean. There wasn't a speck of dust on any shelf. Fresh cured meats hung from the ceiling above the checkout counter. Behind the register was a wall filled with pictures of Jesus, the Virgin Mary, and various saints. Signora Bianchi sat in a chair waiting to gleefully greet her customers.

Elvira entered the store. It was clear to the rest of the patrons that she was an outsider. She looked confused and had trouble reading many of the food ingredient labels that were all in Italian. She asked people standing around for help, but none of the other customers spoke English well enough. Signora Bianchi walked over to Elvira and tapped her on the shoulder. Her Italian accent was thick and hard to understand, but she spoke fluent English.

"Do you need help sweetheart?" Signora Bianchi asked.

Elvira's face lit up. She was happy to hear that someone in the store spoke English and was friendly enough to help her.

"Yes please!" she said excitedly. "I need help picking out ingredients for this pasta recipe I came up with."

Elvira pulled a piece of paper out of her pocket with the recipe on it. She handed it to Signora Bianchi. Signora Bianchi put the paper close to her eyes as physically possible. After reading it for a few moments, she tore it to shreds.

"No," Signora Bianchi said.

Elvira gasped in shock. Signora Bianchi grabbed a piece of paper and a pen from the checkout counter.

"May I ask what you are trying to make?" Signora Bianchi asked.

Elvira crossed her arms. She became defensive. "Well, I was planning on making a pasta dish for my boyfriend."

Signora Bianchi raised her eyebrows. She had a feeling this was why Elvira was here. Signora Bianchi was around seventy-five years old and wise. She was not only known for her import store, but the great advice she gave her customers.

"Tell me *Gioia*, is this boyfriend of yours is Italian?" she asked.

Elvira nodded. Signora Bianchi wrote down a new recipe. She motioned for Elvira to come close to her. Elvira had to crouch down because she was seven inches taller than her.

"The way to every Italian man's heart is through his stomach," Signora Bianchi snickered. "I write down my families' recipe for Bolognese sauce. I haven't shared this recipe with anyone in my entire life. I've kept it secret for years, even from my own husband. God rest his soul."

Signora Bianchi made the sign of the cross. Elvira was confused by Signora Bianchi's kindness. She just ripped up her recipe and then randomly divulged a family secret to a stranger.

"I don't understand," Elvira said. "Why would you give away such an important family secret to a total stranger?"

Signora Bianchi pinched Elvira's cheek playfully. "Because he told me to," she said.

At this point, Elvira thought this woman was senile. Elvira thought Signora Bianchi may have some form of Alzheimer's disease.

"Signora, who's he? There's nobody else here?" Elvira asked politely.

Signora Bianchi pointed to a picture of Jesus behind the counter. Elvira suddenly understood what she was trying to say. Elvira was so shocked by this response, she had to sit down. Jesus played a large role in Elvira's life. Christianity changed her forever. She turned to a life of faith after Jesus revealed himself to her with a spiritual sign. She felt extremely close to her religion and its values.

Signora Bianchi grabbed Elvira's hand and held it tightly. She whispered into Elvira's ear. "You've suffered long enough dear. Now it's your turn to be happy. I put Michael in your life for a reason."

Elvira turned pale and felt faint. If Elvira stood, she would have probably fallen to the floor. She couldn't believe that Signora Bianchi said Michael's name. Elvira knew deep in her heart that Jesus was trying to reach out to her. That maybe there was a higher meaning to her relationship with Michael. That maybe this was all fate.

Signora Bianchi kissed Elvira on the cheek and guided her out of her seat. She took Elvira around the store and helped her pick out the items needed to make the sauce. They placed everything in a large plastic basket.

As they walked around the store, the radio played Tony Bennett's "The Best Is Yet to Come." When the song came on, Elvira stared at the speaker it was coming from. She passed a row of Italian soft drinks and saw a large bottle of Manhattan Special. She smiled.

"I knew it was an Italian drink," she mumbled to herself. "Maybe I'm more Italian than I thought."

Elvira added the bottle of Manhattan Special to her basket. Signora Bianchi spent the next hour with Elvira explaining the directions on how to make the sauce. When they finally got all the ingredients together, Elvira brought the items to the counter. Signora Bianchi bagged everything for her and refused to take any money. The only payment Signora Bianchi desired was a promise from Elvira. A promise that she wouldn't reveal the secret recipe to anyone, Elvira graciously accepted the deal.

Elvira began to walk out the door with her hands filled with heavy bags. She stopped for a moment and got Signora Bianchi's attention.

"Signora Bianchi," she said. "How did you know my boyfriend's name was Michael?"

Signora Bianchi looked confused. She replied, "Who's Michael?"

Elvira entered her apartment holding at least a dozen shopping bags. The weight from the bags was too heavy for her to hold. She lugged them over to her kitchen table. Elvira took the recipe out of her pocket and read it closely.

"How on earth am I going to pull this off?" She asked herself.

Elvira washed her hands in the sink and put on an apron. She picked up the phone and dialed Michael's number.

"Hey Michael, it's Elvira. Can you be at my place around six tonight?" Michael complied, and she hung up the phone.

Elvira placed her hands on her hips and closed her eyes. She took a few deep breaths. Elvira was trying to imagine how the pasta itself should look. She thought of the way her grandmother used to make meat sauce. Elvira thought that maybe she was part Italian. According to Michael she acted more Italian than any of his past girlfriends. Maybe deep down the line, one of her family members hailed from the sunny peninsula of Italy. Elvira loved to drink red wine, she loved to eat food more than the average girl, she wore her emotions on her sleeves, and she even talked with her hands. All the signs pointed to it.

Elvira spilled the ingredients out of the bags. She glanced at the clock to gauge the amount of time she had. Elvira held the recipe close. She didn't want to risk losing it or Michael finding it. She placed a pan on the stove, filled it with fresh Italian olive oil, and turned on the gas. Elvira chopped celery, onions, and carrots. Once the oil was hot enough, Elvira dumped the vegetables into the pan. She stirred the vegetables in the pan until they turned a light brown color. Elvira added four cloves of finely chopped garlic. Signora Bianchi wrote down in capital letters not to let the garlic burn, because that would make the sauce bitter. Elvira pulled the beef, veal, and pancetta out of its packaging. She hated the way it felt between her hands. She quickly threw the meat in the pan and stirred.

While she waited for the meat to cook, Elvira set the table. She laid a checkered cloth over the table. It reminded her of the kind of cloth that they used in those old Italian pizzerias. The bottle of Manhattan Special stood at the center of the table with two glass cups. Elvira knew how excited Michael would be to see that she remembered his favorite drink. Two brightly colored, deep dish bowls were placed on each side of the table. If Elvira was going to all this trouble to make Michael a sauce, she felt that he should at least have a large bowl of it.

She said to herself, "He better eat that whole damn bowl."

There was a burning smell in the air. Elvira ran back over to the stove to check on the sauce. She could see that it was a little browner than it was supposed to be. She got nervous and quickly tended to the last few steps. Elvira bought a few cans of fresh tomatoes. She hated using tomato paste because it was too thick. She attempted to open the can of tomatoes with a can opener, but it broke halfway through. Elvira placed a knife in between the part of the can that was open and pried it apart. The liquid in the can of tomatoes exploded from the force of the pull. She was covered in red stains from the tomato juice. Elvira pulled the tomatoes apart with her hands and placed them into the sauce pan.

Elvira glanced at the clock once again. She only had an hour left to complete the sauce. The more she hurried, the larger the mess she made of herself and the kitchen. Elvira quickly finished the rest of the recipe. She placed one cup of whole milk and red wine in the pan. The recipe said to use white wine, but Elvira hated white wine. She would never have dated a man who preferred white over red. Elvira capped off the sauce by spreading salt, pepper, oregano, and basil over the pan. She covered the lid. The recipe said to let the sauce sit for at least sixty to ninety minutes.

The next step was for Elvira to boil the pasta. She filled a large pot up with water and set the heat on the stove as high as possible. She placed a large amount of salt into the water, so the pasta wouldn't stick together. Elvira loved salt, she could never use enough salt in her cooking. The water came to a boil and Elvira placed fresh linguine in the pot. The hardest part of her job was done. She looked across the kitchen and smiled. Although the meal was made, the kitchen looked like a bomb hit it.

Michael looked sharp for his date with Elvira. He had a feeling she had something planned for him. He could hear it in her voice over the phone. Michael was excited by the idea that Elvira had a surprise for him. He wasn't used to getting surprised. Once Michael finished getting ready, he took Elvira's present out of a drawer. He placed it on his bed and stared at the present for a few minutes. Michael was deep in thought. He paced back and forth around his bed.

Elvira's birthday was on Christmas Eve, which was a little under a month away. Michael planned to surprise her with tickets to see Tony Bennett. He also planned to give her the dress as a present to wear to the concert. The only issue was that the concert was a week before her birthday. Michael didn't want to ruin the surprise and have nothing to give Elvira on the day of her actual birthday. Michael loved planning surprises, but hated waiting for them. A part of him wanted to give Elvira the present tonight. He couldn't wait to see the look on her face when she opened the box. Michael lived for those moments. Making Elvira happy is what made him feel the most alive.

Michael sat at his desk and wrote out Elvira's birthday card. He picked a card that was bright blue with a small ribbon wrapped around it. The words on the card were so beautiful, almost as if they were stripped from Michael's heart. He still didn't think the words on the card were enough. Michael took a fancy piece of paper out of his desk drawer and began to write. He wrote for at least the next hour pouring his heart out onto that small paper. He folded the paper into a rectangle and taped it to the inside of the card. Michael took the card and placed it between the large bow on the box. Michael left his apartment for the first time, feeling truly vulnerable. It was clear that Elvira had Michael's heart. She was the only woman who broke down the barrier he built to shut out everyone around him.

Michael stood outside Elvira's apartment door with the present under his arm. He knocked on the door a few times. There was no answer. After a few moments, Michael knocked again.

He heard a faint yell. "Coming!" Elvira said.

There was a smell of burning in the air. Elvira opened the door. A slight hint of smoke flew out of her apartment. Elvira looked like a total mess. Her hair was frizzy, there was tomato juice all over her face, and she was still wearing the dirty apron. Michael stepped into the apartment and looked around. He looked at Elvira for a few moments in shock. Michael saw the table set with a glass of Manhattan Special already poured for him. There were two deep dishes of linguine with Bolognese sauce that looked so fresh it was still steaming. Elvira could see the excitement radiating through Michael's body. Her reaction to his happiness was genuine.

"You did this all for me?" Michael asked.

Elvira nodded with excitement. The smile on her face was unbreakable. Her cheekbones rose. Her eyes squinted and glistened with purity. Michael walked over to the table and picked up the bottle of Manhattan Special.

"You remembered my favorite drink too?" he asked.

Elvira nodded once again. Michael placed the present down on the table. He picked up a rag off the counter and wet it in the sink. He walked back over to where Elvira was standing and stood close to her.

"Look at you," he said. Michael ran his fingers across her face. "You look like you just performed open heart surgery."

Michael wiped the tomato juice off her face with the rag. Elvira looked completely shy and timid. She batted her eyes at him as he cleaned her face.

"I can't even describe how much this means to me," Michael said. "No one has ever gone to this kind of trouble for me before. You remembered everything I liked. You listened to me. Even though you said you couldn't cook, you still learned how."

Elvira opened her mouth to say something. Michael placed one finger over her lips. In this moment, her eyes looked pure. Michael could see the love she had for him in her soul. He kissed her. Elvira closed her eyes. She fell deep into a passionate trance. This kiss was different from the rest. This kiss wasn't playful, innocent, or sexual. It was pure passion. There was only one feeling behind this long kiss. It was love. Michael and Elvira both felt it. There was trembling in their hearts, a burning fire of passion in their bellies, and a calmness of the mind. Their worlds stood still. Nothing else mattered but the two of them being connected.

When they broke free of their trance, Michael mumbled. He said, "I love you."

"What was that?" Elvira asked.

Michael spoke so low that she could barely hear what he was saying. Michael paused. His fear of intimacy kicked in. He couldn't bring himself to say those three words. The anxious thoughts once again took over his brain, barring him from true happiness. He asked himself questions. "What if it's too soon? What if she doesn't love you back? What if her feelings change one day? What if she hurts you? What if you hurt her?" Michael knew he loved Elvira. He fell in love with her the same day he met her. Michael had suffered so much loss in his life. He had been treated poorly by his own family and the women he loved. His only defense mechanism was to shut out his feelings. To run away from the truth, rob himself of happiness because he'd rather feel the pain sooner than later. Michael's mind was completely broken. His spirit, demoralized.

Elvira watched him struggle. She knew exactly what was going on. Elvira had to overcome those same fears. They had two different life experiences, but the result made them feel the same way. Elvira was battling the same demons as Michael. She knew Michael loved her. It was written all over his face. He was never good at hiding anything. Michael tried so desperately to spit out those three magical words. He wanted to say them, because that's what he felt in his heart.

Elvira placed her finger over Michael's lips, mimicking what he did to her. She wrapped her arms around the back of his neck. Michael put his head down with shame. She gave him a small neck massage with her thumbs. This instantly released all the tension from Michael's body. The touch of her skin was better than any medication a doctor could prescribe. Michael looked up at her again. Elvira grabbed his hand and placed it on her chest, over her heart. She laid her two hands on top of Michael's. Without saying any words, Elvira let Michael know that she knew what he was trying to say. She let him know it was okay to have anxiety and fear. That it was okay to be afraid of the unknown. This small action was also Elvira's way of letting Michael know that she was in love with him too. They had a bond, unlike any other couple. They felt each other's pain, sorrow, and happiness. Words never had to be spoken. People often claim that love is unequal. That usually, one person in a relationship cares more than the other. While that may be true for some, this wasn't the case for Michael and Elvira. They loved each other equally. Their bond, as soulmates, allowed them to.

It took Michael a few moments to process what was going on. Then, he suddenly understood. Michael realized that maybe he wasn't alone. That Elvira was probably just as afraid. There subtle way of saying I *love you*, helped quell both their fears. The day would come where they both overcame those fears. Their relationship would grow to heal them both.

"I have a surprise for you," Michael said happily. Michael walked over to the table. He handed the box and card to Elvira.

"We can wait until after dinner, or you can open it now if you want," Michael said. Before Michael could even finish those words, Elvira sat on the floor and unwrapped the present. Michael sat next to her. First, she took the card out from between the ribbon. She loved the way Michael wrote her name on the card. He tried so hard to be neat, but his handwriting was naturally sloppy. Elvira opened the card and read it out loud. The words continued to roll of her tongue as tears slowly streamed down her face. The words on the card were so beautiful. She found a note inside the card. Elvira glanced at Michael.

"I couldn't fit all that I wanted to say on the card," Michael said. "I decided to write you a little note."

That little note was about a page long. Elvira read the note closely. You could see she was trying to absorb every single word. As she read the note, Michael could see the mixture of emotions in her face. Her reactions flowed accordingly with Michael's words. She looked up at Michael when she finished. Elvira tried with all her might not to cry. Michael said nothing and pushed the box over to her.

Elvira untied the bow with one quick pull. She savored every moment. She placed the bow aside and ran her fingers over the wrapping paper, then tore it to shreds. Michael sat beside her, smiling and filled with joy. He waited anxiously to see her reaction. Elvira saw the name of the department store on the box and instantly knew what the gift was. Still in complete shock, Elvira threw the cover of the box over her shoulder. She pulled the dress out and held it in her hands. She ran her fingers through the smooth silk.

Elvira got up off the floor and ran into her room. She never received such a gift. Elvira laid the dress across her bed. She examined the kind of dress Michael chose for her. The dress was classy, but also sexy. Elvira could tell that when Michael chose this dress, he examined her body. The dress fit her curves perfectly, showing off the shape of her body. Elvira was having a mixture of emotions, but one feeling was the most prevalent. A heat rushed over her body, she was really turned on. Her instant reaction was to tease Michael. She wanted to put the dress on and show off her body to him.

"Look at me Michael," she said to herself. "This could be all yours."

She ripped her sauce stained clothes off and put on the dress. Elvira stared at herself in the mirror. She ran her fingers down the sides of her body and struck a pose. Michael waited patiently in the kitchen for her to return. Elvira poked her head through the door leading into the kitchen.

"Are you ready?" Elvira asked.

"I've been ready my whole life," Michael replied.

Elvira entered the room. Michael stared at her in amazement. Elvira ran over to Michael and hugged him.

"I don't even know how to say thank you," she said. "How did you even afford this? This dress must have cost you a fortune."

Michael shook his head. "Money is no object with me. The minute you told me that you were never given presents before, I knew I was going to do this. You deserve so much more than this. You deserve the world."

Elvira put her head down. "These beautiful things you say to me. No man has ever said anything close. It's hard for me to take in all of what you say and accept it. It's hard for me to believe I'm this amazing. What about all the bad things about me?"

Michael lifted Elvira's head with his finger. "There aren't any bad things when you care about someone this much. Besides, in my eyes, you're perfect."

Elvira held out Michael's chair for him. "I want you to try my pasta," Elvira said. "The recipe is a secret. Let's just say I found out I was a little more Italian than I thought."

Michael sat down. He covered his pasta with fresh cheese Elvira bought. She stood next to Michael eagerly waiting for him to take the first bite. Michael twirled the linguine with his fork. From the moment the pasta touched his tongue, Michael would know the quality of the sauce. He was very picky with any kind of red sauce. Michael figured it was Elvira's first time making sauce. He assumed she'd be rusty, but he was sorely mistaken. Elvira answered yet another one of Michael's five burning questions, she learned how to cook an amazing dinner made with such tender love.

"Tell me the truth," Elvira said. "How bad is it? I'll understand if you want to order Chinese instead." Elvira knew the sauce was going to be amazing, she trusted Signora Bianchi's judgment. She was toying with Michael because she felt confident in her cooking.

Michael's eyes opened wide. He pointed to the dish of pasta. "You really cooked this?" he asked.

Elvira nodded confidently. "Yes, I did."

"This has to be the greatest Bolognese sauce I've ever had. It's like you imported it from Italy. I think my *nonna* would even be jealous of this recipe."

Elvira sat across from Michael and tried the pasta herself. She was completely amazed by her own cooking. Elvira never thought she'd be able to pull this off. Signora Bianchi really saved her.

"So, tell me Michael," she said. "Do you still want to marry an Italian girl? You know the olive skin, brown eyed, girls? The long curly brunette hair—they'd cook for you all day and night."

Michael was almost done with his dish of pasta by the time Elvira finished her sentence. He wiped his mouth with a napkin and placed it back on the table then reached for his glass filled with the Manhattan Special.

"My whole life, I wanted to find that perfect Italian girl. The one who I could bring home to my family. She would impress them all. I probably talked my friends' ears off about that so-called Italian girl. But then I met you."

Michael paused for a few moments to drink. "I don't need the olive skin and dark eyes. The long curly hair. The whole deal. I found my Italian girl in you. You're my Italian girl. You act more Italian than any of them ever did."

Elvira blushed. She loved to hear that she was Michael's Italian girl. Elvira was never one to enjoy pet names, but the one Michael gave her worked. Elvira was very competitive. She loved hearing she was better than all the Italian women in Michael's life.

Elvira folded her hands on the table. "How could you be so sure?" she asked. "I can't speak Italian. I can barely cook. Why am I your Italian girl?"

Michael smiled. He loved when Elvira teased him like this. "Well, I guess you're right. I can't be sure. I have no clue what I'm going to do with these Tony Bennett tickets then."

Michael took the two tickets out of his pocket and placed them on the table. The surprises never ended with Michael. Elvira never knew what he had up his sleeve next. He was sneaky when it came to gifts. Elvira grabbed the tickets and stared at them for a few moments. She looked at Michael with the biggest puppy-like eyes. The dress was hard for

Elvira to accept on its own, but now this? She had a hard time believing this was even reality.

"How could I get you a dress and not give you a place to wear it?" Michael asked her. "Happy Birthday Elvira. I know it's a few weeks early, but the show is three weeks away. I didn't want to spring it on you last second."

Elvira said nothing. All she did was look at Michael. She had never felt loved and appreciated before in this way. This was all foreign to her. It was almost as if she didn't know how to react. Elvira's mind was racing. She was having feelings of happiness and love. At the same time, her past rushed back to the forefront of her mind. Elvira said to herself. "Am I really this special? He's doing all this because he loves me. How could he love me this much?"

The anxiety showed on Elvira's face. She was having a difficult time accepting all of this. Elvira looked deep in thought. All she did was stare at the tickets. Michael got out of his seat. He kissed Elvira's forehead.

"That mind of yours," he said. "That's what I love the most about you. The way you think. The way you act. The way you walk. The way you talk. The quirks you have. Your personality. It all starts right there."

Elvira got out of her seat. She kissed Michael slowly and then wrapped her arms around his body. She hugged him tightly. Michael and Elvira stood there, embracing each other. *Skin hunger* is the need to hold someone, the need to be close to a body, to hug, to touch and to feel. Michael and Elvira were both emotional people. Wherever they went, they were always holding hands, kissing, or hugging. Whenever one left the other's arms, they instantly missed each other.

Tears streamed down Elvira's face. She wept in his arms. "It's ok," Michael said. He rubbed her back with his hand. "Let it out."

Elvira cried into Michael's chest. She thought of all she's been through in her life. Elvira wanted to say so much to Michael in this moment. Through all the crying, she could only get out a few words. "No one has ever made me feel this special."

Michael tried to hold back his tears. He never liked to cry. Michael always felt that he should be strong for those around him, especially the woman he loved. When it came to Elvira, he couldn't help it. Michael cried along with her. He understood her pain. "I know this is a lot for you to take in. It will take time, but one day you'll see what I see," Michael said.

7
CHAPTER

Elvira and Allison practiced yoga at a studio called Nirvana. They took a yoga class together every Sunday morning. It was a great way for them to unwind and start the week with a clear mind. Yoga helps a person become more mindful and self-aware. It not only exercises the body, but the mind as well. Elvira loved her yoga classes because they complimented her naturally easygoing personality. It helped center her mind and accept life as it is. Elvira decided to bring Allison because she was stressed with her job. It eventually became a Sunday tradition between the two. Elvira and Allison would go out to brunch after their practice.

The two of them sat down at a little café across the street. The café looked like a total hole in the wall. It could have passed for a vacant storefront. Elvira loved to explore new places and restaurants. The restaurants that looked like dives always ended up having the best food. It was a philosophy she stuck by. Elvira and Allison both ordered coffee and bagels.

"You seemed pretty chipper today," Allison said. "How was your weekend?"

Elvira smiled. She never liked telling Allison too much right away. "It was a normal relaxing weekend. Pretty uneventful if you ask me."

Allison already knew Elvira was lying. She blushed the minute Allison asked her about the weekend.

"I know you're lying to me" Allison said. "You slept with Michael, didn't you?"

Elvira always got a kick out of Allison's dirty mind. She always wanted the nasty details. Sometimes she could even be worse than a guy.

"No!" Elvira said defensively. "We didn't sleep together yet."

Allison continued to question Elvira. "Then what are you all smiles about?" she asked.

"You remember that dress I told you about? The one I tried on in the store on my date with Michael? He went back and bought it for me. He wrote me this beautiful birthday card. On top of it all, Michael said I needed a place to wear the dress. He bought us two tickets to see Tony Bennett at Radio City Music Hall."

Allison said nothing. She was in total shock. From the beginning she had Michael pegged as a want to be writer, a loser who didn't have much going for him. Allison realized she was mistaken. She was happy that Elvira finally found a good guy.

"This guy impresses me," Allison said. "I honestly thought he was gunna be just another asshole. I guess you finally hit the jackpot."

Elvira paused. She felt bad for Allison. Allison didn't hate all men, but she had a very poor opinion of the ones she dated. "Michael has a friend you know," Elvira said. "I think he's Italian too. Michael kind of described him as annoying, but I think you guys would get along."

Allison thought about Elvira's proposition for a moment. "An Italian huh? I've never dated an Italian man before."

"It's a life changing experience," Elvira joked. "At least for me it was. Michael has so much passion. He kisses me slowly, like he wants to savor every moment. He knows when to be gentle and rough with me. He pinned me against the wall, and I just couldn't control myself. It was like we both lost it. He doesn't look half bad naked either. I wanted to eat him alive."

Elvira bit her lip again just thinking about the moment. Allison's jaw dropped.

"Wait...you want to eat him alive?" Allison asked. "I've never heard you use that saying in our fourteen years of friendship. You saw him naked? When were you planning on telling me this?"

Elvira laughed. "If I told you how it even happened you wouldn't believe me. It all started after we bumped into each other."

"I guess the universe really wanted you guys to do it," Allison joked.

Elvira and Allison both believed that every person had a destiny. That God has a plan for everyone. That everything in life happens for a reason. Good or bad, these moments bring a person to the next step in their life. This would eventually shape them towards the person they needed to be. The hard part of it all is figuring out what the signs are. Sometimes the signs can't be avoided, other times people miss them. When it all boils down, if the universe wants something to happen, it will.

* * *

Elvira didn't get home until late in the evening on that day. It had to be at least around nine o'clock at night. There was a thin layer of fog in the air. Elvira was only a block away from her apartment. She never liked walking alone at night, it scared her. She looked down at the ground. There seemed to be a large shadow following her. She quickly turned around and saw nothing. Elvira hurried towards her apartment building. She raced up the steps, to the door, and turned around one more time. There was a man standing at the bottom of the steps. He stood halfway into the light. Without even seeing a full picture, Elvira instantly knew who it was. It was a familiar face. A face she wanted to forget, a face that reminded her of a horrible time in her life.

Fear struck Elvira's heart as this man appeared to be moving closer to her. She desperately tore apart her purse to find the keys to the door. She opened the door and slammed it shut behind her. Elvira ran up to her apartment. She tried to call Michael, but she kept dialing the number wrong. Her hands were still trembling from the trauma. When she finally got the number right, it took a while for Michael to answer the phone.

As Elvira called his phone frantically, Michael was in the bathroom shaving. He couldn't hear the phone over a record playing. Michael cut his neck accidently and bled a large amount. He washed his face and held a steamed cloth to his neck. As he exited the bathroom, Michael heard the phone ringing. He shut off his record player and ran over to the phone. Before Michael could even give a greeting, he could hear Elvira crying.

"Michael!" Elvira wept. "I need you to come here right away."

Elvira continued to cry. Michael's entire demeanor changed. His mind entered survival mode. It resembled an animal's protective instinct. Instead of becoming filled with fear and anxiety, he stayed calm. He could hear by the tone of her voice that this was serious.

"Slow down," Michael said calmly. "What happened? Are you hurt?"

Elvira couldn't find a way to tell Michael who was outside her home. Fear took over her mind. She wasn't thinking straight.

"There's a man outside my apartment," she said. "He followed me home and almost into my apartment building. I got inside before he could reach my door. I think he's drunk. Please come here! I don't know what to do."

"Don't leave your apartment. I'll be right there." Michael ran into his bedroom. He put on any clothes he could find. Barely dressed, he ran towards the door. He was wearing an open button-down shirt and dirty jeans.

He exited his apartment building and ran down the street. Michael was athletic, but in no way a runner. Elvira's apartment wasn't very far from his. Michael ran so fast, he looked like a track star.

John McGrath marched around the sidewalk next to Elvira's apartment building. He had an intimidating presence. His hair was finely combed and wavy. He sported a thick beard. Elvira peered out of her blinds to stare at him. John was completely intoxicated. He held an empty Jack Daniel's bottle in his hand. John seemed to be moving around too quickly for a drunk. His eyes were bloodshot, and his pupils dilated.

John shouted at the top of his lungs. "Elvira!" he yelled. "Open the fucking door."

Michael finally turned the corner onto Elvira's block. He heard the screaming from at least a mile away. Michael slowly walked down the block towards John. The anger in his heart that had been suppressed for so long was ferociously present. He stood tall and clenched his fists. His white face turned puffy and red. His teeth were clenched. Michael instantly knew who this man was. Michael stood a few feet away from a staggering John.

"I took you off the street!" John yelled. "You were nothing more than a helpless whore until I found you."

John's words made Michael cringe. He couldn't believe that a person could bring themselves to say such horrible things. When John talked, it felt like someone was sticking an ice pick in Michael's ear.

"Let me take a wild guess," Michael said. "You're the ugly, piece of shit, drug addict, guy that Elvira used to date. You know, the one who abused her? That's you right?"

John slowly turned around. He stared at Michael with his beady red eyes. John resembled a rabid attack dog. He was practically foaming at the mouth. John was looking for someone to hurt, and he found his target.

John snarled at Michael. "Who the fuck are you?" He threw his body in Michael's direction and lunged at him. Michael moved out of the way. There was no fear in Michael's eyes. John was taller and larger than Michael. Yet, Michael remained completely unfazed.

Michael pointed at John. "You must feel real tough right?" he yelled. "You enjoy hitting women? It must make you feel like a man, threatening a woman who can't defend herself. Well you wanna know what? Now I'm here. You picked the wrong day to get into a drunken rage. Let's see what a real man you are. Pick on me."

Michael always had pent up anger, but never acted out violently. He was never the kind of person to provoke a fight. The day Elvira told Michael what John did to her, Michael was mortified. Michael held a hatred in his heart for John ever since. He saw, first hand, the extent of what John did to Elvira and the toll it took on her.

John laughed at Michael. Michael's words barely registered in John's brain. There was no reasoning with or changing a person who could never see what they did wrong. A person who was so evil, that they simply didn't care about how their actions affected others.

"I'm gunna let you in on a piece of advice," John said smiling. "She was a whore when I met her and she's a whore now."

Elvira was standing outside her apartment door listening to the entire conversation. John's words brought tears to her eyes. Michael watched as Elvira cried. His face filled with fury. Veins popped out of the side of his skull. Michael looked like a ticking time bomb.

John turned around. He noticed that Elvira was present. He laughed at her crying. "That's right. Cry you fucking..."

Before John could finish his sentence, Michael grabbed him by the shoulders and slammed him against the side of the building. The entire side of John's face scraped the brick on the wall. Michael pinned John against the wall with one arm. His hand squeezed John's face together so he couldn't continue speaking.

"Don't you ever talk to her like that again," Michael said. "Don't look her way. Don't speak to her. I never want to see you around here again. If you think this is bad, you have no idea what's going to come next." John smiled. His teeth were filled with blood. Michael released John. He fell on the concrete sidewalk.

As Michael walked away, he heard Elvira scream. Before Michael could even turn around, John had already hit him with the empty bottle of liquor. Michael instantly fell to the floor. Blood dripped down his face from the glass shards. John climbed on top of Michael's chest and choked him. Elvira ran over to help Michael. She tried to pull John off his body. She scratched, bit, and pried away at John. She tried anything in her power to move him. With one swift push, John knocked Elvira down to the floor.

Michael's eyes were filled with the blood that dripped down from his forehead. He could barely see. Michael waved his hands frantically trying to break free of John's grip. He gasped for air that was leaving his body. Michael felt his life slowly slipping away. John saw the life leaving Michael's body. He was excited by the feeling and tightened his grip further.

In what Michael thought would be his last few moments on earth, he saw a flashback of the dark times in his life. Michael suddenly remembered the years of abuse he faced in his home. The days his father hit his mother, the endless name calling and shaming he faced by his own family. He remembered throwing this body into harm's way. There were many times in Michael's life where he wanted to give up. Times when he begged God to let him live as another person for just one day. Michael hated himself. The way he acted sickened him. He was always kind to others asking for nothing in return. He only faced constant abuse from those he loved. Michael tried to change the person he was and gave in to the people who harmed him. He shunned the world he once looked at purely. He built a wall around his heart deciding to never let anyone get too close.

As his eyes closed, Michael's mind was clear. He couldn't see or hear anything. Michael was numb from all the pain. He could only think of one thing. Michael saw a vivid image of Elvira. He saw an image of the day Elvira placed his hand on her heart. The day Elvira let him know she loved him. This time around, Michael didn't want to give up on life. He had someone to fight for. Michael wanted to find a way to stay alive. Elvira needed him.

Suddenly, Michael's eyes opened wide. Through the blurred vision from the blood, he could see John was still on top of him. Michael moved his arms around the sidewalk floor. He tried to find anything he could grab. Michael felt a sharp object. It was a piece of glass from the broken bottle. Michael grabbed the glass and stabbed John in his thigh.

John screamed in pain. "You stabbed me! You fucking stabbed me!"

John released his grip from Michael's neck then desperately searched for the piece of glass that punctured his skin. Michael rolled away from John trying to catch his breath. He still didn't have enough strength to get off the floor. Michael frantically looked for Elvira. He saw her holding her shoulder in pain on the floor. She sat wrapped in a ball.

Michael finally began to breathe normally. He wiped the blood from his eyes on his shirt and crawled off the floor. John removed the piece of glass from his skin. Michael saw John attempting to get off the floor and tackled him. They rolled around the sidewalk scuffling, punching, and hitting each other. Michael got the better of John and pinned him down. With all the strength he had left, Michael continually hit John in the face.

"How could you hurt her?" Michael yelled. "I'm never going to let you hurt her again."

When Michael subdued John, he went to check on Elvira. Her eyes were a cold blue. Her skin was extra pale. Her hands couldn't stop shaking. Elvira held Michael's face. Within seconds, she was covered in the blood dripping off Michael. They helped each other inside her apartment, slowly walking up the steps towards her door. John lied on the sidewalk moaning in pain.

Michael barely made it up the steps to Elvira's apartment. She guided Michael to her bedroom. He quickly collapsed on her bed riddled in pain. Elvira saw the amount of pain Michael was in and snapped out of her shocked state. She decided not to call an ambulance because they would question Michael and John about the fight. She rummaged through her apartment for a first aid kit. She was forced to compromise with sterile alcohol and old rags.

Elvira kept gently smacking Michael in the face, so he wouldn't fall asleep. "C'mon my love," Elvira said holding back tears. "You need to stay awake. It's very bad when you fall asleep after getting hit on the head."

Michael gave an unconvincing moan of pain as a response. Elvira continued to try and keep him awake. She stroked the side of his face. "I have some leftover pasta," she said. "I know you can't wait for that.

Michael mumbled with a small grin. "Pasta."

Elvira used a wet rag to clean the blood off his face and hands. With tweezers, Elvira combed through Michael's hair and picked any of the remaining glass shards from his skull. The bottle never penetrated Michael's skull, it just happened to cut him at an awkward angle.

"This is going to burn a little," Elvira said. She poured the alcohol on his cut. Michael screamed in pain from the burn. The jolt from the burn woke him up. While he was conscience enough, Elvira helped him remove his bloodstained clothes. Elvira brought him orange juice to help raise his sugar levels back to normal. Once she force-fed him the juice, she placed a small blanket over him.

Michael appeared to have finally fallen asleep. Elvira curled up next to Michael in bed. She gently placed her head on his chest next to his heart. Elvira listened to his heart slowly beat. She was too afraid to fall asleep in case Michael got sick. Halfway through the night, Michael placed his hand on Elvira.

He mumbled to her. "Are you hurt?"

Elvira shook her head. "I banged up my shoulder a little, but I'll be ok. It's just a bruise."

Michael attempted to find the humor in all this and lighten up the situation. He could always make Elvira laugh no matter how upset she was.

"You know. It's funny," Michael said. "I think we met like this. Right after I got beat up in the coffee shop."

Elvira tried not to smile. "It's not funny," she said coldly. "You got hurt because of me. You almost died because of me."

Michael sat up. "It's not your fault."

Elvira looked at Michael's bruised neck. She cried hysterically. "The last person I ever wanted to hurt was you."

Michael held Elvira's hand. "I would do the same thing over again in a heartbeat. I hate that guy. I've never had so much hatred for a person in my entire life."

Elvira sobbed. "But why?" she asked.

"Because he hurt you," Michael said. "Now he'll never hurt you again."

The guilt of getting Michael hurt consumed Elvira. She was convinced it was her fault. She had a bad habit of blaming herself often. Elvira couldn't find any words to say. She only continued to look at Michael and sob.

Michael tilted Elvira's head towards his. "I'm in love with you Elvira," Michael said.

Elvira was silent. She didn't move, she didn't speak, she even held her breathe. She noticed Michael's heart was beating faster. It was clear he was getting nervous.

"I almost died tonight," Michael said. "I felt the life leaving my body. A few more seconds and I probably wouldn't be sitting here next to you. My body was ready to give in. I felt ready to throw in the towel, but something kept me going."

Tears filled Michael's eyes. Following his code, he tried to stay strong for Elvira. He held in the tears. "All I could think about was you," Michael said. "I asked myself, how could I leave this earth without telling her I'm in love with her? I knew I needed to tell you that you're my world. That I wake up and fall asleep to the thought of you. That I wish I woke up next to you every single morning. If I really could, I'd watch you eat cashews until the end of time. I love when you laugh really hard and your voice gets all raspy. I love the way you randomly play with your feet in the crease of a couch. I love how you drag me into random public bathrooms and sing for me. How could I ever leave this earth without saying all this?"

Elvira felt Michael's heart beating even faster. It felt like his heart was about to burst. For once, Michael didn't care. He let his anxiety stir. He let the intrusive thoughts of doubt invade his brain. He embraced the vulnerability and intimacy. Michael finally put all his cards on the table, he was all in.

Elvira still remained silent. Michael's intimate words finally registered in her brain. She took in all of what he said. For the first time in her life, Elvira felt truly and unconditionally loved. There was no fear in her eyes or heart. Michael's words finally helped Elvira accept that she was a beautiful person, on the inside and out. His words made her realize she truly deserved his love and she was his world.

"I don't know what I would do if you left me," Elvira said. "After what just happened, I stayed up throughout the night thinking. What would I do if you weren't here? I would have never gotten the chance to tell you all that I feel. I would have never gotten the chance to tell you that you changed my life forever. That no one has ever looked at me the way you do. That I want to keep you all to myself."

Elvira paused. Michael and Elvira lay on the bed facing each other. She looked directly into Michael's eyes. "You make me feel safe and protected. You make me feel like I'm the only woman in the world for you. Whenever I think about you, the first thing that comes to my mind is your eyes. Every time you look at me, I feel you staring into my soul. It's the most sensual feeling. I can never listen to Tony Bennett or any of the classics ever again without thinking of you. I love that I can be my quirky self around you, and that you're always eager to learn more about me. I love that I can tell you anything, and never feel judged. When you called me your Italian girl, my heart skips a beat. I think it's adorable when you get neurotic and overthink just about anything. I wish you could cook chicken thighs for me every night. Before I go to sleep, I pray for you. I pray that Jesus helps guide you to where you are today. When I go to bed with the thought of you, you always visit my dreams. Most of all, I love your mind. Those words that roll off your tongue, it's like you ripped them from your heart. The way you think is inspiring. You inspire me to be myself."

Elvira kissed Michael. "I forgot to mention that I'm madly in love you."

Michael gently grabbed Elvira's chin and kissed her. Within moments, the kissing became more intense. They fell into lust. Elvira felt ready to give herself to Michael. She saw him as a wounded warrior, a warrior who fought to the death for her. Elvira had never felt more erotic. Michael had succeeded in doing something few men could do. He combined the emotional and physical part of sex with the sex of the mind.

Elvira climbed on top of Michael and stroked her body over his. She rolled her hips on his pelvis and kissed him. She stared down at Michael.

"You're hurting me," Michael joked. "I don't think I have enough strength to go through with this."

Elvira rolled off Michael. She lied down and turned her back to him. "Fine," she said. "Maybe some other time then." Elvira smiled deviously.

Michael pulled Elvira toward him with force. "I'd wake up out of a coma to spend the night with you."

Michael suddenly sprung to life. Michael kissed her lips intensely. The way she tasted was sweet. It almost felt like he was eating candy. He kissed her cheek and moved further down her body. She grew weak when Michael licked her neck, one of her sweet spots. Michael unbuttoned Elvira's shirt. Button by button her breath grew deeper. He kissed her collar bone and then slowly moved down to her breasts. Michael enjoyed pleasing a woman to the fullest extent. He felt it was something men often neglected.

Michael grabbed Elvira's hair and pushed her head back on to the bed, then pinned her hands. He rendered her helpless. She allowed herself to be his, to be completely dominated. He kissed her breasts. Elvira closed her eyes. Her breath was heavier as Michael shifted his attention. With her hands still pinned, Michael kissed her nipples, taking his time with one of the most sensitive parts of a woman's body. Elvira felt Michael's warm skin press against hers. She trembled when Michael's hands reached down to unbutton her pants. Michael's fingers entered her. He could feel how wet she was, her body was yearning for his entry. Michael took his time undressing Elvira. Kiss by kiss, he passed her belly button. With one finger, Michael pulled her panties off her legs. He kissed her inner thighs on each side, teasing her. Elvira grabbed Michael's back with her hands.

There wasn't a thought in Elvira's brain. All she could feel was Michael's head between her thighs. His warm tongue, reaching inside her as her eyes rolled to the back of her head. A mind-blowing rush of pleasure swept through her body. She savored every second of Michael's love. Michael got a thrill from hearing Elvira moan and screech. She wasn't the quiet type and he loved it. When Michael pulled his head up to gasp for air, Elvira pushed him onto his back.

Elvira jumped on top Michael, digging her nails into his chest. Michael loved the way Elvira touched him, she always held him close. Her passion was real, not fabricated. Elvira removed Michael's boxers using only her feet. The body heat and sweat made it easy for Elvira to slide across Michael's body. Elvira teased Michael and wouldn't be content until she saw him beg to have her. The same way Michael made her beg for more. She used her waist to tease him, rolling her hips on his groin. Michael tried to stay composed and not give in. Elvira saw this and decided to push him even further. She kissed him intensely, leaving a small bite mark on his lower lip. With both hands, she gently grabbed Michael's face and pushed it to the side. Elvira licked Michael's neck, making sure to leave her mark wherever she went. She worked her way down his chest, then groin. Elvira looked at Michael as she tasted him. She wanted to see the pleasure in his eyes.

Michael kneeled above Elvira, who was now lying down. The two of them savored the moment they would become one person. Not moving his vision away from her pure eyes, Michael climbed on top of her. Elvira placed her hands around Michael's back. Her neck rested on his shoulder, anticipating the moment. As he entered her, Elvira's grip tightened. Elvira dug her nails into his back. The passion radiated off their skin. Their connection was strong, their feelings written on the wall, and their bodies in synchronization. Elvira grabbed the side of her bed sheets, clawing away at anything she could get her hands on. She shook.

Michael exhaled heavily. "Are you ok?"

Elvira barely spoke. All Michael heard was sighs of pleasure. In between them, she gasped. "Don't stop."

They spent the entire night making love, enjoying every second. Heat rushed over their bodies. It was unlike any before. They both began to shake. A dominant force took over their minds. They moved faster, soaking up what they knew would be the last moments of their awe-inspired night. They were both out of breath, their pupils completely dilated, and their hearts racing. Michael's and Elvira's toes curled. They both let out a scream. Their orgasms were earth-shattering. Michael and Elvira never had such a feeling before in their entire lives. It was indescribable and unparalleled.

The events that occurred that night changed their lives forever. Michael and Elvira were finally brought together physically, mentally, and spiritually. They both collapsed on the bed. Elvira curled up next to Michael. He placed his arm around her, holding her close to his body. He ran his fingers through her hair as she fell asleep. Michael had already slept, so he wasn't very tired. He spent the rest of the night just watching the love of his life sleep. Michael thought she looked beautiful while she peacefully breathed.

With his one free hand, Michael took off the gold amulet he was wearing. The amulet had an engraving of St. Anthony, the patron saint of Michael's family. This amulet was passed down in his family to each firstborn male. It was an Italian tradition. Michael pulled it off his neck and made the sign of the cross. He kissed the amulet and whispered to himself.

"St. Anthony, I know I haven't prayed in a long time. I haven't exactly been a model Christian, but now that's going to change. I know all of this was Jesus' doing. All that I have been blessed with was from God himself. He has been protecting me my whole life, I just refused to see it. He was testing my faith, time and time again. After every failure, he gave me a second chance. Then I met her, this woman sleeping next to me. She's my angel on this earth. I like to believe I'm her angel too. That God put us together for a reason. Did you know that she prays for me every night before she sleeps? You probably do, because I know Jesus listens to her. She inspired me to renew my faith. From this day on, I'm going to bring God back into my life. Not only for me, but for her. For the both of us. Thank you, Jesus, for saving me. Thank you for showing me there can be heaven on this earth."

Michael had never said such a heartfelt prayer in his entire life. He had endured so much pain, that he lost his faith. Slowly, Elvira helped change that. She not only inspired him creatively, but spiritually. She helped renew his faith in God. The way she talked about Christianity was contagious. Seeing what it had done for her made him eager to learn. With a few prayers of her own, Elvira restored Michael's faith in God.

The sunlight entered the bedroom. Michael checked on Elvira to see if she was awake yet. He kissed her cheek while she was sleeping. Elvira smiled. It looked like she was dreaming. Michael slid away from her. He walked around her apartment in search of a pen and paper. He found an empty notepad lying on her bookshelf. Michael got back into bed and wrote. He decided he was finally going to pursue his dream of becoming a writer and had just the right inspiration for a story. The story was going to be about how he finally found love. About the trials and tribulations, he faced in his life. How in the end, all his suffering ended up being worth the pain. Most importantly, he wanted the world to know how lucky he was. How lucky he was to have Elvira in his life. Michael wanted their relationship to be immortalized. That when they both moved on from this world, it could serve as an inspiration to others. Michael filled the notepad with ideas, experiences, traits, and story ideas. Creativity flooded his mind. Great sex and a little love could inspire anyone.

Elvira awoke from her deep sleep. She felt around the bed in search of Michael. He laughed.

"Don't worry I'm right here," he said.

Elvira turned around. "I thought you might have run away on me," she joked.

Michael kissed her. "I'm not going anywhere. Especially after last night."

They both laughed together. "Now what are you up to?" she asked. Elvira glanced at his notepad. "Have you been writing this whole time?"

"I couldn't sleep," he said. "So many thoughts were rushing through my brain. Then out of nowhere, I came up with this idea for a novel."

Elvira clapped. "Ah! I can't believe it. I can't wait to read your novel. What's it going to be about?"

Michael smiled. "It's going to be about us," he said. "Our story. All of this is just so amazing. A love like this only happens once in a lifetime. I want it to be immortalized."

"I love being your inspiration," Elvira said. "It's like we're going to have a baby together. This novel, I mean, is going to be our baby."

Michael laughed. "You really are quirky. Those are the things I love about you the most. When you say stuff like that. But yes, it's going to be our baby."

Elvira bit Michael's arm as he teased her. He jumped. She laid her head on his chest and turned to look at him. "How do you think our story is going to end? We're technically writing the story as we're living, so you'll have to make up an ending."

Michael pointed to his notepad. "It's funny you said that," he said. "That's actually the first thing that came to my mind. I wrote the ending. I know exactly what's going to happen."

He handed Elvira the notepad. She glanced at the first few pages of the Michael's novel. She immediately handed it back to him. "I don't want to read it," she said. "I want you to read it to me."

Elvira felt it would be more intimate if Michael read her his novel. She enjoyed hearing him speak. She loved his voice. Elvira wanted to hear Michael himself read the words off the pages. Michael put his chin to his chest with shame. He shook his head.

"I hate reading out loud because of my stutter," Michael said. "Every time they used to call on me in high school to read, I dreaded every second of it. I'd hate myself for not being able to read a paragraph without a stammer. Until this day, I have trouble even reading a few sentences out loud."

Elvira kissed him. "Do it for me," she asked. "Please?"

Michael had no choice, he couldn't say no to Elvira. He mustered up all his courage and read. Elvira listened attentively to every word Michael said. She closed her eyes and pictured the story. When he finished, Michael didn't stutter a single word through three whole pages of reading.

"I probably stuttered at least two or three times," Michael said.

Elvira shook her head. "I didn't hear a single stammer," she said. "I actually think you read it perfectly! You're good at reading out loud. When you come up with more, I want you to read every word to me. I would rather you read it to me."

Michael was amazed he didn't stutter. Stuttering affects the emotional part of the brain. When a person who stutters is excited, happy, sad, or nervous that's usually when it starts. He didn't stutter when he told Elvira he loved her. Now, he didn't stutter while reading out loud. This was an issue he struggled with his entire life. Elvira was the cure to the speech impediment that had been ailing him since childhood.

"I'll read you every word," Michael said confidently. "I have to ask. What do you think of my writing?"

Elvira paused. She looked at Michael for a few moments, creating suspense. "I don't know how to tell you this," she said. "But, I love it! I absolutely love it! I had no clue you could write like that."

"You're not just telling me that because you love me?" Michael joked.

Elvira laughed. "Trust me, if I hated it, I would tell you. I'm not easily impressed. An ex-boyfriend of mine was a movie producer. All I did was tell him he sucked. I hated his work. He was always in it for the money."

Michael stayed silent for a few moments. He crossed his arms. "You had a boyfriend who was a movie producer?"

Elvira saw the jealousy in his eyes. She could see that even mentioning a past boyfriend made him angry. The prospect of sharing her with anyone drove him crazy. Elvira loved it when Michael got jealous; it was a turn on for her.

"Oh stop," she said. "I see that jealous look on your face. I didn't even like him. I only dated him because he wouldn't leave me alone. Besides, I never loved him. I love you, Michael. He isn't even worthy of being mentioned in the same sentence as you."

Michael was the kind of man who needed large amounts of attention. He loved the way Elvira hung all over him. How she always wanted to hold his hand and lay on him. The way she professed her love for him made him feel extra special. Without her even saying a word, he could always tell how much she cared about him by the look on her face. She was transparent.

"What did you think of the way I ended our story?" Michael waited patiently for her response.

Elvira thought for a few moments. She said, "In the ending we run away together. We run away to another country. Leaving this old world behind to start a new life together. You never said where."

"Italy," Michael said. "A little town called Positano. It's on the Amalfi Coast. We would have an apartment with a balcony view. It would overlook the Mediterranean Sea. There'd be fresh fruits growing in our backyard. We'd wake up to the smell of fresh espresso in the morning and fall asleep with a warm buzz from red wine at night. We'd grow old together. Who knows? Maybe we'd even have a real baby.

As Michael spoke, Elvira closed her eyes. She imagined the magical moment with a vivid image in her brain. She took a deep breath and then opened her eyes.

"It's perfect," Elvira said. "You'll love me even when I look old? When I'd be all wrinkly? When my hair is gray? When I'm sick? You'll even love me when I get annoying and picky?"

"I'll love you until end of time," he said.

Michael and Elvira slowly leaned in for a long kiss. A thought came to her mind. She pulled away. "I think you should add to your ending," Elvira said. "I don't think that's the real end of our story, just part of it."

Michael was confused. He didn't know what could be better than a life in Italy, where everything was perfect. "What do you think the ending should be?" he asked.

Elvira smiled. She was confident in her answer. She replied, "I think the ending should be that we'd be in heaven together. In heaven, you get everything you want. Our souls can spend the rest of eternity together. We'd never have to be separated, there'd be no pain or sickness. Only happiness, only us. No matter what happens to us in this life, we'll find each other there."

Michael never thought about heaven before. That in heaven, maybe you do get everything you want, there's a life of peace after this one. What Elvira told Michael that day was right from her heart. Spending a life in heaven together truly means immortality. It meant that Elvira realized she was Michael's soulmate. It was the best way of saying "I love you."

"That's probably the most beautiful thing anyone has ever told me," Michael said. "I think that will be our ending. That's our story."

8

CHAPTER

Manhattan was a little extra quiet on this day, which was a rare event. The weather was windy and cold. It was lightly snowing. Michael aimlessly walked around the city, attempting to clear his head. He could never just put his pen to the paper and write. Writing for Michael was like bleeding all over the page. What he wrote needed to be from his heart. To have that, a clear mind was essential. He happened to be walking past Washington Square Park when he saw a flag waving on a lamppost. New York University sported purple flags along the areas that were considered parts of its campus. Michael followed the long line of flags until he reached a large building with huge glass doors. There was darkness around the entire building aside from those two doors. It was almost like someone was guiding him to enter the building. The light was paving his path.

Michael stumbled upon the admissions department. He approached a friendly secretary behind the desk.

"How are you doing today ma'am?" Michael asked courteously. "I'm interested in becoming a student here at NYU. Can I have information on your undergraduate programs?"

The secretary smiled. She was extremely friendly and helpful. "You came at the right time. Admissions for the spring semester is going to close within the next few weeks. If you fill out this paperwork we can get your application in."

The secretary invited Michael to have a seat. She had a peculiar aura around her. For some strange reason, Michael felt safe. It was a protective vibe he was getting from the secretary, it could be considered along the lines of a comforting parent. She handed him brochures that showed the various programs the university offered.

"We offer over fifty undergraduate programs," the secretary said. "Look through these and see what interests you the most."

Michael combed through the brochures and stopped when he saw the psychology program. He smiled.

"Can I have the application to the psychology program?"

The secretary nodded. "We have one of the most prestigious psychology programs in the country."

"Well, I'm glad to hear that," Michael said. "I'll be back with the completed application soon."

Michael shook the woman's hand and thanked her. He got out of his seat and walked towards the door. The secretary tried to get Michael's attention before he left. "Excuse me sir," the secretary yelled.

Michael turned around. "Yes?"

"You picked the right school Michael. Elvira is going to be happy here."

All the color drained from Michael's face. He stared at the secretary with a blank look. His brain was trying to process what the secretary had said. Michael thought he just heard Elvira's name. Michael didn't believe there was any way this secretary could have known he was getting an application for her. How could she know he wasn't interested in being a student?

"I'm sorry, I didn't hear you," Michael said. "Could you say that again?"

The secretary repeated herself. "You picked the right school, I think you're going to be happy here."

Michael started to think he may have just been hearing things. He lightly tapped his ears a few times and exited the building.

Michael spent the day traveling across Manhattan getting brochures from various schools. He wanted Elvira to have a wide variety of options. He knew it was her dream to become a psychologist. Elvira pushed him out of his comfort zone. She gave Michael encouragement and confidence. She was one of the first people to truly believe in him. Michael only wanted to do the same for her. Elvira was one of the smartest people Michael had ever met. Her intelligence was all natural, she could have never gone to school a day in her life and she would have still been just as smart. He could hear it by the way she talked.

Elvira spent her entire day in the bookstore near her home. She sat down in an aisle that was secluded. Elvira enjoyed sitting on the floor as opposed to a table. She loved the smell of the paper in the air and the feel of book pages turning between her fingers. Elvira's favorite kinds of books were classic novels. The kind most people would find hard to understand. These were the type of novels that take up three or four pages describing how someone crossed the street. These tiny details were her favorite part of reading.

Elvira loved the artist in Michael. She saw the writer within that was screaming to tell a story. From the first day they met, Elvira knew that Michael was uneasy. Elvira believed talented minds, were always the most troubled. Michael wasn't troubled in the rebellious sense, but instead in a sweet way. Michael was searching for a higher meaning, a reason to be inspired and a reason to live. Elvira treasured the fact that she served as that inspiration for him. That she was the woman who brought him to life. She was the woman who helped him pursue his dreams. Elvira was truly his muse.

Every writer could always improve. The more they read, the more they write, the better an author they would eventually become. Michael had one tiny problem, he never read. When he did read, it was a magazine or a history textbook. He never read novels or stories that would exercise the creative part of his brain. Elvira wanted to encourage Michael to read more so his writing could improve. She knew that if a book came as a gift from her, Michael would be more inclined to read.

Knowing Michael so well, Elvira combed through the bookstore for a read he would enjoy. Hundreds of novels flashed through her mind. Elvira and Michael were both old souls. Their taste in trends were far older than their actual age. They both enjoyed the idea of living in a time that was more classy, elegant, and traditional.

Elvira's mind continued to race. She didn't want to give Michael anything that was too hard to read. She searched for something more enjoyable, so that it would turn him on to similar genres. Suddenly, a choice surfaced. Elvira raced across the bookstore to the historical fiction section. She scrolled her fingers across the bookshelf until she found her novel of choice. The last copy of The Great Gatsby stood on the shelf untouched and dusty. Elvira wiped dust off the cover of the novel.

The Great Gatsby was the perfect fit for Michael to begin his journey reading. It took place in the 1920s, an era of true class. Women dressed to the nines. They sported short dresses and short hair for the first time. Their clothes were flashy. They danced the Charleston to loud jazz music. Men wore full, three-piece suits. Tuxedos were essential on special occasions. Finding a drink was difficult, but not that hard. Speakeasies were the place to be. On top of it all, The Great Gatsby was a love story. It was the story of a tragic love, but Elvira knew Michael would enjoy it.

London Lennie's was one of top ranked seafood restaurants in all of Queens. It was the practically the size of the entire block. Large golden letters hanging above the door bore the restaurant's name. There was always a smell of fresh broiled fish in the air. A tank of lobsters that customers could choose from sat near the door. The restaurant looked rustic, like an old pub in England. Michael had been going there since he was a child. The owner originally started with a small storefront that sold fresh fish. After years of hard work, he expanded his business and opened a seafood restaurant that now served the finest fish in New York City.

Michael sat at a table waiting for Elvira to arrive. He had a folder in his hands filled with brochures from colleges across the New York City area.

Elvira entered the restaurant and looked especially beautiful. She was wearing a bright pink jacket that had a flamingo on it. Elvira always wore clothing that was out of the ordinary. She loved being different from everyone else. There wasn't one definitive sense of style Elvira had. She could be wearing anything from farmer's overalls, an elegant dress, sweatpants, or a shawl. He never knew which Elvira he was going to get, and that was just the way he liked it.

Elvira smiled at Michael from a distance. Every time Michael saw her, his heart was beating rapidly. Without fail, this happened no matter the amount of time spent with her. It was like Michael was going on his first date all over again. That one special feeling never faded away. As she walked towards him, Michael's heart pumped faster. She sat down at the table with a small box in her hand.

Michael smiled at her. "You look exactly like a Pink Lady from *Grease*."

Elvira ran her fingers through her hair. She laughed. "Tell me about it, stud."

A little box Elvira was holding caught Michael's eye. He tried to act like he didn't notice. Michael wanted Elvira to mention it first. He didn't want to ruin any surprise she had for him.

Michael handed Elvira a menu. "I ordered two dozen oysters for us to start."

Elvira nodded. "Are they Blue Point oysters? All the rest taste too fishy."

Michael smiled at her. "My God do I love you," he said. "Of course, they're Blue Points, no other kind of oysters could compare."

The waiter brought the oysters to their table. Elvira took a small bottle of wine out of her purse. She poured the wine into an empty glass on the table.

"Don't tell me," Michael joked. "You're carrying wine in your purse now to?"

Elvira laughed. "I've been stuck on this one kind of red wine," she said. "It's Italian. I can't drink any other kind of red wine now."

"You need to keep me updated on these weekly trends," Michael joked. "I wanna be in on this too."

Elvira poured Michael a glass of the wine she was carrying. They both split the oysters evenly, having twelve each. They smelled nothing like fish and tasted completely fresh. Elvira seasoned her oysters with salt and pepper while Michael preferred to use hot sauce.

After they finished eating, Elvira was ready to reveal her gift to Michael. She held the box near her ear and shook it a few times. "I did a little shopping today," she said. "I saw something and thought of you."

Michael was giddy. He could see how much thought went behind everything Elvira did. Michael and Elvira were always on each other's minds. A day didn't go by without them thinking of one another. There was too much in the world to remind them of each other.

Michael waited patiently holding back his excitement. He waved around the folder in his hand.

"You're not the only one who did a little shopping today," Michael said. "I have a little surprise of my own."

What Michael had in that folder was going to change Elvira's life forever. He was going to encourage Elvira to do something she never thought she could accomplish alone. Elvira just needed a little push, the same way Michael did. Love and encouragement go a long way, especially when it's from your soulmate.

"I'll go first," Elvira said playfully.

Elvira handed Michael the box. Michael let the excitement overtake him. He opened the box and pulled out the novel Elvira bought for him. He ran his fingers over the cover.

"I want you to read it," Elvira said. "I probably thought about over one hundred books that I could have gotten you, but this one stuck out the most. I know you're an old soul, just like me. It's a book about the 1920s. I think you'll really enjoy it."

Michael stared at the book in awe. He mumbled to himself, "*The Great Gatsby*. It's funny you picked this book, I was supposed to read this around fifteen years ago in high school."

Michael turned the cover over. On the dedication page, there was a note from Elvira.

Dear Michael,

I know your dream is to become a writer. One of the best ways for a writer to improve is by reading more often. I figured if this book came from me, it would encourage you to read more. No matter what happens, just know that I'll always have faith in you. Whether you become a famous writer or not, your words will always mean the world to me. I love everything about you. These past few months have been the most amazing of my entire life, and I hope we get to have many more.

After reading the note, there were tears in Michael's eyes. Small gestures like this meant the most to him. Money never mattered to Michael. In his mind, it was just paper. There was so much more to life than worrying about expensive things. What comes from the heart matters the most. When a person does what they love, their whole world starts to fall into place. Michael and Elvira were starting their journey down that very path.

Michael held his hand out. Elvira placed her hand on top of his. Michael brought her hand up to his lips. He kissed her.

"I'm going to finish this book by the end of the night," Michael said. "You'll always be the reason why I'm inspired to write. Thank you, my love."

Michael always held that book close to him. He never let that book out of his sight. That small gesture meant more than any gift a person had ever gotten him.

Elvira pointed to Michael's folder. "Now what could you possibly have in there?" she asked. "I never know when it comes to you. You're always so very sneaky with your surprises."

Michael laughed. "There's really no one way to explain it. It's like the gift you gave me. I want you to follow your dreams. Your happiness means the most to me. I crave seeing that beautiful smile on your face."

He handed Elvira the folder. Elvira excitedly combed through all the papers. Page by page she turned the papers over. Elvira saw applications from schools across the entire New York area. She was left completely speechless. She stared down at the papers for a few moments in silence and then glanced up at Michael.

"These are all applications for schools," she said. "There's information on psychology programs in here."

Michael smiled. "I remember you telling me that you wanted to study psychology. I went to all the colleges that offer psychology programs in the area. I have a feeling NYU may be the best choice. I had an oddly spiritual experience there, but it's up to you of course."

Before Michael could even finish his sentence, Elvira jumped out of her seat. The papers flew everywhere in a gust of wind. She ran to Michael and hugged him, almost knocking his seat over. Elvira hugged Michael tightly. She never wanted to let go. Elvira always needed a strong man in her life. She could be as delicate as a flower or as fierce as a lion. Elvira needed someone to support her going to school, it was a scary journey. It wasn't going to be easy, but Elvira knew Michael would support her though it all.

As the days passed, their love for each other grew. Michael and Elvira weren't only lovers, but best friends. Together, they picked up the pieces of their messy lives. For once, their lives were both on track to being steady. With Michael's support, Elvira would reapply to school and pursue her dream of becoming a psychologist.

Michael placed his hand on his head. He began to breathe heavily. "I can't put my finger on it, but I feel really weird," he joked. "I think these oysters are doing something to me."

Elvira laughed. She saw right through Michael's ploy. "Oh, really now?" she said. "You know what, I'm starting to feel a little off as well. Maybe it is the oysters."

Michael snickered. "You know, they say oysters are an aphrodisiac," he said smoothly. "Maybe that's what's going on."

Elvira teased Michael. "I'm pretty sure that's a myth," she said. "But nice try Casanova."

Michael loosened his shirt's collar. "I don't know about that," he joked. "The way I'm feeling is starting to tell me otherwise. I think we should take advantage of this special moment."

Michael and Elvira locked eyes. They waited to see who would break to make the first move and run for the door. They both wanted to fulfill their strong urges, but neither made a move. It didn't take long for Michael to break. He took money out of his pocket and threw it on the table. He grabbed Elvira's hand and they ran towards the door of the restaurant. In a whirlwind, they weaved between the waiters and waitresses carrying food.

Michael sat in his bed reading *The Great Gatsby*. He was already halfway done with the book. Michael had a stigmatism in both his eyes, which left him with blurry vision when reading small print or staring at something for too long. He was forced to wear these thick framed glasses. Elvira walked into Michael's room and searched his dresser for a shirt. She had just finished taking a shower and was wrapped in a towel.

Michael looked up at her. "You know, you're quite distracting," Michael said smiling.

Elvira chuckled. "I have no clue what you're talking about."

"How do you think I can finish this book while you're standing over there soaking wet in a towel?" Michael said snickering.

"Well, now you know how it feels. Remember that day you took a shower in my apartment?" Elvira smiled thinking about the moment. She fired back. "Besides, why can't you concentrate on two things at once?"

They laughed together. Elvira put on Michael's shirt and crawled in the bed next to him. She watched him quietly read.

Elvira pointed to Michael's glasses. "You have glasses?" she asked.

"Yes, they're my reading glasses," he said. "As you know, I don't read very often. That's why you haven't seen them."

"I like them a lot," she said. "I like what you got going on over there."

Michael let his glasses fall to the tip of his nose. He looked at Elvira seductively.

"Do I look like a writer now?"

Elvira bit her lip. "You look like one of those sexy author types."

Michael took off his glasses. He held them in his left hand. "You know, when I become famous, you're going to have to share me with the rest of the world."

"I'll never share you," she said. "You're all mine. Forever and always."

"That's what I like to hear," Michael replied confidently.

Elvira kissed Michael goodnight. She turned over and tried to get some sleep. Elvira always had trouble falling asleep. She would toss and turn until she found the right position to sleep in. After that, she'd turn the pillow back and forth to try and find the cold side. In the midst of Elvira's complicated sleeping process, she suddenly farted. She didn't fart intentionally, but let it unknowingly slip. She pretended to sleep with her back turned to Michael. Elvira prayed he didn't hear her fart.

Michael slowly turned his head away from his book. He noticed Elvira was silent and didn't move. Michael figured she was probably too embarrassed.

Michael held in all the laughter. "Did you hear something?" Michael asked.

Elvira didn't say anything. She continued pretending to sleep. Michael peered over Elvira's body and looked at her face. She appeared to be sleeping, but Michael could tell she was acting.

"You know I could have sworn I heard a fart," he said. "I know for a fact it wasn't me."

Michael kept looking at Elvira's face. He saw a small crack of a smile during her fake sleep. Michael moved closer to Elvira's ear. His whispered, "You little liar."

Elvira uncontrollably laughed. When Elvira thought something was really funny, her laugh was like a mini-Hollywood production. She threw her whole body into it. When she smiled, all her teeth showed. Her voice got high and raspy. Michael laughed right along with her. There was no wrong that Elvira could do in Michael's eyes. He loved her the way she was.

9

CHAPTER

Allison was an intelligent woman, just like Elvira, also made a life for herself in New York. Allison worked as a physician's assistant in the same office as Elvira. She did well for herself and lived in an upscale home just outside of Queens. Allison commuted from Great Neck, an area that was known to people who were financially well-off. Great Neck was a quiet town. It was never too busy or too slow. It had just the right amount of the hustle and bustle of Manhattan. At the same time, it still felt like an escape.

Allison was messy and unorganized. There were papers sprawled out all over her home. Clothes laid all over the floor, Allison didn't have a clue whether they were clean or dirty. Elvira and Allison sat at a table together. Like the rest of Allison's home, the table was messy. The two of them were filling out Elvira's applications for college. Elvira asked for Allison's help because she already went through the process. Allison combed through the applications to see which schools Elvira was going to apply to.

"Are all these applications from schools in the city area?" Allison asked.

Elvira shrugged her shoulders. "I'm pretty sure they are. Michael got them all for me. He went to each school personally. He didn't know which one I would prefer."

Allison continued to comb through the applications. She pulled out the application for NYU. "NYU is by far the best school here," Allison said confidently. "I'm not so sure about the others. Did you ever consider broadening your horizons?"

Elvira gave Allison a confused look. She had trouble believing what Allison was saying. "You mean schools outside of New York?"

Allison nodded. Elvira was angry that Allison had even brought up the idea. She worked hard to build a life here. She finally found some stability and a man who completely adores her. Elvira didn't understand why Allison would want her to throw that all away.

"Don't give me that look," Allison said. "I know what you're thinking. Humor me though, what happens if you don't get into NYU? You want to go to the best school, don't you? You're a smart woman. Going to a city school is going to be a waste of a great mind."

As much as Elvira didn't want to hear it, Allison was right. Elvira wanted to attend the best school possible. She had been given another chance at life, and now was her time to seize the opportunity.

"I guess I could apply to a few schools outside of New York incase. I don't know what I'm going to tell Michael though."

Allison sighed. "Elvira, I know you love him. From what you told me, Michael seems like a great guy. That means he'll only want the best for you. Besides, this is all a backup plan. Don't say anything for now, wait and see if NYU accepts you first."

Elvira innocently agreed. She didn't think much of the decision at the time. There was no harm in applying. "What schools do you think would fit me well?"

Allison picked a piece of paper up from off the floor. She wrote down a list of five more schools she thought Elvira should apply to.

"Check out these schools, see which one you like the most," Allison said. "I know for a fact they have some of the top psychology programs."

Michael sat at a desk in his apartment. There were two candles lit next to him. He enjoyed the smell that came from candles, it calmed him. The lights in his apartment were dim. When Michael wrote, he needed complete and total silence. He paced around his apartment thinking for a few hours. When he found the perfect pattern to put his ideas together, Michael wrote it all down. Michael always carried a notepad with him. Whenever an idea passed his mind, he had to write it down. The notepad had random phrases and memories scribbled everywhere. It was barely legible. The notepad had pages full of unforgettable moments in his life and Elvira's. Moments he felt needed to be included to get the story of their love across properly. Before Michael even wrote his novel, he was confident it was going to be a smash hit. This feeling had nothing to do with cockiness, Michael wasn't even confident in his work. He was confident that people would want to read a story of a love that truly did exist, a story of two people being brought together by unforeseen circumstances. How those two people changed each other's lives. Michael was confident in the reader's ability to understand what love means.

When Michael finished scribbling on his notepad he ripped off the pages from the legal pad and taped it to the wall in front of him. It was a technique Elvira suggested. He always took whatever suggestions she had into consideration. To Michael, her opinion was gold. He leaned back in his chair and thought about the pages taped to the wall.

Michael closed his eyes. He took in all his feelings. It was important that Michael allowed himself to feel. His feelings needed to show through his writing. Michael's mind was troubled and complicated. Everything he did was always a process. Some would say he had a touch of obsessive compulsive disorder. He was a classic over analyzer. Michael's obsessive qualities were a blessing and a curse. It helped or hurt him depending on the situation. His disorder always forced him to picture everything he went through multiple times in his brain. Michael's mind was always running. It acted like a movie projector, replaying events over again every day. That's why he enjoyed film so much. It was the only way he could escape his own mind. Michael related everything in his life to a movie. The little projector running in his head never stopped.

Michael walked over to his closet and tore it apart. He threw everything inside onto the floor. He was searching for a rusty metal box with an old typewriter inside. Michael hadn't touched it in years.

"Ahha!" He dragged the metal box across the floor and opened it. The typewriter looked untouched. The typewriter was a gift he received many years ago. His grandfather, who he referred to as *nonno*, gave it to him. *Nonno* helped him through many dark times in his life, offering wisdom and advice. Although *nonno* shared the same old school Sicilian mentality as his father, he saw Michael's talent. He realized it was worth Michael taking the risk of pursuing this dream. Since he passed away, Michael hadn't touched the typewriter. He lost the one father figure he had, and it threw him into a deep depression. Michael let the typewriter collect dust in the bottom of his closet, not daring to disturb the demons he put away. With encouragement from Elvira, Michael finally felt it was time to start writing again.

As Michael wrote, his heart bled. He unearthed his own dark past. Putting his thoughts onto paper made his life seem much worse than it ever was. Reading back the words aloud rehashed the horrible experiences he faced. Writing could be emotionally strenuous when the story is based off life events.

The candle's wick slowly burned away as the time passed. Hours had gone by, and Michael refused to stop writing. A wave of creativity was flowing through him. Happiness, sadness, and fear pumped through his fingers as he wrote. His words dripped off the page with pure emotion. By dawn,

Michael had a pile of papers beside him. His phone started to ring. Michael was so tired that his body completely ignored the sound. He collapsed on his desk and fell asleep. Through all the thinking and emotional strain, Michael finally produced the first fifty pages of his novel.

Elvira spent her entire night calling Michael's apartment. He didn't attempt to contact her the entire day. They never went more than a few hours without talking. Elvira thought that something bad happened to Michael. Her naturally calm and laid-back attitude suddenly shifted. Fear took over her mind. Hundreds of thoughts and possibilities swarmed her brain. She worked herself up to the point where she couldn't rest without knowing Michael was safe.

A vicious snow storm raged that day. By the evening, the weather got worse. The darkness and the snowy wind made it virtually impossible to see. Elvira bundled up for a winter expedition. She put on a scarf, a hat, and a puffy winter jacket. Elvira didn't care how bad it looked, as all she wanted was to survive the cold. Resembling an Eskimo, Elvira marched through the storm, down Ditmars Boulevard. The wind was blowing furiously, making the cold weather piercing. The streets were completely lifeless. Cars were abandoned in the middle of the road because it was too dangerous to drive. Luckily, Elvira only endured this weather for a few blocks. She finally reached Michael's building. Her face almost blistering from the cold, she shook all the snow off her body and frantically ran up the stairs.

Elvira knocked on Michael's door three times. She desperately waited for a response, but there was no answer. Elvira shook the door's knob with both hands and the door slowly opened. She poked her head inside and looked around.

"Michael?" she said. "Michael are you here?"

Elvira searched his apartment for any signs of life. She walked into Michael's bedroom and spotted him slumped over his desk. Elvira immediately noticed the pile of papers and his typewriter.

Elvira smiled. "He was writing," she said.

Elvira pulled a chair next to Michael's desk. She watched him sleep. Elvira whispered in his ear. "For a minute, I thought I lost you."

The sound of a gunshot couldn't have woken Michael up. Elvira ran her fingers along the typewriter. She wondered why Michael never mentioned it. Elvira picked up the first pages to Michael's novel and held them in her hand. Mindlessly, she stared at the cover page. She was split between reading it now or waiting for Michael to read it to her. Elvira brought the novel into the kitchen and placed it on the table. While she decided, Elvira brewed espresso.

Elvira opened the kitchen cabinets to find Michael's *maginet* pot. She never used one before, but she always watched Michael when he made coffee. She struggled taking the pot apart. The bottom half of the pot often got stuck. Elvira banged it on the counter a few times, and the bottom half loosened. She grinded the espresso beans and covered the grinder with a towel so the sound wouldn't wake Michael. As the coffee pot brewed, Elvira anxiously stared at

Michael's novel. She turned over the cover page and read the first sentence.

Michael woke from his deep sleep. He stretched his back and arms. His back cracked from being hunched over a chair though the night. Michael noticed the pages to his novel were missing. He scrambled through all the papers on his desk, desperately searching for his work. He remembered leaving the pile stacked on his desk the night before.

The sound of the coffee pot bubbling reached Michael's bedroom. He slowly walked toward the kitchen to investigate the noise. Michael peeked over the wall and spotted Elvira sitting quietly at the kitchen table.

Michael was never a morning person, but the very sight of Elvira could change his whole attitude. His grumpiness fled. "If I called the cops right now, I could get you for breaking and entering," Michael joked. He pointed to his novel. "Also, theft of my property."

Elvira jumped when she heard Michael's voice. "I came by because I didn't hear from you all day. I thought something bad happened."

Michael wanted to hear that Elvira worried about him. He wanted to know she cared. He loved the idea of her running over to see if he was okay. Michael never had that before. The other women he dated couldn't have cared less if they hadn't talked to him for a day.

Michael turned the gas on the stove off. He poured two cups of coffee, one for himself and one for Elvira. He sat across from her. Elvira pushed the novel over to him.

"Did you read it yet?" Michael asked.

"I fought with myself over it. If you didn't just wake up, the temptation might have gotten to me."

"I'm not going to read it to you," Michael said sternly.

Elvira's instant reaction was sadness. She anxiously wanted to read Michael's novel.

"Why not?" she asked sadly.

"Because I want to finish it first. I want you to fully absorb it all in one sitting."

Elvira pouted. "Well, that's lame." She said.

Michael laughed. "You're just going to have to be patient. I'll be finished with it in a few months."

10

CHAPTER

Michael and Elvira lived the next few months in total happiness. No relationship is perfect, but they made it work. A relationship is like playing tennis. You're always on your feet, and you need to be ready to flow with the changes. Good chemistry with your partner is important. The game never gets dull and every serve always offers something new.

The dreadful New York winter finally started to subside. Spring was approaching. Flowers were just beginning to bloom. At this very moment, life was peachy, they finally found stability. Unfortunately, their happiness didn't last for long. There is no life without conflict. Even the best relationships go through highs and lows. Michael and Elvira's relationship was about to face its first test. Not every relationship is meant to last. One major event would prove if Michael and Elvira could withstand their first emotional hurdle.

Elvira waited restlessly at the entrance to her apartment building. She had an odd feeling her acceptance letter to NYU was going to get delivered today. She had gotten accepted to every school she applied to. NYU was the last one on her list.

It was also her top choice. There wasn't any doubt in Elvira's mind, she was confident.

The mailman entered her apartment building. He put letters in the apartment mailboxes. She waited for him to finish putting all the mail in their designated boxes. Elvira ran over to her mailbox and combed through the letters. The last letter of the bunch was from NYU. The purple envelope stuck out. The envelope was small. This worried her, but she tried to stay hopeful.

Elvira tore open the envelope. She read the letter with a bright smile on her face. She wanted to see the word "Congratulations" in the first paragraph. The first person she planned to call was Michael. He was the one who pushed her to take this leap of faith. Elvira knew he'd be so proud of her. While this fantasy would seem all but a perfect ending to their story, fate had other plans. Elvira was not accepted to NYU and faced a difficult decision that could severely strain her newfound love. She dropped the letter on the floor and dragged herself to her apartment.

Allison was the first person Elvira called. She rushed over to Elvira's apartment to help figure things out. Allison felt at fault for Elvira's pain, she was the one who encouraged her to apply to schools out of state. Allison just wanted the best for her friend, but she did realize she may have caused her more harm than good. Allison sat on Elvira's couch hugging her best friend.

"I'm sure Michael will understand," Allison said. "You're overreacting."

Elvira stopped crying. She gave Allison an angry look. "If he just decided to leave and write in some random place without telling me anything, I'd kill him."

Allison's face dropped. "I guess you have a point," she said sadly. "When are you going to break the news to him?"

"He's taking me to Long Island tomorrow," Elvira said. "I'm going to have to tell him right away. Michael knows me too well. He'll know something is wrong."

Allison shrugged her shoulders. "Try to break it to him slowly. You never know, he might take it really well."

Tears streamed down Elvira's face. Her eyes were red and puffy. Her skin was extra pale. Elvira became physically sick over anticipating what was next to come.

"I know him," Elvira said sternly. "This is going to break his heart."

Port Washington was a small town on Long Island that offered unforgettable views. There was always a slight breeze. A row of small shops and stores were spread across the area near a harbor. The harbor was adjacent to the legendary Louie's Oyster Bar & Grille established in 1905. It offered a beautiful view of the docked ships while dining.

Michael borrowed Billy's car for the trip to Port Washington. As Michael and Elvira passed through the small town, she took in all the sights. She loved the atmosphere the town had. A gaggle of geese crossed the street, marching towards the harbor. Michael stopped the car to let them pass before he entered the harbor's parking lot.

"Look at the baby geese!" Elvira said excitedly.

"I wonder what a group of geese is called," Michael said.

"A flock?" she replied.

"No," Michael said. "I think there's a specific word for it."

Port Washington served as the inspiration for East Egg in *The Great Gatsby*. Michael recently finished the book. He wanted to show Elvira that he did his homework on the background of the story.

Michael drove up to the water as far as he possibly could. For a few moments, they soaked in the awe-inspiring view. The sun was just about to set. It gave the sky a bright orange color. The shadows of the boats reflected on the clear blue water. It was so quiet, that they could hear the creaking of the boats floating.

Michael and Elvira explored the harbor. They walked to the outermost part of the pier. Together, they stared out into Manhasset Bay.

Michael pointed across the bay. "You see that small spot right over there?" he asked her.

Elvira nodded. "Yes, I do."

"This is where the green light is supposed to flash in the book. Where we are standing right now is East Egg. Jay Gatsby waited on the other side of the Manhasset Bay for Daisy's green light."

Elvira smiled. "I see you finished the book already. What did you think?"

"I loved it," Michael said. "It gave me the inspiration to come here and see this very spot for myself."

The wind lightly blew through Elvira's hair. It was slowly getting darker outside as the sun set. Elvira was deep in thought. She stared aimlessly at the water. There was no place in the world she'd rather be. Elvira tried to hold back her tears, she was fearful that this could all come to an end.

"Wouldn't it be nice to live here?" she asked. "Only a few minutes away from this beautiful view."

Michael shrugged his shoulders. "One day," he said. "Your time will come."

Elvira sat on a bench nearby. She couldn't hold in her sadness any longer. Elvira wore her emotions. Michael could sniff out exactly how she was feeling with little effort. She put her head down, attempting to hide her face.

"We need to talk," Elvira said. "I've been hiding something from you."

Michael's entire demeanor changed. He knew what Elvira wanted to say was going to be serious. Michael could tell by the tone of her voice. He always anticipated the worst possible outcome. Whenever Michael was at his happiest, something came along to take that happiness away. He always felt the rug was swept from under him. Some would say those are the highs and lows that come with life, but Michael always took it personally.

"Ok," Michael said softly.

Elvira couldn't find the words. She knew that no matter what way she put it, Michael was going to take this harshly.

"I didn't get into NYU," she said sadly. "I got into every school besides NYU. The thing is I applied to a few schools out of state."

Michael sat down next to Elvira. "Why would you apply out of state? I didn't give you any brochures from a school out of state."

Elvira saw that Michael was upset. "Allison suggested I applied for a few top programs outside of the city just in case I didn't get accepted to NYU. I did get accepted to this amazing program in California. It offers me so many more opportunities than the schools around here do."

Michael was speechless. He couldn't believe what he was hearing. He didn't feel sadness or anger. Michael didn't feel anything. He was in a state of total shock. This is the last thing he would have ever expected Elvira to do.

"Tell me you're not considering doing this?" Michael asked.

Tears streamed down Elvira's face. "I'm considering it Michael."

Michael said nothing. He didn't move or speak. All he did was sit. Michael couldn't even look Elvira's way. He was afraid to make eye contact with her. Painful intrusive thoughts rushed right into his mind.

"I think we should go," Michael said calmly. "This probably isn't the place to discuss this."

Elvira nodded in agreement. She originally planned on waiting, but the anticipation was eating her alive. Michael and Elvira drove home in total silence. They didn't say a word to each other. The two were at a loss for words.

Michael parked his car in front of Elvira's apartment building. Elvira exited the car first and walked up the steps alone. Michael sat in the car by himself for a moment, he took a deep breath. Before he followed her, Michael grabbed a small folder from the backseat of Billy's car.

Elvira sat on the couch hugging a pillow. She didn't have the strength to even look forward. A heavy weight kept pushing her chin to her chest. It was the first sign of a serious depression that was unfolding. She felt it creeping up on her. Michael entered her apartment abruptly. He slammed the door behind him. Elvira jumped from the loud sound. She had never seen him this bent out of shape. He always appeared calm to her.

"How could you ever consider doing this?" Michael said loudly.

Elvira didn't move. She didn't even look at Michael. She could hear the anger in his voice. "I'm already thirty-one years old. This is a once in a lifetime opportunity for me. I may never get the chance to do this again. It's a very prestigious program. They're going to set me up with a career. It would only be for one school year."

Michael sat in a chair across from Elvira. He put his head in his hands. Michael looked defeated.

"I can't believe you're doing this to us!" he said.

Elvira felt attacked by Michael's words. She also felt a little hurt that he was reacting so poorly to something she really wanted to do. Instead of offering a solution, Michael kept blaming her.

Elvira fired back at him. "Don't pin it all on me. This was your idea in the first place."

Michael got up out of his seat. He waved his arms frantically. He screamed, "I didn't want you to move across the God damn fucking country!"

Michael's yelling scared Elvira. She had never seen him act this way before. Michael's entire demeanor changed. His teeth were clenched together tightly, his face red, and his eyebrows scrunched together.

Elvira stood nose to nose with Michael. She tucked her fears away. She was on the cusp of her own fit of rage. Like Michael, Elvira was fierce. She was not the kind of woman to double-cross. It was a side of her personality Michael had not yet seen. "Don't look at me like that," she said. "It's my life not yours. I can do whatever I want."

Michael's eyes bulged. He couldn't believe what was being said. There was so much anger pumping through his blood, he didn't know how to use the energy. The anger was a reaction to the sadness he was feeling. This situation was out of Michael's control, and he knew it. He felt that life was once again finding a way to kick him down.

Michael turned away from Elvira. He walked towards the door, attempting to defuse the argument. He waved her off. "It's nice to know that you didn't include other people in your life plans," he said.

Elvira grabbed his arm tightly. She whisked him around to face her. As angry as Elvira was, she didn't want Michael to leave. "You're making this decision a lot easier with the way you've been acting," Elvira said sternly.

Michael's anger continued to grow. He couldn't understand why Elvira would leave. In his mind, she already made her decision. Michael was starting to convince himself that Elvira didn't care about him and all of this was a lie. This feeling was an irrational one, but it came from a deep place in Michael's mind. Throughout his life, he had always been pushed aside and kicked to the curb by those he loved. This clearly wasn't true with Elvira, and Michael knew that in his heart. However, this special situation made his negative thoughts a little more real. Michael was fighting a battle in his mind, and the negative thoughts were winning. They were forcing him to react impulsively.

"You know what," Michael said. "Why don't we call it quits? If you leave everything is going to change. How could we survive being away from each other for one whole school year? We'll both go crazy. Do me a favor and make it easy on me. Leave sooner. Let's rip this off like a bandage. It would be better for the both of us."

Elvira stared at Michael with a blank face. Her heart was broken. She never expected Michael to say something like that. The looming depression Elvira felt took over her mind. She cried uncontrollably. Michael's words felt painful to hear, Elvira would rather him drive a knife through her heart. The feeling she was having was unbearable.

In between her sobbing, she said, "I thought we'd never have to say goodbye, but I guess this is it."

Elvira ran into her bedroom, shoving Michael out of the way. He chased her, only to meet the door slamming within an inch of his face. Michael banged on the door to get Elvira's attention.

He pleaded. "Elvira, please open the door!"

There was no response. All Michael could hear were faint cries. Elvira cried into her pillow, so Michael wouldn't be able to hear. He continued to bang on the door.

"I love you," he said calmly. "I only reacted so harshly because I love you. I never thought I'd lose you this way."

There was still no response from Elvira. All the color drained from Michael's face. There was no more swagger in his step. The new colors of the world he saw so vividly were fading away. Michael reverted to the old version of himself. He was once again a lost soul. Michael slowly walked away from the bedroom door. His body felt limp, with little strength in his bones, Michael dragged his feet across the wooden floor. He didn't feel the need to pick up his feet while walking.

The folder he brought into Elvira's apartment rested on the kitchen table. Michael opened the folder. Inside was the manuscript of his novel. The novel wasn't anywhere near complete, but he planned to surprise Elvira with the first one hundred pages.

Tears streamed down his face. He mumbled to himself, "I hope this isn't the last Chapter in our story."

Michael threw the manuscript down on Elvira's kitchen table. He abruptly walked out of the apartment, slamming the door behind him. In the hallway, Michael let out a large scream. Behind the scream wasn't anger, but sheer pain. A wave of anxiety crashed over his body. Michael felt completely out of control. His hands were shaking, and he couldn't catch his breath. Michael worked himself up into a full-blown panic attack. Without thinking, Michael punched

a hole right through the wall in the hallway. His hand pro-
fusely bled from the cuts and scrapes of the sheetrock. When
Michael met Elvira, he promised himself his anger would
never get this far out of control again. He already saw himself
slowly regressing.

Elvira heard the bang and ran out into the hallway.
Michael was not there, but she noticed the fist-sized hole in
the wall near her apartment door. She was surprised to see
Michael this angry and upset over her. He was the one who
asked to part ways. As she walked pass the kitchen table,
Elvira noticed Michael's novel. She violently grabbed it and
held it close to her body.

She screamed, "Why do you always make it impossible
for me to hate you? Even when you're not here, you still find
a way to make me love you more than I already do. Why did
you have to say goodbye?"

Michael found himself right back where he started this journey, drinking to mask his pain. He walked into a local biker
hangout. The bar was lit with red light bulbs. It made the
dirtiness and eeriness of the bar even more profound. The
criminal-like bikers were playing pool in the corner of the
room. They were tall and wore leather vests with a patch
that read, "Satan's Horde." Their beards were dirty, and an
awful smell of body odor reeked off their skin. Michael found
himself in a lion's den. The bikers could smell that new blood
was in the room. He didn't have raggedy biker hair, he never
wore leather, and he didn't ride a motorcycle. Michael was
an outsider.

The bikers watched every step Michael took. He walked over to the bartender and ordered a whiskey. The bartender waited for the approval of one biker across the room. He appeared to be the leader of the gang. He had the name, "Lurch" stitched on his vest. Once Lurch gave an approving nod, the bartender made Michael his drink. Michael quickly downed the whiskey and ordered another. The bartender complied.

After a few more whiskeys, Michael was finally starting to feel numb. The alcohol was coursing through his blood. Lurch grabbed Michael's shoulder and squeezed it. He sat down next to him.

"You look like you walked into the wrong bar," the biker said laughing.

Michael smiled. "I guess you can say I don't fit in too well here."

The rest of the bikers laughed along. Lurch raised his hand, and his gang went silent. Lurch continued to pry at Michael. "You look troubled. Why else would a guy like you be in a bar like this?"

Michael finished his drink and threw money on the bar. He sensed the danger. "Thanks for the hospitality, love what you've done with the place."

He attempted to get up out of his seat, but Lurch sat him back down with one swift push.

"Where do you think you're going?" Lurch asked. "Relax, we're all friends here."

A few more bikers surrounded Michael. Lurch placed another whiskey in front of him.

"Drink it," Lurch demanded. "This one's on the house."

Michael slowly sipped the whiskey. He was trying to buy himself more time.

"Let's try this again," Lurch asked. "What are you doing in my bar?"

Michael sat calmly in his chair. He continued to sip his whiskey. He tried to saver every last drop. "I don't want any trouble. I came here to have one drink, then leave. You know, to take the edge off from a rough day."

Lurch laughed deeply. "I know why this guy's here. It's written all over his face." A biker standing behind Michael patted him on the back reassuringly.

"You're here because of a woman," Lurch said loudly. He moved in closer. Michael could feel Lurch's breath on his face. "Did she break your heart? Let me guess. Maybe you caught her with another man? Maybe she used you? Oh, or it could be that she doesn't love you anymore?"

As Lurch continued to speak, Michael could only hear a constant ringing. The ringing got louder as Michael's anger grew. Lurch was trying to get a rise out of Michael, and he was winning. Michael knew he was outnumbered and in trouble, he tried to hold in his anger.

Lurch pushed Michael. "Is that it?" he asked.

Michael didn't reply. His eyes were glazed over.

Lurch grabbed Michael and shook him endlessly.

"Is that it?" he asked again. "Is she a..."

Before Lurch could answer with an insulting word, Michael took his whiskey glass and smashed it over Lurch's face. Lurch screamed in pain from the shattered glass that punctured his skin. A biker standing behind Michael tried to hit him with a pool stick. Michael ducked out of the way and Lurch got hit instead. Lurch fell to the floor in pain. Michael made a run for the door followed by an army of bikers.

Michael stumbled outside the bar. He ran towards the alleyway and jumped inside a large dumpster. The bikers ran down the street, not even attempting to search the alleyway. Michael waited in the dumpster for at least twenty minutes.

His head peered out of the alleyway to make sure there wasn't a biker in sight. Michael made his way to the nearest pay phone and called Billy to pick him up. He sunk to the bottom of the pay phone booth holding back tears. Using a spare key, Billy was forced to pick up his car where Michael last parked it.

Billy angrily drove up onto the sidewalk and swung the door to his car open. He scolded Michael.

"You idiot," Billy yelled. "You take on a whole entire biker gang over your girlfriend? You think that's a solution to this problem?"

Michael sat in the car completely emotionless. He looked at Billy with a blank stare.

"You've never felt this kind of love," Michael said. "Don't be cynical, picture having the love of your life pried out of your arms. The one person that made me feel alive is gone."

Billy finally could see how troubled Michael was. He could hear it through the tone of Michael's voice. Billy noticed the painful look Michael had in his eyes. His best friend was a shell of the man he once knew. The very minute that Elvira said she was going to leave, a piece of Michael left with her.

"Mike, I know you're in pain. I see it all over your face. But what would ever make you wander into that bar? That's the most dangerous hangout in Astoria. Those bikers could have killed you!"

There were tears in his eyes, and he didn't want Billy to see. Michael stared aimlessly out the car window. He tried to deepen his voice to hide the weeping.

"I wish they did hurt me. I wish I woke up in a hospital bed and Elvira was standing over me. She'd be crying for me, saying how much she loved me. That she couldn't leave me here alone."

Michael continued to hide his face from Billy.

Billy sighed. "You're fucked up kid."

Michael answered aggressively, "What's that supposed to mean?"

"I've never seen you like this," Billy said. "I don't think you'll ever love another woman more than Elvira. I see it in your eyes."

* * *

Elvira was in bed surrounded by layers of blankets and pillows making her feel more comfortable. Elvira always got cold easily, she never enjoyed the winter months. She was always that one person to wear a light jacket in the middle of summer.

Sitting on Elvira's nightstand were always three different pairs of reading glasses. They all had the same prescription, but she liked to switch between the styles of rims. One pair of glasses had a traditional black frame, and another had light purple tinted rims. Her favorite pair, the quirkiest kind, had zebra striped rims with a small red tint near the front of the lens. They were the most absurd color and style, she loved them, they made her stick out.

The manuscript rested on Elvira's lap as she stared down at it, constantly debating on whether to read it. Elvira knew that if she read his novel, she would want to run over to Michael's apartment and jump into his arms. She knew it would make her leaving that much harder. It took a full hour to make her decision. In that hour, she constantly picked up and put down the manuscript. She turned the pages back and forth, just to glance at the first word. Her emotions got the best of her, and Elvira finally gave in. She grabbed a pencil to make notes.

What Elvira read changed her meaning of the word and feeling of *love*. She now knew that what she fell into with Michael was something so rare and special that there were very few people on this earth to ever experience it. Through his words, Michael made Elvira see what he was feeling. Michael remembered everything Elvira had ever told him. From the major events in her life, to the smallest little detail of her personality, Michael captured the entire essence of Elvira's being. The words dripped off the pages with emotion. The thing that stuck out to Elvira the most was how amazing Michael painted her out to be. By reading his novel, she saw herself through his eyes. She saw the way Michael viewed her. The feeling was so overwhelming, it was almost uncomfortable. Elvira couldn't believe that in Michael's eyes, she was completely perfect. Elvira always thought she was the farthest thing from it, but Michael saw something else. Every person has imperfections, but Michael overlooked all of Elvira's. To him they were just parts of her personality. Every day, Michael knew he could get a different side of it, and he was always eager to see what she'd throw at him next. Their relationship just worked, they adored each other.

Elvira felt an entire flood of emotions. Her love for Michael had never been stronger. She doodled on the cover of the manuscript like a schoolgirl. Elvira drew a little elephant, because of the famous saying, "elephants never forget." It reminded her of the way Michael remembered every detail of her life story. The manuscript felt heavy in her hand. It was probably just as heavy as Michael's heart that same evening.

Elvira picked up her phone and eagerly dialed Michael's number. She tried calling multiple times, but there was no response. Elvira was confident that Michael would answer the phone. She figured he wasn't home yet. Sadly, she wasn't wrong.

Michael forced Billy to take him to another bar. He would have done just about anything to numb the massive pain in his heart. At nearly three o'clock in the morning, Michael was belligerently drunk. Michael and Billy were the last two people in the bar. The bartender made the last call over an hour ago. Michael's body was slumped over the wooden bar. Billy kept trying to keep him awake. For once, Billy stayed completely sober. He knew Michael needed to let this all out. Someone had to see him through this.

Billy pushed Michael's motionless body. "Mike, we have to go. The bar's already been closed for over an hour."

Michael slowly picked himself up. He mumbled in a drunken stupor. "She's leaving me," he said. "Why does she have to leave me?"

"I know that buddy, but there's nothing we can do about it now," Billy said.

Billy put Michael's arm around him to help him walk. Michael stumbled off the bar stool and almost fell to the floor. Billy pulled him up.

Michael continued to repeat himself. "She's my world," Michael slurred. "...my Italian girl."

"What the hell are you talking about?" Billy said. "Did someone spike your drinks? You're not making sense."

Billy had enough of Michael's drunken talk. He dragged him out of the bar and shoved him into the backseat of his car. Michael slipped in and out of consciousness.

Billy mumbled to himself, "I told him not to get hooked again. Then what does he do? He goes out and finds the love of his life."

Michael heard Billy's snide comment. Even though he was highly impaired, he still had enough sense to not let Billy get away with saying it.

"She's different!" Michael screamed.

Billy answered condescendingly, "Well I guess you see that might not be true now."

Billy helped Michael up the steps and into his apartment. Michael stumbled over to his couch and collapsed onto it face first. The phone started to ring. It was practically dawn and the sun was just starting to come up. He wondered who would be calling Michael at this hour.

Billy answered the phone with an annoyed tone. "Yeah."

"Who's this?" Elvira replied.

"It's Billy. Anyone who calls Michael's phone should know who I am."

Elvira never met Billy, but she could already sense why Michael said he was annoying. His voice was a little high pitched and screechy. He sounded quite grumpy on the phone. Also, Elvira knew Billy never liked her. The way Michael described it, Billy was jealous that she was around.

"It's Elvira. You know, Michael's girlfriend?"

"You know whatever you did last night made my best friend turn into a total maniac?"

"Excuse me?" Elvira replied.

"After he got into a fight with you, he started a fight with a gang of bikers. He said something about looking to get hurt so that you'd come and see him. He didn't think there was anything he could do to get your attention after that fight. Mike kept mumbling on about his words going too far. Now he's drunk and passed out on his couch."

Tears filled Elvira's eyes. She held them back, so Billy wouldn't hear the sadness in her voice. "He broke up with me because I'm moving to California for school."

Billy decided to take this situation into his own hands. Michael never thought with his head, only his heart. He knew that when Michael woke up and found out that Elvira called, he would make up with her. Billy decided to think for the two of them. He knew they couldn't survive a long-distance rela-tionship. Billy saw a grim future for his best friend and Elvira.

"Do me a favor sweetheart," Billy said. "Don't call here again."

"What!" Elvira yelled.

"Listen, I know that sounds harsh, but think about it. If you really love Michael, you'd let him go. I've known this guy since we're five years old. I've never seen him love anyone more than you. I don't think he'll ever love another woman the same to be honest. But, I do know that he wouldn't be able to handle a long-distance relationship. If you feel the same way he does, neither could you. I'll tell him you called if you want, but my advice to you is to forget about him. Forget this phone call. Forget any of this ever happened. It's too painful."

"Hey Billy?" Elvira replied candidly.

"Yeah?"

"Fuck you."

Elvira slammed the phone down then threw it onto the floor. She had a full-blown adult tantrum. Elvira stomped around her apartment, throwing herself onto her bed. The tears that came down her face wouldn't stop. Her heart was pumping so fast, Elvira could feel a hard pounding on the left side of her chest. She couldn't catch her breath because she was sobbing so much. She continually slammed her fists down onto her pillows. Elvira was in total denial of what was happening, but deep down inside she knew Billy was right.

11

CHAPTER

Elvira only had a few hours left in New York, her true home. The city that broke her and built her back up, the city that allowed her to live a full life, and the city she would eventually find love. Michael and Elvira had not spoken to each other in over a month. Billy never told Michael that Elvira called the night they broke up, and Elvira never called Michael back.

The weather was gloomy. The sky was a pale grey even though it was still early in the morning. The clouds covered any sunlight from bleeding through. This giant cloud that covered the sky followed Elvira around. Her apartment was filled with plastic wrap and cardboard boxes. One large suitcase stood in the center of the room. Allison and Elvira continued to pack the knickknacks left lying around. Elvira searched her bedroom to make sure she didn't leave anything. Sitting on Elvira's nightstand was a picture of her and Michael. They were both smiling. Elvira sat on his lap while Michael wrapped his arms around her waist. They were sitting on her stoop. Elvira smiled, and thought back to the moment that changed her life forever. She rubbed the dust off the picture and placed her fingers over Michael's face. She took the picture out of the frame and placed it in her pocket.

Elvira lugged her suitcase down the steps of the apartment building. Allison followed carrying a box. The weight of the suitcase was too heavy for her. She didn't have the strength to carry it. Elvira watched as her suitcase tumbled down the rest of the steps. The suitcase spilled open after hitting the cement. Elvira cried as she picked her clothes off the street. Allison gently rubbed her back. Allison could see her best friend was completely lost. For the second time in her life, she was running off to another big city all alone.

Elvira buried her face in Allison's shoulder. "He hasn't spoken to me in over a month," she cried. "I'm never going to see him again."

Allison picked Elvira's head up. She looked at her with an assuring grin. "Nothing is ever final in life, don't talk like you know what's planned for you."

Elvira's sadness suddenly turned to anger. She wiped away her tears and grinded her teeth together. Her voice deepened. "He's probably out with his tall, olive skinned, dark haired, Italian whore drinking Manhattan Specials." She paused for a moment. "I'll kill him!"

Allison tried not to laugh. "What's a Manhattan Special?"

Elvira buried her face in Allison's shoulder again. The sadness came roaring back. She screamed out, "You wouldn't understand!"

Allison truly didn't understand. Michael and Elvira's relationship was unique. They were both two quirky people who had an odd sense of humor. Their relationship worked in a way that was confusing to others. It takes a special couple to share their type of bond. For the sake of their conversation, Allison pretended she did understand exactly what Elvira was going through.

"Stop it!" Allison yelled. "From what you told me, that man loves you. Nothing is ever going to change that. He's just upset."

Elvira collected her thoughts. There was one final thing she had to do before leaving New York.

"I need one favor from you before I leave," Elvira said.

Elvira carefully planned this since she fought with Michael. She couldn't leave New York without making some sort of attempt to contact him. Elvira knew the quickest way to Michael's heart. It wasn't through a phone call or even a quick visit. The key to Michael's heart was her soul. Elvira was prepared to bear her soul to Michael the only way she knew how.

Michael's apartment was covered with empty bottles of gin. He had grown fond of Martini's since taking up drinking again. Drinking a Martini gave him a feeling of serenity. He felt like Humphrey Bogart, a man who he looked up to. His desk was covered with stacks of paper. During their breakup, Michael lived only to write. He stayed cooped up in his apartment glued to his typewriter and the endless bottles of gin. Between the drinking and the failed attempts to mend his broken heart, Michael almost finished his novel. He was only missing the ending–the ending of their love story. Michael wanted the novel to be based on reality, since the old ending couldn't be used. He wanted to see what fate was going to deal him next.

Sitting at his desk, Michael poured himself more gin. He reached into his desk drawer for a pack of cigarettes. He lit his cigarette, filling the room with smoke. Michael took his glass of gin and walked over to the mirror. With his cigarette and drink in hand, Michal talked to himself.

"What would you do Humphrey?" he asked. "Is Elvira happy without me? Should I let her be happy and move to California? Should I run over to her house and stop her from leaving? Maybe she should fly away on the plane without me? After all, that's what you did."

Michael finished his drink. With the cigarette glued to his lower lip, he read his novel aloud. For the next hour, Michael acted out each part in the novel. He was a one man Broadway show. He laughed, cried, and even sang along to the emotional parts of their story. More than half the lines in the novel were direct quotes from the two of them. Reading it aloud made him remember how much Elvira loved him, and how much she probably still loved him.

In the middle of Michael's performance, he heard someone banging on his door. Not a single person had visited him since Elvira left. Michael sheltered himself. He didn't want any disturbances while he wrote.

Allison waited at Michael's door impatiently. She banged the door repeatedly until he answered. The door swung open. Michael looked completely disheveled. He was wearing bright colored boxers and a wrinkled tank top. His breath reeked of cigarettes and alcohol. Michael looked like a shell of the man he once was.

"Who are you?" Michael asked.

"I'm Allison Williams," she replied. "Elvira sent me."

Michael grunted. He pretended to be disinterested.

"Let's not be petty," Allison said. "I can see through that gin drinking, cigarette smoking, tough guy, act that you think you're putting on."

Michael shook his head. He knew this wasn't the man he was.

"What of it?" he said shortly.

Allison handed Michael a small box.

"Elvira is leaving for California today. She left this for you."

Michael took the box and opened it. Inside, he found a cassette tape.

"What's this?" he asked.

Allison crossed her arms. "Play it, you big dope!" she yelled.

Michael placed the tape in the cassette player. Within the first few seconds of hearing Elvira's voice, his heart sank. Elvira put together a recording of their favorite songs. He knew how harshly she judged her voice. Elvira found it difficult to share her voice. She was always particular about who heard her sing. Elvira always questioned if her voice sounded up to par. Michael was one of the few people to hear her sing without a microphone, or any sort of enhancements.

Allison stood over him as Elvira's voice belted out "It Had to Be You." Allison watched as the tears streamed down his face. Followed by "Because of You." Then came their song, "Strangers in the Night." Michael sobbed, uncontrollably.

By the time "I've Got a Crush on You" played Allison could barely keep her own emotions at bay. She saw, first hand, how much Michael loved Elvira. How deeply he adored every aspect of her being.

As the tape continued to play, Michael didn't move an inch. He closed his eyes and absorbed every single word. Michael could hear Elvira calling out to him through the music. He heard the words Elvira so desperately wished she could say. Without even speaking to her, Michael knew exactly how she was feeling. He turned around to see if Allison was still behind him. With tears in her own eyes, she watched the pain course through Michael's veins.

Through his tears, Michael mumbled. "Where is she?"

"We were loading up the cab before I left. If you hurry, maybe you can catch her."

Michael ran into his room and threw together an outfit. He scooped together the scattered pages of his novel, scrambling to put them in order. Without even saying goodbye to Allison, he ran out the door. Allison watched as Michael practically threw himself down the steps.

"I need to find myself an Italian," she said to herself.

Elvira waited outside her apartment building for Michael to arrive. She held out hope that the cassette tape would have broken his silence. The cabbie was parked on the sidewalk. He was becoming more impatient by the moment. Elvira glanced at her watch. Her flight was in less than an hour. If she didn't leave for the airport in a few moments, she would miss her flight. Elvira didn't have enough money for another plane fare.

"Lady, I don't have all day!" the cabbie yelled. "What the heck are you waiting for?"

Elvira sighed. "Someone was supposed to meet me here to say goodbye."

"Well they ain't here," he scathed.

Elvira looked down the block one last time. She didn't see anyone coming and decided to get into the cab.

"Take me to LaGuardia Airport," she said.

The cabbie started the car. The meter in the cab began running. Elvira was emotionless. At this point, she couldn't even cry. Elvira became so numb, that she didn't think anything mattered anymore. After all the trouble she faced throughout her life, this pain was only expected.

Out of breath and gasping for air, Michael ran down Elvira's block. Michael saw the cab pulling away. He ran even faster, pushing his body to the absolute limit.

"Elvira!" he screamed.

Michael waved his hands frantically in the air. "Elvira!" he screamed again.

Elvira heard a faint sound. She glanced out the side of her window.

"Did you hear something?" she asked the cabbie.

"It's the piece of shit cab you're sitting in," he replied.

The cab left a trace of smog in the air. Michael tried to catch up to the cab, but his body gave up. As he reached Elvira's apartment building, he collapsed. There wasn't much oxygen left in his lungs. He lied on the cold stone steps, gasping for air. The pages of his novel scattered all over the floor. Michael didn't even try to pick them up, he didn't see a point.

Elvira was never going to read them. She was never going to see the beautiful world he created for the two of them. A heaven-like place where they could both be sheltered from the cruel boundaries of their minds, where only the two of them mattered, and they could truly run away from it all.

Michael's mind went blank. All he could feel was a relentless anger. Michael didn't know where to direct it, there was no person to blame but himself. He wasn't in the right frame of mind, and often had trouble realizing that. Michael started to blame the one being that he felt had control over everything.

He pointed up to the sky. "Why did you do this to me?" Michael screamed. "Why does everything I love get ripped right out of my hands?"

Michael grabbed his St. Anthony chain and ripped it off his neck. He held the chain with a tight grip.

"Was it all just a tease? Did you dangle the love of my life in front of me? Oh, let me guess. Maybe it's another test of my faith?"

Michael got up off the steps then he picked up the scattered pages of his novel. Michael cursed the God that protected him. The God that showed him love and forgiveness. The God that gave him a soulmate. Michael was in such a tremendous amount of pain, that he forgot all that God did for him. That's why humans are flawed. Many people are quick to blame God for the hardships they face in their lives. They're quick to pray while things are bad and forget to give thanks when things are going well. They don't acknowledge there is a God until it benefits them. Yet, God loves us all anyway. Michael's mind was clouded by anger and hurt. He wasn't looking at the bigger picture. God had a plan for him, but it was going to take time to unfold.

* * *

California wasn't what Elvira expected it to be. Los Angeles was a downgrade from New York. It was murkier, uglier, and more dangerous. She committed to the California University's Rutherford Institute of Psychological Studies. Elvira used all the money she saved over the years to lease an apartment.

Elvira's new apartment was small. There was a tiny bathroom in the corner, the living room was the length of a mattress, and the kitchen had a teeny-tiny stove. Elvira didn't have any extra money for furniture. All she had were the clothes on her back and one suitcase. Allison was kind enough to store the rest of Elvira's belongings in her home until she finished school. With almost nothing, Elvira called this shabby apartment her home. She was used to having nothing, throughout her life there were plenty worse situations she found herself in. There were times where she had less than this. Elvira felt blessed just to have a mattress to sleep on. Not having material items never bothered her.

Elvira stacked all her clothes in a corner of the room. Lying at the bottom of her suitcase was Michael's manuscript. She kept it under her bed. Elvira liked the idea of having Michael's novel close to her while she slept. It was a simple way of bringing him here with her. Every night before she went to sleep, Elvira reread the novel. It made her feel like he was sitting next to her. When she read, she escaped into a world where their relationship never changed. The story never got old. Elvira wondered if Michael decided to continue writing his novel. She wondered if Michael gave up on their story. She wondered if Michael still loved her.

Elvira quickly realized Los Angeles could never be called home. It was nothing like New York. Elvira only had two semesters and then she would have enough credits to complete her college degree. Her school's program was extremely challenging, but it was nothing she couldn't handle. Elvira was a great student and a fast learner. What hurt the most were the nights she spent alone. She missed having Michael cook her breakfast in the morning. She missed doing yoga with Allison every Sunday. She missed the rush of seeing the bright Broadway lights in Manhattan.

Elvira consumed herself with schoolwork to mask the pain, but she was never able to fool her mind. The looming depression she had been feeling was slowly creeping up on her. Her depression was especially hard to control. It couldn't be compared to the depression of an average person. Without a supporting cast, Elvira set herself up for trouble.

The days dragged on, and the demons in Elvira's mind tightened their grip. She thought that Michael didn't care about her. She questioned whether or not Michael had already moved on. Elvira even dared to believe that he was already seeing other women. That he grew tired of her quirky personality and wanted to find someone more *normal*, that very word made her cringe.

The days flew by since she gave him the cassette tape. Elvira hadn't received a single phone call. She knew if Michael wanted to find out where she lived, that he would hound Allison for the answer. This depression slowly took over her life. She barely ate one meal a day, the idea of food made her sick. Elvira spent half the night studying, and the other half struggling to sleep. She managed to sleep around three hours a night. The loss of sleep, loss of appetite, and loss of the quality of life would catch up to anyone. It was clear Elvira was struggling to find inner peace.

While it's easy for any person to become depressed over a relationship, this sadness was an entirely different animal for both Michael and Elvira. When you meet your soulmate, you feel what they feel. You carry that person with you wherever you go whether it's in the super market, a concert, or walking down the street. Having this unique ability could easily be a blessing and a curse. Those who love, often suffer. Imagine feeling whatever your soulmate feels: the happiness, the sadness, the anger, and the hurt. During happy times, it could be a blessing. When you're in the middle of a messy breakup, like Michael and Elvira, this feeling becomes painful.

Elvira could feel in her bones how depressed Michael was. She could feel that he was destroying his body with alcohol. She could feel his mind was battering him with negative thinking. On top of feeling Michael's depression, she felt her own. Elvira was completely helpless. She didn't know how to help Michael or even help herself. Elvira turned to the one thing that never failed her. She turned to her faith, and her beloved Jesus Christ. She unpacked her crucifix and placed it on the wall above her bed. She prayed.

"Jesus, I come to you filled with pain and anxiety. I come to you at a troubling time in my life. You've seen me through much worse, but once again I look to you for salvation. I come to you, not to pray for myself, but for the love of my life. My prayers tonight are for Michael. If you have to help one of us, please let it be him. I pray that you guide and protect him. I pray that you lead him to happiness, whether it's with me or someone else. I'll be happy, if he's happy. I know that Michael is a troubled Christian. I know he's questioned his faith in the past and maybe even today. Please, give him a reason to believe. Give him a reason to have faith in you, Jesus. Give him a reason to be happy. I know he's beating himself up. Help relieve him of his anxiety and depression."

12

CHAPTER

Michael anxiously sat by the phone in his apartment. Before Allison left his apartment, she placed her phone number next to Elvira's cassette tape. Michael wasn't stupid, he knew why Allison left her number there. Allison was probably the only person who could contact Elvira. Every fiber of Michael's being wanted to make that phone call and get Elvira's number. His crippling anxiety was the only thing that stopped him. Michael filled his mind with potential fears and as he played out the situation. His thoughts were screaming loudly. What if she doesn't want you to call? What if that was her way of saying goodbye? What if you waited too long? What if I can't convince her to come home? What if I made this all up in my head? Michael violently grabbed his head and dug his fingernails in his skull. He couldn't take the overthinking anymore. It made him sick. His eyes filled with tears from the pain. He felt like his insides were rotting. Michael was creating an entirely different world in his mind. One where everything was made up and he forced himself to believe horrible things about the woman he so deeply loved. It was truly an alternate reality.

The depression finally sunk in. It found its way into Michael's thought patterns. His views on reality were skewed. He now saw life through this dull, black and white lens. There was nothing more to life than the way he negatively viewed it all. Michael was losing his soul once again. A part of him was missing. There was no bandage big enough to cover the hole in his heart. There was no woman beautiful enough to take Elvira's place. If Michael even attempted to fill the void, it would only damage him further. He knew there was only one Elvira Vaughn. He knew that there was only one woman on the planet who could totally captivate him. She was truly one of a kind, a rare diamond that fell into Michael's lap at a little café in Astoria. Every diamond is unique and never one that is cut the same. There's always something different about it. A jeweler can make a perfect cut, but a diamond will always be different. There's never one in the same, even if it may look so. Michael always felt he came across the rarest diamond of them all. He could never put a price to it. "My Elvira," as he liked to call her, could never be compared to the rest of the diamonds out in the world.

Michael was out of work for months. Since leaving his last job, Michael was living off money he saved for a rainy day. He decided he'd never work a desk job again. Elvira inspired him to pursue his dreams, to become the artist he so desperately wanted to be. While he wrote the novel, his money slowly depleted. That rainy day fund was whisked away by a storm that lasted months. He was only left with a few hundred dollars in his savings account. Finances were the last thing on Michael's mind, and he neglected them completely.

It only took a few weeks before Michael was on the street. He was evicted from his apartment and forced to move in with his parents. This added to Michael's depression. He didn't care about the money, but he cared about being around his family. Michael didn't want to bring back any childhood memories. His early days in middle school were torture. High school was a little better, but not at all easy. Michael was always facing trouble. Nothing ever came easy to him in life. There was never a break, or a brief stroke of luck. In school and at home, Michael was battered by those around him. Moving back into his home made him feel like the small, helpless boy he once was.

Angelo Coniglio laid across his large, comfy, sofa chair. That was his favorite spot, a place he hardly moved from. He stared at Michael, sleeping on a couch beside him.

"This is what a writer amounts to," he mumbled under his breath. "Bum."

Michael grew a thick beard and his hair was longer and messy. He wasn't a bum in spirit, but he definitely was starting to resemble a person who was unmotivated. His mother instantly noticed Michael's change in behavior. Without a clear sign, Carmela knew his depression started with a woman. She didn't dare inquire, she could see that whoever this woman was, Michael was in love. How did Carmela know all of this by looking at her son? The answer is simple, a mother's intuition even more so, an Italian mother's intuition. Carmela brought Michael a steaming hot espresso. She gently nudged his lifeless body.

"Wake up sweetheart," Carmela said. "It's already one o'clock in the afternoon."

Angelo grunted. "Let the bum sleep," he said coldly.

Michael angrily stared at his father. He kissed his mother on the cheek and took the espresso.

"Billy is waiting in the dining room for you," Carmela said. "He mentioned something about a nice girl that you should take out."

Michael still remained silent. He walked into the dining room. Billy sat at the table with his hands folded.

"You look like shit," Billy joked.

"Fuck you," Michael said.

Carmela overheard Michael. She walked into the room, smacked him on the back of the head and then walked away. She was always eavesdropping.

"What the hell is your problem?" Billy asked.

"How the hell can you set me up on a blind date? After what happened to me? Are you crazy?"

Billy smiled at Michael. "This one is different. I know you're going to like her. She likes old movies. She's really a sweet little thing."

Carmela poked her head into the room. "Is she tall?"

Michael cracked a smile. "What is it with you and my dates being tall? Who cares? Dad is short."

Billy laughed at the two of them arguing. "Being here makes me feel like I'm at home," he joked. "Sorry Mrs. C, she's not tall at all."

Michael motioned for Billy to come closer. "Come over here buddy."

Billy naively walked closer to him. Michael swiftly smacked his face. "Don't ever set me up on a blind date again."

Billy tried to stay calm. He wanted to tear Michael's head off, but he knew Michael was going through something really rough. "If you don't take this girl out for a coffee, you're not allowed to borrow my car anymore. I'll never pick you up again. Look forward to taking the bus everywhere."

Michael sighed. "I'll take her out for coffee, but that's it. It's going to be a friendly thing. I never want to hear about it again."

Michael ironically found himself back in the Astoria coffee shop. He sat at the same table where he met Elvira. He hadn't visited the coffee shop since she left as it was too painful for him to go. It didn't feel right to be there without her. The coffee shop, and even Astoria, didn't feel like home anymore.

When Summer walked into the coffee shop, she instantly knew who Michael was. She sat down across from him.

"Sorry, that seat is taken," Michael said.

"For a date?" Summer asked.

"Yeah, how'd you know?"

"Because I'm your date," she said. "I'm Summer."

"Wait." Michael paused. "How did you know I was your date?"

"Billy told me to look for the depressed writer type."

"Asshole," Michael mumbled.

Michael's date was short and had brown hair. Her name, Summer, fit her perfectly. Michael leaned back in his chair. He wasn't nervous, there was no pressure because this date didn't matter to him. Michael was relaxed, there wasn't any anxiousness about him on this day. Michael didn't want to impress this girl, so he acted like himself. He didn't hide anything and was totally open with Summer.

"What kind of coffee would you like?" Michael asked.

"Could I actually get a hot chocolate please?"

Michael bought two piping hot drinks. Summer nodded her head with appreciation. She sipped her hot chocolate. Michael sensed Summer was reserved. She enjoyed listening more than talking. Her words were short, and she used them sparingly. Michael wasn't used to quiet, he was always talking. Elvira was well-known to be chatty. There was never a dull moment between them. Summer was a completely different change of pace.

"What's with the depressed writer deal?" Summer asked.

Michael shook his head.

"Don't listen to a word Billy says. But yes, I am a writer. I'm almost finished with my first book. All I need to do is change the ending."

Summer had a unique knack for reading people. She could easily sum up a person's character within moments of meeting them. Summer analyzed Michael. She closely listened to every word that came out of his mouth.

"What's the book about?"

Michael didn't feel threatened by Summer. She gave off a pleasant energy. Michael never told anyone about his novel. This was the perfect opportunity to get the opinion of a total stranger. His novel would face its first test. Michael worried about the reader picking up on his feelings. He wanted the reader to know how much he loved Elvira. Michael wanted the reader to know this wasn't another cheesy love story.

"It's about two people who heal each other. They both lived troubled lives, but in different ways. All they needed was love, not just an ordinary love, but a genuine kind. They find each other in the unlikeliest way and fall in love. Together, they heal each other's wounds. They show each other what true love feels like. They grow to share this wonderful storybook life experience together. They get to experience the feeling of having a soulmate, something that most people never get to have."

Summer could instantly tell the passion behind Michael's writing. The way he described it sounded too personal. There was something more to the story that Michael was hiding. She knew a story like this couldn't be pulled out of thin air. How could Michael write a story about this kind of love without ever experiencing it? It was a woman's intuition.

"That's beautiful," Summer said. "It sounds like a novel any girl would love to read."

She took a sip of her hot chocolate. Summer continued, "I have to ask, where did the inspiration come from?"

Michael looked away from Summer. He didn't want to reveal that his novel was more of an autobiography of his feelings with a small fantasy twist, than an actual story.

"It's based off a friend of mine. He really loved this woman. I've never seen a love so pure, so true. He loved her with everything he had, even more than himself."

Summer saw right through Michael's charade. Billy told her Michael was recently single. She knew that this was a story about a woman Michael loved. Summer was also smart enough to see no woman could ever hold a candle to Michael's "novel girl."

"You're hiding behind this novel," Summer said. "The novel is about your soulmate, not your friend's."

Michael crossed his arms. "How do you know that?" He said childishly.

"The way you look when you described the story. I could hear it in your voice. I could see it in your eyes. It's written all over your face."

"I don't know what to say," Michael replied.

"For you to write a novel about a woman is the most romantic thing I've ever heard. From what Billy told me and from my own opinion, you could have whatever girl you want. You're handsome and have the whole artist thing going for you. You're a beautiful person."

Michael hardly heard compliments like this in his life. He didn't know how to accept them. The only other woman to ever talk about him in that way was Elvira. He sat in total silence. Michael barely looked at Summer.

"Don't take this the wrong way," she said. "I feel bad for any woman that ever falls in love with you."

"Why?" he asked defensively.

Summer smiled. She reached across the table and grabbed Michael's hand. "Because no woman will ever compare to her. A part of you will always be with her. Any woman would be able to tell. A woman wants to be loved by a man completely. A woman needs all a man's love. Not just a part of them. There would always be some part of you, that's attached to her. It makes me cringe, because I wish I was her. I wish a man loved me that way."

Michael tried to speak, but Summer silenced him.

"Please don't say anything about how amazing she is. I'm already jealous enough."

Summer got out of her seat and kissed Michael on the cheek. She rubbed his arm.

"I hope you find happiness, because you deserve it. Only you can write your own ending."

She picked up her drink and walked out the door. Michael wasn't feeling well. He felt like Summer rubbed salt in a wound that was still fresh. She rehashed feelings he'd been suppressing for months. Michael chased her down the street. When he caught up to Summer, he tapped her on the shoulder.

"What if she doesn't love me anymore?" Michael asked desperately. "Then what?"

Summer placed her hand on Michael's face. She rubbed his cheeks with her thumb.

"I'm intuitive," she said. "I can sum up a person by looking at them. I judge them based on the vibrations they give me. When you spoke about her. I felt this heaviness on my chest."

Michael shrugged his shoulders. He didn't understand.

"Heaviness?" he replied.

Summer placed her hand over Michael's heart. "I felt a heavy heart. She loves you Michael, I know it. I felt it."

Summer walked away from Michael, leaving him shell-shocked. A total stranger ripped all his innermost personal feelings, right out into the open. He felt too vulnerable.

Michael might as well have been standing naked in the middle of Ditmars Boulevard.

* * *

Elvira sat on her mattress wearing only a tank top and shorts. She was determined to do well in school. To make extra time for massive amount of readings, she woke up early morning and went to sleep late at night. Her apartment didn't have any air conditioning. The weather in California was getting warmer by the day. Beads of sweat dripped down her face. She placed a cold rag over her forehead and wiped the sweat away then took a deep breath. She was having a hard time studying so she picked up the phone and dialed Allison's number.

"I miss you so much," Elvira said.

"What's wrong babe?" Allison replied. "You sound a little down. I thought you'd be happy. You're pursing a dream!"

Allison didn't understand what Elvira was going through. Her bouts of moods were hard to deal with. The depression of losing the man she loved magnified her feelings. She didn't have a shoulder to lean on. She missed the way Michael loved her with his nurturing, kind, tender, and passionate love.

"There's something missing."

Allison rolled her eyes. "Go out and meet a guy already! You did everything you could. You left the cassette tape and he never called back. What more could you do?"

Allison was always bitter when it came to the idea of love. Life wasn't a romance novel. To her, none of it existed.

"Have you seen or heard from him at all? Did you pass his apartment like I asked?"

"I did," Allison said. "His name isn't on the doorbell list anymore."

Elvira felt nauseous. Her stomach was filled with pain. There was no way for her to reach Michael anymore. She craved his love, his attention, the sound of his voice, and the way he made her laugh. Elvira knew that she would never be able to find that kind of connection with another man again. She worried if Michael would find another woman—more beautiful, younger, and even more interesting. Michael built her up, and Elvira started to tear herself down. She was regressing and began to blame herself. Elvira thought she was too much. That she scared Michael away. She was once again, failing to realize how much he loved her.

"He moved on I guess," Elvira said.

Michael needed to reflect on his coffee date with Summer. What she said bothered him. He had a hard time understanding his own feelings. Michael hadn't even scraped the surface yet. His mind was filled with racing thoughts. He didn't know how to feel. Michael decided to go out for a long walk to sort out his thoughts.

Michael enjoyed exploring the neighborhoods of Queens. He spontaneously took the bus to Maspeth, a town that was known for being quite ethnic. Many Polish, Italian, and Asian immigrants settled there. All different walks of people passed him as he walked down Grand Avenue. Not a single person looked Michael in the eye. New Yorkers weren't the best at making eye contact. They also weren't known for being friendly.

In the midst of people rushing by each other, an Asian family stood apart from the rest. They seemed to be kind, loving, and open. The family attentively watched their small daughter walk up the street. She was around seven years old. She was bright eyed, happy, and full of hope, as most children are. The energy she gave off was comforting.

Michael trudged down the street, he barely noticed the small girl attempting to block his path. The little girl stepped in front of him and pulled a paper heart out of her pocket. She waved her hand back and forth, holding this paper heart. Michael stopped and stared at her. He couldn't tell if the little girl was offering this paper heart to him. Michael tried to walk around her, and the little girl stepped in front of him again, once again blocking his path. She lifted her arm and held out the paper heart again. Michael looked to her family for approval. Her mother and father nodded with bright smiles. Michael took the heart and smiled to show thanks.

The heart had a written message on the front, it said, "Jesus loves you." Michael instantly denied the possibility of this being a holy sign. He knew people spread the word of Christ all the time. The family were probably devout worshipers. Michael turned the heart around. The back had another message, it said, "Peter 5:7 Cast all your anxiety on Jesus, because he cares for you." Out of all the Bible quotes to choose, Michael was handed a quote about anxiety, an issue he suffered with daily. He wondered why the little girl was so adamant that he took the heart from her. Someone or something clearly wanted him to see that heart. Michael refused to believe that this was a message from Jesus. It was too farfetched.

Michael ran to the nearest pay phone and called Billy. Subconsciously, he knew why the little girl handed him that paper heart. Michael knew what the message meant. He just refused to believe it. He figured Billy would occupy his mind for the rest of the day.

"It's Mike," he said shortly.

"How did the date go?" Billy asked.

"We'll talk about it later. What are your plans for today?"

"I'm actually headed over to my friend's record store. He's going out of business and is giving away a bunch of free records. You wanna come?"

"Sure, I could use a few new records."

Billy greeted him outside the store. The front door and windows were boarded with wood. Billy led him inside through the back door. Michael walked in and knew Billy lied. This was an antique store, not a record store. It was filled with items that almost looked ancient. There were hundreds of rows of antiques. The furniture looked Victorian. The glass sculptures were from France. The store even had a cash register from the early 1930s.

"This isn't a record store," Michael said.

"I know you love music. I figured you wouldn't come out if I didn't say that. You need to stop isolating yourself. You've avoided me for too long."

Michael grunted. He knew Billy was right. He loved antiques, so he decided to stick around.

"You see Mike," Billy said. "There's a small box of records on the floor over there. Go check it out."

Michael worked his way through the dusty store. He bent down to his knees and pulled the box of records from underneath an old bookshelf. He combed through each record, trying to find anything he might be interested in. The records Michael came across were at least thirty years old. They were called 78s because they played at a speed of 78 revolutions per minute. He saw records from the great opera singer, Enrico Caruso. Michael knew any collector would pay a ridiculous amount of money for original Caruso records, depending on the rarity. He quickly put them aside. The last record was a Frank Sinatra hit. It was still wrapped in plastic. It didn't look aged and it clearly was untouched. Michael pulled it out of the box and read the name aloud. The record was called, *Sing and Dance with Frank Sinatra.*

"Come check this out," Michael yelled to Billy.

"You find anything you like?" Billy asked.

"Am I crazy or does this record look brand new?" Michael said.

He handed Billy the Sinatra record. Billy saw the plastic wrapped around it. There were no creases on the side of the record. The edges weren't bent from sitting in the box. It looked completely pristine.

"Holy shit," Billy said. "This does look brand new."

Billy brought the record over to the owner of the store. The owner was an old Italian man. His name was Claudio Bartolomeo. He'd been collecting antiques for fifty years. Claudio had a minor stroke and decided to suddenly retire.

He realized there were more important things in life. Claudio wanted to spend his last years on this earth with his family in Italy. There wasn't enough time to sell everything in the store, so he decided to give the antiques away to his friends.

"When did you get this record?" Billy asked.

Claudio examined the record. His eyes lit up when he saw the title.

"Ah," Claudio said. "A young lady brought this in not too long ago. She looked exotic. She had short blonde hair. I never got her name."

Michael practically jumped out of his skin when he heard Claudio describe the woman. He quickly pulled a picture of Elvira from his wallet. Michael handed Claudio the picture.

"Was it this woman?" he asked anxiously.

Claudio examined the picture closely. He adjusted his glasses. "No, it wasn't. The woman in the picture is too tall," Claudio said.

Billy tried to change the subject. He didn't want Michael to think about Elvira anymore.

"Is this new? It's wrapped in plastic and there's no damage," Billy asked.

Claudio shrugged his shoulders. "I told the lady we don't buy records. I even said the store was closing. She insisted on the record staying here. Who am I to argue with her? I took it and placed it in a box."

"That's really odd," Billy said.

Claudio looked through the songs on the back of the record. He read them aloud.

"I remember the good old days. I used to love hearing these songs. I used to sing "I've Got a Crush on You" to my wife. God rest her soul." Claudio made the sign of the cross and looked up into the air.

"What did you just say?" Michael said nervously.

"About singing to my wife?" Claudio asked.

"What was the name of the song?" Michael replied anxiously.

"I've Got a Crush on You?" Claudio said. "It's on the record."

Claudio handed Michael the record. He looked for the track on the back of the record.

"Can I take this and the Caruso records?" Michael asked.

"They're all yours," Claudio replied.

Michael marched out the door with the records in hand. Billy chased him.

"Are you insane?" Billy asked. "What the hell has gotten into you? What's the big deal about that record?"

Michael stopped in the middle of the street. He grabbed Billy by his shoulders and shook him. "Something's happening to me," he said.

Billy looked at Michael cross-eyed. "You're scaring me."

"You don't understand. Someone's following me. Trying to contact me."

Billy ripped Michael's hands off him. "Spit it out, you freakin nut."

"You promise not to laugh?"

"Yeah," Billy sighed.

"Jesus is trying to speak to me."

Billy burst out into laughter. He laughed so hard, tears were streaming down his face. He almost curled up in a ball right on the sidewalk.

"Stop kidding around," Billy said.

"Look at this Billy. A little girl handed it to me today." Michael showed Billy the paper heart.

"You know how those Jesus lovers are, they always hand out this stuff."

Michael crossed his arms. "Read the back," he said calmly.

Billy read the back of the heart. He stared at it in silence. Billy knew Michael suffered from anxiety since they were children, growing up together. He understood the battle Michael fought. Billy knew how hard it was for Michael to lead a normal life. He was always questioning, second-guessing, or fearing something.

"I see what you're talking about, but I still think it's farfetched."

"Oh, yeah?" Michael said. "Claudio mentioned a woman with short blonde hair coming into the store and dropping this off." Michael held up the Frank Sinatra record. He continued, "I never told you, but Elvira left me a tape singing a song on this track. That was also the first song she ever sang to me."

Billy laughed it off again. "C'mon Mike, you can't be serious. Is Elvira at least religious?"

Michael stood nose to nose with Billy. He wanted Billy to see how serious he was about this. "Christianity is her whole life," he said. "Jesus is everything to her. I know she prays for me."

Billy pushed Michael away from him. He knew Michael was always a little nutty, but this time he really thought Michael had a screw loose.

"What do you want me to say Mike? You want me to say that Jesus chose to speak to you, out of all the millions of people in the world? You're not very saintly."

Michael shook his head. "How about this! On that coffee date today, your friend, Summer walked into the coffee shop and knew who I was, right away. She knew, just by looking at me, that I was madly in love with another woman. She told me things about myself I didn't even know. You're telling me that's a coincidence? Or maybe Summer reads minds?"

To keep Michael happy, Billy decided to play along. He didn't want Michael to think he was losing his mind even though Billy thought that was a possibility.

"So, go along with it," Billy snickered. "If you feel this strongly about it, go to church. Head over to St. Patrick's. Pray to Jesus. See if he hears you. Ask for a sign yourself."

The color drained from Michael's face. He was afraid to face God. After the way he'd been acting. After all the horrible things he said about God. How he blamed God for enabling his personal suffering. Michael felt God was going to judge him. He wasn't ready to face him yet.

"I don't know if I can go through with it," Michael said. "I don't know if God is going to forgive me for what I've done."

"Did you murder anyone?" Billy asked.

Michael shook his head.

Billy laughed. "Then I'm sure you're on the big man's good side."

13

CHAPTER

St. Patrick's Cathedral was one of the most beautiful places for a Catholic person to worship. People of all walks of life, from all over the country, and all over the world came to worship there. Even if a person wasn't Catholic, or even Christian, it was a landmark to see. During the holidays, it was nearly impossible to get a seat at this church.

Michael walked down Fifth Avenue, slowly approaching the cathedral. The massive work of gothic styled architecture seemed daunting to him. The long stone steps appeared to be endless. Michael stood at the foot of the cathedral, waiting for the moment he'd take his first steps into the church. Even though Michael was afraid, there was a part of him that knew this was right. A part of him felt he had to do this. That it would be good for his soul. That maybe, God would be able to forgive him, and bring clarity to his life. Michael hoped that God would be able to wipe away the demons in his mind. The demons that forced him to think negatively about himself and those he loved. The demons that forced him to believe he wasn't good enough for anyone.

Slowly, Michael's spirituality was growing. Michael felt more open to the idea of everything happening for a reason. That God had a plan for him all along. As Michael took his first step onto the staircase, he felt something guiding him. Michael sensed an odd presence. It almost felt like someone was holding his hand, pulling him to the top of the steps. His feet were weightless as he couldn't feel the stone beneath.

The large wooden doors were suddenly less intimidating. When he opened the door, it wasn't heavy. The door didn't feel like it was made of solid wood, but feathers. The church was completely empty, not a single soul was in sight. All Michael could see was a long pathway leading to the altar. He soaked in the essence of holiness around him. Instead of feeling fear, Michael knew he was home. His mind was calm. The voice of his demons faded. Every step Michael took, their voices got lower. They were powerless in the house of God.

The rows of pews were endless. When Michael reached the first pew, he knelt on one knee and made the sign of the cross. He knelt and folded his hands. Michael looked around him one more time before he prayed aloud.

"God, please forgive me for I have sinned," Michael said softly. "I come here to ask for your forgiveness. I know you've been trying to reach out to me. I'm sorry I didn't believe it was you. I let the doubts and criticism of others around me, influence my thinking. I'm sorry for not trusting you, for believing that you wanted to hurt me. I should have known that you only want the best for me and that sometimes a blessing seems like a curse."

Michael stopped for a moment to wipe the tears from his eyes. The emotions poured out of him. His hands trembled.

"I need a sign," he cried out. "All these things that have been happening to me. Are they because you're trying to reach out to me? What are you trying to tell me? Is this because of Elvira?"

Michael stared at the crucifix on the side of the altar. He clenched his hands together tightly. He bowed his head submissively. There was total silence in the room.

"I give myself to you," Michael said. "Please, help me learn not to be afraid of love, but instead to embrace it. Guide me to mend those mistakes I've made. To vanish the demons that follow me. Help me think clearly and see what's true. Give me a sign, what's the next step? Guide me, Jesus Christ."

Michael made the sign of the cross then he got up off the pew. As he walked back towards the door, he looked back at the altar.

"One more thing," he mumbled. "If there's one person I want you to look out for, it's my Elvira Vaughn. She had such a hard life and deserved none of it. I often ask myself, why her? Why does someone who has such a beautiful soul have to suffer? At the start of all this, I often asked myself. How do you know if you love someone? How do I know if she really is my soulmate? Then it hit me. When I realized I wanted her happiness, even before me own, I knew. If I had to spend an eternity of suffering so she can smile, I'd make that trade right now. True love is loving someone more than myself."

Michael blessed himself with holy water. He walked out of the church. The colors of the day seemed brighter than before. The vibrant colors of the world were fading back into Michael's view. He continued his walk along Fifth Avenue. His mind was oddly clear, he could easily absorb the world around him, and felt open and free.

A man selling souvenirs was shouting sales pitches at people. All the people walking by simply ignored the salesman. To them, he was another guy trying to make a quick dollar. The salesman had a table full of little statues, keychains, and small pictures of New York City. Standing behind him was a metal wrack of hats.

"Excuse me sir!" the salesman said.

Michael stopped his walk. He pointed at himself.

"Me?"

"Yes!" the salesman yelled. "It's your lucky day."

Michael felt bad for the salesman. He probably didn't have much money. Everyone ignored him on the street. All he was trying to do was make a living. Michael complied and walked over to the man.

"Why's it my lucky day?" Michael asked. "I haven't been feeling so lucky."

"Well that's about to change," the salesman said excitedly. "Today is a special day."

There was something different about this salesman. Michael didn't feel like this man was trying to sell him anything. He wondered why the man chose to call him out of the massive crowd of New Yorkers.

"Ok," Michael said skeptically.

The salesman turned around. He rummaged through the rack of hats. The salesman grabbed a beige hat with a long salmon ribbon.

"If you have a special lady in your life, this is the hat for you!"

The salesman handed Michael the hat. He held the hat in his hand and gently let the fabric run through his finger. Michael instantly recognized it. It was the exact same hat that he bought Elvira. He knew this was another sign, and that it was God's way of telling him that his prayers were heard.

Michael thought to himself. "What are the odds a street vendor calls me aside and tries to sell me the same hat I bought Elvira in a department store?"

He handed the hat back to the salesman.

"Thank you, sir," Michael said. "I already bought this exact hat for the woman I love."

The salesman smiled. "Then what are you doing here? Go to her my son."

Michael knew who the salesman really was. There was no running away. Faith had found its way back into Michael's life. It was calling out to him. There are many people, who would have a hard time believing this was happening. They all wouldn't dare to think that God played such a close role in our daily lives. Michael finally learned to accept that, and all it took were a few signs.

"You've been following me," Michael said calmly.

The salesman shook his head. "I haven't been following you. I've always been with you. It only took you this long to see."

The wind blew the hat out of the salesman's hand, dancing down the street and onto the sidewalk. Michael grabbed the hat then looked back over in the direction of the salesman, only to see that he disappeared. Michael asked Jesus for a sign, and he gave it to him. As Michael thought back, there had been many occurrences like this one, but he ignored them all. He blocked it out because he didn't have enough faith. Living a life of faith isn't for everyone, but Michael trusted God. He trusted Jesus and the Holy Spirit.

In that moment, Michael made a decision. He promised himself he'd stop drinking. There would be no more wallowing in self-pity. Instead, Michael took a leap of faith. He was going to chase after love, instead of hiding from it. There was one thing Michael had to do, and that was win the love of his life back. Michael knew he was living a storybook romance. All he needed was a real perfect ending. Instead of praying for something to change, Michael took it upon himself to create his own destiny. He knew God was guiding him along the way. There was only one-way Michael was going to end his story with Elvira. Michael had to finish his book and live out the original ending he wrote. That ending, was a destiny he always promised her.

Finishing his book was one of the most emotionally strenuous things Michael ever had to do. He felt that he couldn't concentrate in his parent's house. There was always fighting and screaming. He needed a place where there was peace and serenity. He needed a place where he could feel at one with the world, and not worry about a single thing. Michael made a list of all his most favorite places to visit, but none seemed right. He couldn't concentrate anywhere. Michael knew that the place he wrote had to be special. It needed to hold significant meaning in his life and Elvira's. One place finally came to mind. The simple thought of its view made him smile.

Every single day, for two weeks straight, Michael took a train and bus to the Port Washington Harbor. It wasn't an easy travel there from Astoria without a car. The commute was around two hours daily, but Michael didn't care. He had nothing but time. Michael brought only a notepad and a pen with him for every single one of those days. He sat silently at a bench facing the water and wrote. The fresh spring air had a sweet smell. Michael soaked in the view around him. He loved to watch the ships in the harbor rock back and forth. Geese crossed the road, holding up a line of traffic. Couples walked around holding hands. Then there was Michael, sitting alone, looking out into the bay.

As Michael got off the bus, he religiously inhaled the fresh air. Before he wrote, he walked to the outermost part of the harbor. He stared out into the bay and looked back on all the people. Michael hoped he would get off the bus and see Elvira, sitting at a bench on the harbor, waiting for him to find her. Even though Michael knew she was far away, he still hoped she'd be there. Michael was met with the same disappointment, every day. Elvira never showed up. The Port Washington Harbor held a special place in Elvira's heart, as it did Michael's. He knew how much she loved that area. The town was artsy and musical, just like her. She always professed to Michael how she'd love to live there one day. Michael always felt that she'd eventually make it happen.

The emotions the harbor brought out helped Michael finish his book. Michael created an unforgettable ending, one that left himself in tears by thinking about it. It wasn't corny, or cheesy. It wasn't funny, or even sad. The perfect word to describe it would be, beautiful. The beautiful part about it all was that it was true. The novel, the feelings, the spirituality, the signs, and now the ending would all be derived from truth. Michael wrote about his experiences with God, about Jesus coming to him in the form of a salesman, and how his fears tried to deter him from true happiness.

There was nothing left to do but type the rest of his novel, piece it all together, leave everything behind. The anger, the sadness, and the parts of his life he never put to bed. He left all his past relationships where they were, in the past. Michael knew he couldn't bring any of this into the relationship with Elvira. It was time to let sleeping dogs lie. That included, leaving his family behind. All the drama, the pain, and the influence they held over Michael. It all didn't matter anymore.

Michael needed money to get to California. A phone call to Elvira couldn't fix this. He had to show his love in a special way. That was the only way she'd take him seriously, is if he flew to California. Michael had to show he was willing to sacrifice so she could pursue her dreams to. That's what he should have done all along. Michael knew he should have been more open to the idea of moving to California with Elvira, instead of letting her go off to another big city alone.

He was no better than any of the other men who hurt her. Michael was only human, and he hoped Elvira would understand he made a mistake.

The only way Michael could make money, was to sell his novel. That was never going to happen. The novel wasn't about making money. It was about letting Elvira know how special she is and the impact she had on his life. He would never become a sellout. Michael wanted to immortalize their relationship for the whole world to see. There wasn't enough time for Michael to find a job and make some quick cash. The longer he let this drag out with Elvira, the worse it was going to get. He needed at least a few hundred dollars.

Michael dragged a garbage bag full of his worldly possessions to a pawn shop. He was willing to sell anything and everything he owned to get enough money for a trip to California. All he needed was a one-way ticket as there was no going back for him. The idea of a one-way ticket made him smile, it made him finally see things a little more clearly now. The pressure of life burdened him. He only had one thing on his mind that kept him going, the love of his life, Elvira Vaughn.

George Whaley, the owner of the pawn shop, didn't give Michael any pleasant vibes. He had long greasy hair and wore a large gold ring on his finger. There wasn't a single wrinkle on his shirt or pants. He was dressed sharply, almost a little too sharp for the kind of store he was running. George approached Michael as he entered the store. His walk resembled the hungry pounce a lion makes on its prey.

"Hi, I'm George Whaley."

Michael nodded. "I got a whole bag of stuff here. I need an appraisal."

George had a demonic smile on his face. His greedy intentions were evident. He could smell Michael's desperation. George was ready to make some money, and he didn't care if he had to rip off Michael to do it.

"Place the bag on the counter," George said reassuringly. "It's your lucky day, I'm going to give you a great deal."

Michael wasn't going to fall for George's tricks. He could see George was trying to rob him, but Michael didn't have much of a choice. He needed money fast, and he knew that George had the advantage going into this sale. Michael spilled everything in the garbage bag onto the counter. George took a small magnifying glass out of his shirt pocket. He examines Michael's belongings. George rummaged through all the items, grunting and pushing things aside.

"There's not much I can work with here," George said.

He pulled a calculator from a drawer in the counter. George typed in some numbers, pretending he was coming up with a good price.

"For you," George said. "I can do one hundred dollars."

Michael's eyes bulged. He didn't expect George to start that low.

Michael shook his head. "I can't do it. This is everything I own. You want me to throw my life belongings away for a measly hundred bucks?"

George laughed. "Listen buddy, you brought me crap," he said. "Total crap, there's not even anything remotely worth something. I gotta make money to."

Michael packed the items back into the garbage bag.

"I'm not selling any of this for that price," Michael scathed.

George shrugged his shoulders. "Suit yourself."

The last item lying on the counter was the Caruso records Michael took from the antique store. George barely went through everything and tried to lowball Michael for it all. He didn't come across the Caruso records yet. They instantly caught his greedy eyes. George put his hand over the records. He was practically salivating.

"Are these original Caruso records?" George asked.

Michael nodded. He could tell George was interested in these records.

"Why yes, they are," Michael said confidently. "But, they aren't for sale. Especially not at your prices."

George patted Michael on the shoulder. "Wait a minute," he said. "Let's talk about this buddy. I'm sure something can be worked out."

Michael pulled the record out of George's hands. He grabbed the calculator and typed in a number. He pushed the calculator over to George with one finger.

Michael smiled. "This is what I want for the two Caruso records."

George shook his head angrily. "Are you insane?" he asked. "You want me to pay you five hundred dollars for records?"

Michael crossed his arms. "It's about to get higher if you keep questioning me."

George grunted. "I can do two hundred. Not a penny more."

Michael shook his head. "They're worth much more, five hundred. Shall I charge you an extra five hundred?"

George took a wad of one hundred-dollar bills from his pocket. He threw the money at Michael.

"Here," George said.

Michael took the money and put it in his pocket.

"God sees everything," Michael said. "Don't be too greedy, or it's going to catch up to you."

14

CHAPTER

Carmela Coniglio sat at her kitchen table. Michael sat across from her. He held her hand. Michael told Carmela all that happened to him throughout the last sixth months. He was always close to his mother. Carmela was the first person to know everything that happened to him. If he got a new job, or met a nice girl, it was always Carmela who had the inside scoop. Michael let Carmela know that he was planning to run away, for a long time. That he didn't know when he was getting back. Michael promised his mother that if his novel ever got published, she'd get a big check in the mail. If the check wasn't much, Michael swore he wouldn't keep a dime of it himself.

"Why do you have to leave me?" Carmela wept.

Michael wiped away the tears from his mother's eyes. "I have to go," he said sadly. "I can't really explain why, but I do."

Carmela smiled. "Michael," she said. "I gave birth to you. I know you're leaving to go chase a woman."

Michael smiled. "I could never hide anything from you Ma," he said. "She's the most amazing woman in the world. I know you'd love her, and she'd love you."

"I know she is," Carmela said. "I've never seen you talk about another woman this way."

"I'm glad you think so," he said. "Your opinion means the world to me."

Michael kissed his mother goodbye. It was the last time he was going to see her. It broke Michael's heart to leave his mother alone. She didn't have the best life at home. Carmela held Michael's arm. She laid her head on his shoulder.

"All those years you cried," Carmela said. "Isn't it worth it now?"

"What do you mean?" Michael said.

"All the heartbreak, problems in school growing up, and the adversity you faced. Now you know it was all worth it. It was all meant to be. If none of that happened, you would have never met this wonderful woman."

Michael cried in his mother's arms. He thought back to some of the hardest moments in his life. Michael remembered how his mother guided him through everything. His bond with Carmela was special. She always knew her son was one of a kind. All she wanted was for him to be happy. If chasing this girl was the answer, she would support Michael. Carmela would never encourage her son to leave, but she knew Michael had to give this a chance.

"You're right," Michael said. "You've always been right mom."

Michael kissed his mother goodbye one last time. He walked outside of the home he grew up in. Michael stared at it, and reminisced.

His mother called out to him again. "One last thing Michael," Carmela said.

"Sure Ma," Michael replied.

"Tell me she's tall?" Carmela joked. "What's her name?" she continued.

Michael would always remember these moments with his mother. The kind that made him endlessly laugh. His mother was a woman with high energy. She always told the best jokes, and never judged a single soul. Carmela helped mold Michael's personality in the absence of his father. Michael was thankful her good qualities rubbed off on him.

Michael brightly smiled. It was the first time in months he smiled like that. "She's almost taller than me," Michael said. "Her name is Elvira Vaughn."

By hearing her name, Carmela knew she was not Italian. She always knew her son wanted to marry an Italian girl. Carmela was taken by surprise.

"She's not Italian?" Carmela asked curiously.

Michael shook his head. "She's not Italian by blood, but her soul is definitely Italian. She loves Tony Bennett, Frank Sinatra, she cooked me a nice meat sauce, she loves to drink red wine and she even talks with her hands. She made herself into my Italian girl."

Carmela smiled. "Then God bless her."

Billy honked his car horn multiple times. He watched Michael say goodbye at least five times in a row. Billy teased him for being such a momma's boy. Michael marched over to Billy's car.

"How many times are you going to honk that stupid horn," Michael said. "I was saying goodbye to my mother."

Billy waved his hands in the air. "Who the hell says goodbye fifteen times like you?"

Billy was upset Michael was leaving. Outside of Michael, he didn't have anyone else. Michael was his closest friend. They were so close, they could have been brothers. Now Michael was leaving him, and it really hurt. Billy was going to be left alone.

"What's your problem?" Michael asked.

"I'm upset you're leaving Mike. Who am I going to argue with all the time? Who am I going to drink with?"

Michael laughed. "That's what you choose to be upset about? Not being able to drink and argue with me?

"Isn't that what we always do?" Billy said.

They both laughed together. Michael and Billy definitely had differences, but their friendship was genuine. They'd do anything for each other. Even though Billy always teased Michael, he looked up to him. Billy knew Michael never cared what anyone thought of him. He always stayed true to the person he was. He never went along with the popular trends or conformed to what society wanted him to be. If anyone ever had a problem with it, Michael would set them straight. Billy admired him for that.

Michael handed Billy a small piece of paper. "Take me to this address."

"What's in Great Neck?" Billy asked.

"Just drive already!" Michael yelled. "I'll explain on the way."

Allison waited outside her home. She looked intimidating, and unapproachable. Allison was ready to attack on behalf of Elvira. She didn't know what Michael was up to. Allison didn't want Michael to do any more damage. After months of trying to get over Michael, Allison didn't want Elvira starting this painful journey again. Elvira was still healing.

Billy abruptly pulled into Allison's driveway. Michael jumped out of the car and ran towards Allison. He trudged up the driveway, almost falling at Allison's feet.

"I need to know where Elvira is," Michael demanded.

"Why?" Allison asked defensively. "You never called her after she gave you that cassette tape."

Michael slammed his hands down at his sides. "You're really going to question me?" He yelled. "I love her!" he screamed out. "I am fucking madly in love with her!"

Allison raised her eyebrows. She knew Elvira said Michael was a little neurotic, but Allison never expected this. She tried to speak but Michael cut her off.

"I made a mistake," he said. "I'm only human. I've never felt this kind of way before. When you love someone this much it's scary. I have so many feelings I don't even know where to put them half the time. It took me a while to realize I was wrong. I should have moved to California with her. I'm willing to make up for that now. Give me the chance to fix it!"

Michael continued to beg and plead with Allison. She ignored him as he kept retelling the story over again to try and make her see his point. Allison wanted Michael to really learn his lesson. She only acted this way because she didn't want Michael to think Elvira was waiting at his beck and call. Michael was sweating it out and Allison got enjoyment from it. She liked to watch him beg.

"Alright!" she screamed. "Just shut up already."

Allison tucked her hand under her shirt, and into her bra. She pulled out a folded piece of paper and handed it to Michael.

"What's this?" Michael asked nervously.

"It's Elvira's address. Don't mess it up this time. I won't be here to help you again."

Michael unfolded the paper to make sure Allison wasn't bluffing. He hugged her tight, picked her up off the ground, and spun her around.

"Thank you!" he screamed out. "Thank you, thank you, thank you."

Billy screamed from the car window. "What the hell are you doing!"

"Who's that?" Allison asked. "He's got a mouth worse than a truck driver's."

Allison stared at Billy's car. She couldn't get a good look at Billy. Allison seemed to be a little curious about his friend. Elvira always bragged that Allison should find an Italian man. If Allison and Billy got together, it would make perfect sense. With Michael gone, Billy wouldn't be alone. Allison wouldn't hate men anymore if she found a good one. It was a double win.

Michael smiled. "Why, that's my good friend Billy Benfatto. Why don't you come meet him?"

Allison blushed. She brushed her hair using only her fingers. "I don't think I'm in any condition to see him right now."

Michael put his arm around Allison. He guided her towards the car. "Oh please," Michael said. "You'd easily be the most beautiful woman Billy has ever been with."

Allison's cheeks turned red. "You really mean that?" she asked.

"Why of course I do," Michael said.

Billy was instantly smitten by Allison's beauty. She was an extremely attractive woman. Allison wasn't anywhere in Billy's league, but Michael was going to do all the talking. It was easy for Michael to light a fire between them. Billy got out of his car and brushed his hair back with a pocket comb. Michael rolled his eyes.

"Elvira always told me you wanted an Italian man," Michael said. "Here's the perfect one for you."

Allison hit Michael's shoulder playfully. She held out her hand and introduced herself to Billy. After a half hour of talking, Michael pushed Billy to ask Allison out on a date. Billy and Allison were a match for each other. They both complimented each other's needs. Billy needed a woman like Allison in his life. Allison was self-sufficient, owned her own medical practice, and had a dominating personality. Billy was so stubborn and stuck in his ways. He needed a woman with such a strong outlook. Allison would challenge him at every step and break him out of his mold.

Love always finds a way. It hits a person when they least expect it. That could be said for both Billy and Allison, who went on to live a happy life together. While Billy was losing his best friend, he gained the love of his life. If Michael and Elvira never fought, Billy and Allison may have never crossed paths. They could have met, but not under the same circumstances. God truly has a plan for everyone. Good can always come from the bad. In this case, a romance blossomed from Michael and Elvira's fight. There's a silver lining between everything that happens to a person. Not everyone can always see it.

Together, Billy and Allison drove Michael to the airport. They both hugged him goodbye and wished him luck on his new journey. Michael told them his plan along the way. They both didn't think it was a wise idea, but Michael was stubborn. Michael knew that if he had to win back Elvira, it had to be a certain way. He had to prove he was willing to make the most vulnerable, intimate, and life changing decision. Michael didn't think they could make a life for themselves here. He felt they needed a fresh start and a clean slate. To run away to a place where nothing else mattered but the two of them.

With a banged up suitcase, Michael walked into Kennedy Airport. Michael owned whatever was in that one tiny bag. He didn't want anything to remind him of the way things used to be. Material items weren't important to Michael. All Michael ever needed was love. He never wanted to be rich, or even famous. Money can't buy love, health, or happiness. It's always nice to have it, but Michael always thought it was important to live humbly.

The airport was overly crowded on this day. The line to purchase tickets seemed to be never ending. It was at least around a two hour wait. Michael was hoping to be in California by the end of day, but that plan didn't seem like it was going to work out. Michael casually took his place on the line. He was the last of maybe two hundred people waiting to buy plane tickets.

An airport employee tapped Michael on the shoulder. "Are you on line sir?" he asked.

Michael nodded.

The airport employee waved his hand, signaling Michael to follow him. He unlocked a stanchion with velvet ropes. "We've just opened this line sir," the airport worker said.

Michael shook the airport worker's hand with thanks. He offered him a tip, but the airport worker refused. He smiled at Michael and said, "Have faith." The airport worker disappeared into the crowd. People rushed onto the new line as Michael got pushed to the front. At the kiosk, Michael bought a one-way ticket to California. Before the night ended, Michael would arrive in Los Angeles.

Michael was a nervous wreck. He didn't have the slightest clue how Elvira was going to react when she saw him as they hadn't seen or spoken in over sixth months. The simple thought of her smile made Michael giddy. Michael trusted that no matter the outcome, God had the best plan for him in mind.

Elvira found another coffee shop similar to the one in Astoria. It was only a few moments away from her apartment. This new coffee shop, called the Cappuccino Cabana, was the local hangout. It was brightly colored and decorated.

It was one of the first to start the upcoming trends of the 1980s. Neon lights lit the windows. Elvira didn't stick around any longer than she had to. Her mind was too preoccupied between the stress of school and battling her depression. Elvira spent most of her time there studying with a friend.

A bright yellow taxicab left Michael at a street corner next to a row of apartment buildings. Michael looked around. He soaked in what was supposed to be bright, beautiful, and sunny California. Los Angeles was nothing like what he thought it would be. It was more run-down then New York City could have ever been.

The elevator leading up to Elvira's apartment was broken. Michael walked up to the top of the steps. He looked at each door number, trying to see if any matched the number Allison gave him. Michael finally reached Elvira's room. It was the last of the entire row of apartments. He knocked on her door and was greeted with silence. After a few moments, he knocked again. Still, there was total silence. Michael peered through the front window of her apartment and noticed the lights were out.

Michael assumed the best and hoped Elvira was in class. He made his way back down the steps and onto the street. He looked for a place to stay until she got back. Michael stumbled across the Cappuccino Cabana. He could see from afar that it looked lively. A group of young students sat outside the coffee shop. They were smoking cigarettes with denim jackets, raggedy hair, and hoop styled earrings. Michael could tell these kids were wannabe rock stars. They stared at Michael with disdain. The young students could instantly tell he was an older man. Michael ignored the stares and peered through the front window of the store.

Elvira sat at a table, quietly reading a textbook. There was a piping hot coffee next to her. Elvira didn't move from that spot for the past three hours. She studied so much, her eyes were sore from staring at the pages of a textbook.

Elvira was the first person Michael saw. She always stuck out from the rest of the crowd. The way she dressed was different. She always looked exotic. Michael noticed she cut her hair shorter. Her new haircut resembled a Julie Andrews type of style.

The moment Michael saw the profile of her face, the vibrant colors of the world flashed before him. Michael felt like he had been colorblind before this moment. His heart pounded, and his eyes lit up. His hands shook. Elvira was more beautiful than he could ever capture in his memory. Michael quietly stared at her through the window. He gathered his thoughts, trying to figure out what he should say.

A man sat down next to Elvira. She greeted him with a kiss on his cheek. It looked like they were studying together. Michael saw Elvira laughing at a joke the man made.

Michael mumbled to himself. "I used to make her laugh like that."

Elvira looked like she was fine. She didn't look sad, or even upset. Her body language seemed to be comfortable around this mystery man. Michael automatically assumed the worst. His heart felt like it was going to explode. His pulse was so strong that he could feel it pound in his temple. Sadness filled Michael's body and mind. He didn't feel any anger, because in his heart, he knew this was his fault. Michael should have done this months ago. He shouldn't have waited a single second. At this point, Michael wanted Elvira to be happy. It wasn't his intention to walk back into her life and uproot her feelings again. Their time has passed, and Michael missed it. Michael walked away from the window of the coffee shop. His head sunk down to his chest. Michael looked completely defeated. He would now have to live the rest of his life knowing he let Elvira walk away.

Elvira finished drinking her coffee. She closed her textbook and took a deep breath. The man next to her did the same.

"Thanks for helping me study," Elvira said. "I really didn't think I was going to be ready for the final exam."

The man nodded with appreciation. "I should be the one thanking you," he said. 'If it wasn't for your advice today, I probably would have broken up with my boyfriend."

Elvira laughed. "Well, I hope it all works out! I'll see you after graduation."

On the walk back to her apartment, Elvira had an odd feeling in the pit of her stomach. She felt an energy that was calming. There was loving presence nearby. It wasn't a fatherly or a motherly love. She was feeling a type of love that only one person gave her. Elvira felt Michael was close. Shivers of joy swept her body. She raced back to her apartment, to find no one waiting there for her. Elvira thought she was going crazy. In her mind and heart, she knew Michael was near. She felt this deep sadness in his heart. It could be compared to the sadness of an abandoned puppy. Elvira felt Michael's lost soul wandering further away from her.

A custodian was cleaning the hallway of her apartment building. He noticed Elvira frantically looking up and down the hall. He tapped her on the shoulder. Elvira jumped.

"I didn't mean to startle you," the custodian said. "Are you looking for someone?"

Elvira nodded. "Was there a man near my apartment door?"

"I saw a man with a suitcase here. He looked like he traveled a long distance. He peeked into your window and then walked away."

Elvira's intuition was completely correct. She knew the custodian saw Michael. Elvira didn't want to wait in her apartment for him to come back. She needed to see him right away. There were so many things she had to tell him. So much time had gone by, and she wanted to make up for it all. Most of all, Elvira wanted to apologize for leaving him. She wanted things to go back to the way they used to be.

"Did you happen to see which way he walked down the street?" Elvira asked.

"No," the custodian said softly.

Elvira frantically ran back out onto the street. She looked down both sides of the road, trying to determine where she should start looking for him. It would be almost impossible for her to guess where he'd end up, or if he'd even come back to see her again. If she didn't at least try to look for him, she'd regret it for the rest of her life. Elvira thought about the places Michael would think she'd be. There was only one place, and that was her campus. Without hesitating, Elvira ran in the direction of her school, desperately in search of the man she loves.

15

CHAPTER

California University's campus was so large that it could have been a city of its own. The facilities were all modern, sparkling, and clean. Elvira's school, the Rutherford Institute of Physiological Studies, stood in the center of the entire campus. It was adjacent to the quad, a place where events were held on a daily basis. On this day, in particular, California University was having a concert. The quad was filled with hundreds of students ready to party, blow off steam before their final examinations.

Michael didn't have the slightest clue how to get around Los Angeles. He wasn't in the mood to explore or wander off into the city for the day. His heart was too heavy. Michael was still under the impression that Elvira finally started to move on. That she was building a new life for herself in Los Angeles. The idea of that made him want to vomit. He wanted her, all to himself. Michael didn't want to share Elvira with anyone. She let him into her little quirky world. Elvira showed Michael all the little things about herself, things that only someone this close to her would know.

The idea that another man was learning these things about her, made him sick. The idea of another man touching her, made him furious. The combination of the two feelings made Michael uneasy. Michael was jealous. He'd never felt so crazy, jealous before in his entire life. Elvira was his, and she wasn't to be shared.

As the thoughts swirled in Michael's brain, he found himself at the entrance of California University. He didn't even realize how far he'd been walking. Michael wandered too far and found himself lost. He was always poor at following directions. His family used to joke that he needed a compass to go around the block. Michael couldn't even find his way back to Elvira's apartment.

Such a large school seemed daunting to Michael. He was impressed that Elvira had the guts to make this life altering change in the first place. She was much different from him that way. While Michael thought everything through, maybe a little too much, Elvira didn't. She could be reckless. Michael figured this was the school Elvira had been attending. Allison never gave him the name of the school itself. Naturally, Michael was curious to see what she'd uprooted her life in New York for. He walked onto the campus and heard the sounds of a live concert. Michael's first reaction was to follow the music. It was the first thought that came to his mind.

Still running, Elvira finally reached the campus. She continued to glance at every corner of the street in search of Michael. California University was so big, Elvira couldn't figure out where she should start looking. She heard the same music Michael did. Music played such a large role in both their lives. Elvira thought it would be best if she checked to see if Michael was at the concert.

Both Michael and Elvira found themselves lost in a crowd of people. Michael stayed at the corner of the crowd as he felt claustrophobic at times and needed space. From afar, Michael saw Elvira walking into the crowd. She looked nervous and distraught. Michael's instant reaction was to hide behind a group of people. He didn't know if he wanted to see her. Michael was jealous, but at the same time he wanted her to be happy. He questioned if it was his place to uproot her life here in Los Angeles. His thoughts swarmed and found himself in yet another thinking loop. All the negative outcomes swirled through his mind. Michael debated with himself. He dug his fingers into his skull. The thoughts wouldn't stop.

Michael was tired of living his life in fear. He was tired of debating what would have a good or bad outcome. He was tired of wanting everything to be perfect. Most of all, he was tired of having these expectations for what life is supposed to be like. Loving someone is taking a risk whether it's romantic or not. Life is filled with nasty outcomes, and they're unavoidable. Every person makes mistakes, and there's always room for forgiveness. Michael wasn't going to let any of this anticipation and anxiety control his life anymore. It was time he set himself free and learn to roll with the punches life brings. He accepted that there was a chance Elvira wouldn't want to be with him any longer. There's no amount of thinking he could do that would change it. Nothing could be done about it. The only thing he could do was find out for himself, by asking.

In that moment, Michael's anxious thinking stopped. He thought clearly. Michael knew that he meant more than that man in the coffee shop could ever mean to her. He knew that no matter how bad their fight was, that Elvira would still love him the same. Even if Elvira's feelings were hurt, Michael knew that eventually, they would be able to get past it. Love isn't just a feeling—it's a living and breathing emotion. Feeling love doesn't have to mean happiness. It could mean anger, sadness, and jealousy. It could fall under any other emotional category. He knew there was going to be hurt, heartbreak, sadness, and rage in any healthy relationship. There was no longer any reason to be afraid. If their love was true, Michael knew that they would get through anything.

The band went to an intermission. Michael glanced at Elvira then back at the stage. Without thinking, Michael weaved through the crowd. He pushed and shoved any person standing in his way. When he fought his way to the front, Michael stood before a metal barrier holding back the crowd. He threw himself over it and ran towards the stage. The crowd screamed. Two burley security guards chased after him. Michael was caught before he could reach the singer of the band. One security guard tackled him, while the other subdued him.

Michael screamed, "I'm not going to lose her! I'm not going to lose her!"

Both security guards were confused by Michael's statement. They dragged him off the stage. He screamed again, "Please! The love of my life is in the crowd. I need to win her back."

The lead singer of the band called the security guards back over to the stage. They dragged Michael back by his arms. The security guards were so strong, Michael could barely move. They held him so tight, that he lost feeling in both his arms. His body grew limp. The singer put his hand up at the guards, signaling for them to drop Michael.

Michael fell to the floor. He held his arms in pain. The lead singer crouched next to him.

"What the heck are you screaming about," he asked.

"My soulmate. She's in this crowd. I lost her, and I need to win her back. Let me sing to her."

The singer smiled. "This girl really means that much to you?" he said. "You know if I wasn't such a nice guy, you'd be spending the night in jail. Is this chick really worth jail time?"

Michael shook his head. "Does this look like the face of a man who's afraid of anything right now? If I had to, I'd swim with sharks. I'd run into a burning building. I would fly a plane. I would..."

The singer silenced Michael. "I get the point."

Michael picked himself up off the ground. He shook out his arms.

"What do you say?" Michael asked.

The singer shrugged his shoulders. "I can't stop love," he said. "What song do you want to sing?"

Michael hugged the singer. The security guards jumped to grab him, but the singer warded them off with a wave.

"Your Song," he said. "Elton John."

"You're on your own kid, the band doesn't know how to play that song. I sure as hell ain't singing it. You got pipes?"

Michael nodded with excitement. "I think I can do it," he replied. "I used to play the guitar as a kid. Would you mind showing me the notes to the song?"

"All I know is that you better win her back. This is cutting into my time."

The singer had the band crew set up a keyboard and a microphone at the front of the stage. He quickly showed Michael the basic notes to the song. Michael didn't have any time to practice. At his point, he didn't even care how it sounded. Michael wanted to profess his love for her in front of the entire crowd. He wanted to show her how much she meant to him. This was something so uncharacteristic of Michael. He hated crowds. He never let anyone hear him sing or play any kind of instrument. He always felt more comfortable in the shadows, and Elvira knew that.

Michael walked up to the front of the stage. He grabbed the microphone. With all the strength in his body, all the willpower of his mind, and the grace of God, Michael spoke directly from his heart. There was no more hiding.

"The woman I lost is out here in this crowd today," he said.

There was a mixed reaction from the crowd. Some booed Michael while others wanted to hear his story. Elvira looked at the stage with the rest of the crowd. She instantly recognized his voice but was too far away to see him clearly. She rushed towards the stage. A handful of other women followed. They also thought Michael was talking about them.

"To the girl who loves to drink red wine. The girl who eats cashews in the most peculiar way I've ever seen. The girl who loves to read these insanely descriptive classic novels. The girl who's eyes I still can't tell are blue or green. The girl who has to sit in one specific spot every single time we go out to eat. The girl who has a voice of an angel. To the girl I love."

A crowd of women gathered around the barrier. They were all met with disappointment. Michael hadn't described any single one of them. None of them had these very specific qualities about them. All the women in the crowd knew that Michael wasn't talking about them. Elvira clawed her way up the barrier. For the first time in what seemed like an eternity, Michael and Elvira's eyes met.

"This song is for you," he said.

Michael sat down in front of the keyboard. He took a deep breath and cracked his fingers. Without any hesitation or a care in the world, Michael began to play. By the grace of God, Michael played the song near perfect. He didn't skip a note. There wasn't a single thing out of place. Michael sang with passion. The hurt, pain, want, and love could all be heard in his voice. It could be seen by the expression on his face. Without even knowing him personally, the crowd knew that without Elvira, Michael was nothing.

Michael chose "Your Song" because it was the only song that could come close to describing how he felt. Michael didn't have any money. He didn't have a stable career. He wasn't the best at hiding his emotions, they always showed. All he could give Elvira was a promise. That was the best that he could possibly do—a promise to trust him. To trust that sharing a life with him would be the best decision she's ever made. He didn't want to fool her. Michael and Elvira were both difficult and quirky people. They both had strong personalities. There was going to be fighting, disagreement, and hardship. All Michael wanted was for Elvira to give it a chance. Michael could only do so much to convince her. The only option he had was to show Elvira how she made him feel. He did that through the only way he knew how, writing. Michael felt so strongly about Elvira and the love they shared, that he had to write a novel about it. His feelings were so powerful there was no other way to channel them, but to write them down. There wasn't a single way for Michael to tell Elvira how much he loved her. He thought a nice long story might do the job. His novel was the best he could do. That was his gift. Michael wanted to put it all down in words. He wanted everyone to know how wonderful his life was with Elvira Vaughn in his world.

Halfway through the song, the crowd figured out Michael was singing to Elvira. The women around Elvira encouraged her to go on stage. Elvira hesitated for a moment then walked toward the security guards that let her across the barrier. As Elvira walked onto the stage, she didn't take her eyes off Michael. She sat down in a chair directly in front of the keyboard. Elvira watched Michael play. She loved the way the piano sounded. Elvira heard what Michael was trying to say through the words of his song. Her world froze as Michael sang his heart away.

While Michael went through his own emotional roller coaster, he failed to see that Elvira was having her own. Michael didn't have the slightest clue how much he meant to her. Michael was the first man to ever make Elvira feel this special. He was the first man to show her things about herself that she didn't even know. While Elvira thought she was annoying, Michael thought she was endearing. When Elvira did annoy Michael, he felt ambivalent about it. He wanted Elvira to annoy him, because if it wasn't him, she'd be annoying another man. Elvira didn't know what love was until she met Michael. She didn't know what it was like for someone to be so interested in her. She never knew what it was like to receive a thoughtful birthday gift or open a present on Christmas morning.

Elvira never imagined a man cooking for her, taking the time to carefully prepare something for her to eat with such enthusiasm. She especially didn't expect a man to buy her a dress. To envision the curves on her body, a dress he specifically chose for her to wear, a dress that was form fitting, a dress that was sexy and elegant all at the same time. Elvira never thought she'd find a man that enjoyed her being around, a man that loves when she hangs all over him and lays on top of him, a man that loves when she curls up next to him in the middle of the night, a man that runs when she's in trouble, a man that would fight to the death for her without any hesitation. Michael embodied all these things and she couldn't get enough of it. Elvira didn't want anyone else to have him. Michael was hers, and she loved knowing it.

Michael sang the last line of the song. The crowd cheered away as he played the final few notes on the piano. Michael grabbed Elvira's hand. She jumped out of her seat and into his arms. Michael looked at Elvira's teary eyes. He held her face between his hands, wiping away her tears with his thumbs.

He held her close to him, not daring to move. It had been so long since he'd seen her, to have her this close to him felt like a dream. He needed to feel her skin on the tips of his fingers. He needed to wipe the cold tears away from her face. He needed to do all of this to make sure it was all real. Elvira tried to mumble a few words, but Michael silenced her.

"I always thought your eyes were more green than blue," he said softly.

Michael held Elvira's waist, feeling the curves of her body between his hands. Elvira placed her fingers around the back of Michael's neck. They slowly moved in closer, until their lips grazed. They kissed each other passionately, not giving a moment's notice to anyone around them. The crowd around them cheered. People whistled and threw anything they could find into the air. People were celebrating for the two of them. It was easy for the entire crowd to tell that this wasn't an ordinary love, and they all respected it.

Elvira pulled away from Michael. She placed both her hands on his chest and whispered into his ear. "I love you," she said.

"Ti Amo," Michael said. "Scappa via con me."

"What?" Elvira asked.

Michael came to California with a plan. Michael knew Elvira would never be able to call this city home. He had no intention of moving there. Michael only flew to California to win Elvira back. He had another plan in mind all along. Almost everyone who was close to Michael begged him not to go through with it. Michael was about to change his life forever. Not a single person thought what Michael was going to do next was a good idea. Billy, Allison, and even his own mother thought he was crazy. Michael ignored them all. He wanted to follow what his heart told him to do.

Michael's entire novel was based on truth. It was based on experiences Michael and Elvira shared together. More than half the lines in the novel were direct quotes from the two of them. Michael wrote the novel as he lived his life. It was all true. Michael wrote that he was going to do all of this. He wrote about the signs from God, the pawn shop, and his flight to California. He wrote about winning Elvira back in a movie-like fashion. He wrote about singing her a song and professing his love for her in front of a massive crowd. The one last thing Michael had to do was live out the ending he wrote. An ending he promised Elvira the first night they made love. Michael took two plane tickets out of his pocket. He placed them in Elvira's hand.

"I love you," he repeated. "Run away with me."

Elvira held the tickets in her hands. She didn't know what to say. Elvira was worried, because her first reaction wasn't to blurt out the word "yes." Michael took her by complete surprise. This wasn't like him at all. To do something so drastic and unplanned was uncharacteristic for him. Michael was spontaneous, but still calculated. By doing this, he was making a statement. He was asking her to leave everything behind, to leave behind her friends, family and the life that she built for herself and to leave behind the pain of the past, and the troubles of the present.

Elvira didn't know how to answer Michael. He could see in her eyes, that she may have not been ready for such a monumental change. Her final exam was tomorrow and then she would officially have a college degree. She could pursue her dream of becoming a psychologist. It was within her reach. By running away, Michael was asking her to give that up. Wherever they ended up, it would make it more difficult for her to find a job in her field of choice. Elvira managed to convince Michael to give her some time to think it over. She spent the rest of the day showing him around the beaches of California.

Together, Michael and Elvira sat in the sand. The weather was perfect. It wasn't too hot or too cold. A slight breeze swept through the air. The water was clear and slowly crashed on the shore. They both stared at the water as the sun was setting. Michael couldn't stop looking at Elvira. It was the greatest feeling to have her back in his life. He didn't want to take his eyes off her. Michael thought Elvira had the most beautiful profile. As she looked upon the water, the sun shined on the side of her face, making her facial features softly chiseled.

Elvira wore a beautifully printed sundress. It wasn't tight or revealing. She didn't like clothes that fit too tightly. The dress blew in any direction the wind flowed. Michael's clothes were ruffled. He'd been traveling all day. He didn't look very sharp, which was not like him. At this point, Michael didn't care. All he wanted was for Elvira to fly away with him.

"We could have this every day," Michael said.

Elvira's head sunk down. "I know," she mumbled.

Michael grabbed her hand. "So, then what's there to think about?"

Elvira grinded her teeth together then her face twisted. She turned red with furious anger. Even though she was happy Michael was here, she was still mad at him. Elvira spent too much time being upset. She never had the chance to be angry with him. She screamed in the middle of the entire beach. "Do you understand what you did to me?" she yelled. "I've been hurt before, I've felt pain before, and I know what it's like to feel abandoned. None of it compared to you leaving me. None of it compared to you letting me get on that plane. You let me leave. I don't know if I could ever handle feeling that amount of hurt ever again."

Michael saw the pain in Elvira's face. The frustration was clear. Michael hurt her, he was no better than any other man who hurt her. There was going to be times that he made mistakes. All he could do was apologize and try his best to make it right. Michael always painted himself out to be this perfect man, and in a lot of ways he was. He failed to see that he was human too. It was possible for him to make mistakes. It was possible for him to hurt the person he loved the most. Michael had a hard time dealing with that but getting through this would only make their relationship stronger.

"When you said you were leaving, I was paralyzed," Michael said. "My entire life stopped in that one moment. I went colorblind. I didn't get enjoyment out of life the way I used to. I was so scared of the pain that might come." Michael placed his hand over his heart and continued. "You don't have the slightest idea how much I love you. The amount of love I have for you, in my heart, scares me. I love you more than I do myself. If I had to live the rest of my life in pain to make sure you'd smile, I would."

Elvira's heart fluttered as Michael spoke. She felt the anger leaving her body, but she didn't want Michael to get off that easy. Elvira pretended to stay angry.

Elvira pouted. "You didn't even try to stop me," she said.

"What?" Michael asked.

"I sent you that cassette tape and you ignored me. You didn't try to stop me," she repeated.

"I chased after you!" he yelled. "I chased after your cab. I almost had a coronary from running so long."

Elvira held back her smile. She tried not to let Michael see she was laughing. She pictured him running down the street after her cab. She thought it was romantic, but at the same time a small part of her wanted him to suffer.

"You really ran after me?" she asked.

"Of course, I did," he said. "I love you. That's what you do for the woman you love."

Elvira wanted to jump on top of him. He was so adorable. She couldn't help it. She wanted to tear him to pieces with love. Elvira wanted to attack him right there in the middle of the beach. She held back all her emotions. Elvira stared at Michael with a stone face. She didn't want him to think he was fazing her.

"That's it!" Michael yelled. "I can't live my life knowing you're going to be mad at me. I can't live with knowing I hurt you. I can't do it anymore!"

Michael stripped down to his underwear and ran towards the ocean. Michael dove into the water head first and disappeared into the waves. Elvira ran over to the ocean water. She fearfully searched the water for Michael. She stood in the water, only ankle deep.

"Michael!" she yelled out. "You can't swim!"

She was met with no response. There was no sight of Michael. Elvira started to panic. She ripped off her sundress and threw it onto the sand. In only a bra and underwear, she dove into the water to search for Michael. Elvira was an experienced swimmer. She effortlessly swam around, screaming Michael's name. The moment Elvira dove in, Michael surfaced. He desperately gasped for air.

"I got tired of holding my breath," he said smiling.

Elvira swam over to Michael and dunked his head into the water. "You son of a bitch!" she screamed. Elvira pulled his head back up. She grabbed his face. "I thought you were dead."

Michael and Elvira floated in the water together, holding each other. They kissed as the water crashed over their faces. Elvira couldn't pretend to be mad at Michael any longer. She couldn't hide it from him. Elvira loved him, more than Michael ever thought. A day didn't go by where Michael didn't cross her mind. There were too many things to remind her of him.

The day came to an end, and Elvira knew Michael was waiting for her answer. Michael and Elvira returned to her apartment. She tried to soak up every second of the fun they were having. They were going to start to fight again soon, because Elvira decided that she couldn't run away with Michael. She dreaded the moment he would ask her the question. Elvira did everything she could to avoid talking about it.

Michael and Elvira changed out of their wet clothes. Michael peeked over at Elvira's body. He stared at her. Elvira was still soaking wet from the water in the ocean. Michael tried to control himself. He didn't want her to know she had the upper hand. If there was one way to easily manipulate Michael, it was teasing him. He had little self-control when it came to a woman he loved. Michael noticed a small tattoo on Elvira's back.

"Is that a tattoo?" Michael asked. "Since when did you get a tattoo? There was nothing on that little birthmark you have. I know that birthmark better than anyone."

Elvira smiled. She knew Michael had been staring at her. Elvira felt proud of her body. She could see that Michael wanted her. It was killing him that she was changing right next to him.

"I got a tattoo of a pig's tail," she said calmly. "I love pig's tails. There's a little one coming out of my birthmark."

Michael was angry, but he tried not to show it. He didn't like that Elvira went out and got a tattoo after they fought. Michael wanted to be included in that decision. He didn't want her to see that it bothered him. Michael tried to let it roll of his shoulder.

"It looks nice," he said through his teeth.

Elvira walked in Michael's direction. She was completely naked. "You want to get a closer look?" she asked.

Michael started to stutter. "I'm, I'm ok," he said.

"No," she replied. "I really think you should get a better look at it."

Michael and Elvira moved closer to each other. The sexual tension in the room was strong. They locked eyes. Michael and Elvira stared at each other. When Elvira stared at Michael, she looked into his soul. She could see right through him. All his emotions, what he was feeling, she knew him too well. Michael was always the first one to break the staring contest. He couldn't control himself around her. Michael lunged towards Elvira and kissed her. Elvira gave Michael the most intimate and sexual kiss of his entire life, then pushed him away.

Elvira shrugged her shoulders. "Not so fast," she said. "Don't think it's going to be that easy. You've gotta work for it."

"That's not fair," he grunted. "You can't do that to me. I mean, look what you did to me."

Elvira laughed. "I can do whatever I want."

Michael and Elvira put on the rest of their clothes. Michael splashed some cold water onto a rag and pressed it against the back of his neck. He needed to calm himself down after that face-off. Michael never won with Elvira. She always knew how to make him fold. She had this alluring essence about her. It was hard for him to control himself around her.

Michael saw that Elvira was buying herself time. This was going to be a really tough decision for her. Michael was asking her to do something he wasn't willing to do for her a few months ago. He hoped that Elvira would see if he could go back in time, he'd change it all. This time around, Michael needed Elvira to take a leap of faith with him.

"Tomorrow is our flight," Michael said calmly.

"Tomorrow?" she said. "You want me to run away with you one day after you come back? One day after we made up? I have the last test of my entire college career tomorrow morning and you bring this on my plate?"

Michael sighed. "I didn't plan for it to work this way, but yes, I'm asking you to do this. I'm asking you because we're in love."

Elvira threw a pillow at Michael's head. "If you loved me as much as you say, you would have supported my move here!"

"You know," Michael said. "That really hurts me. After all we've been through?"

Elvira crossed her arms. "You can't expect me to pick up and leave."

Michael placed a plane ticket in Elvira's hand. "I think it's best I leave. I'll be waiting on that plane tomorrow night."

Elvira guarded the door, so Michael couldn't leave. She wasn't letting him run out the door and repeat their breakup all over again.

"You can't be serious!" she cried out. "Why are you making me choose? Why are you doing this to me?"

Elvira took a pack of cigarettes off a table in her apartment. She lit one and blew out a puff of smoke. Michael's eyes bulged. Since knowing Elvira, he never even saw her look at a cigarette. Michael figured she may have taken up smoking from the stress of school and their relationship.

"Since when do you smoke?" Michael asked.

"Since we broke up," Elvira replied calmly.

Elvira took another puff of her cigarette. This time she inhaled it, and let the smoke come out of her nose. Michael took the cigarette out of her mouth and threw it on the floor. He stepped on it with his foot.

"What the hell is wrong with you?" he said. "Do you know how badly that's going to hurt your voice? Singing is your life."

"Why would you even care?" she asked.

Michael dropped his suitcase on the floor. He waved his hand in the air. His eyes opened wide. Michael looked like he was going to yell, but he didn't. He grabbed Elvira's shoulders and looked her directly in the eye. She could see the desperation in his face. Michael wanted her to see what he was going through. Without holding back, Michael blurted out words from the bottom of his heart. Words so deeply ingrained in his subconscious, that he didn't even realize he was thinking them.

"You know why I came here?" Michael screamed, "I realized pretty damn quick that the next girl I meet isn't going to have these weird greenish-blue eyes. She's not going to make me bribe some random people one hundred dollars to switch tables at a restaurant, she's not going to love Tony Bennett, and she's not going to endlessly watch movies with me. She's definitely not going to get a tattoo of a freakin pig's tail. I mean, who the hell does that? You have to be crazy to do that?"

Michael paused to take a deep breath. He talked so fast he was stuttering every other word. His stutter came out when he got nervous or anxious.

"She's not going to love how corny, neurotic, or goofy I can be. I mean who the hell is going to put up with me? I'm a total nut case. Who's going to want to deal with all the annoying knickknacks I keep? What about the Buck Seasoning? I've never even heard of that until I met you! I mean you cook God damn Chilean Sea Bass with Buck Seasoning. Where am I going to find that?"

Michael ripped open his suitcase. He took his novel out and pointed to it.

"You see this?" Michael asked. "I finished the novel. I can't even count the bottles of gin I drank to get through it. You think it was fun to write about all this? For a while it was, but it was also painful, to dig down, deep into my mind and heart then put all those feelings onto a page. I didn't write this book because it was fun, or because I want to make money. I could care less if I don't make another dime until the day that I die. I wrote this novel because there wasn't any way I could possible describe the way that I feel about you. There's so many variables that go into it."

Elvira's eyes were red and puffy. She didn't have the slightest clue how to respond to this. Elvira knew Michael loved her, but this kind of love was special. Elvira tried to say something, but Michael continued to rant.

"You deserve the world! Don't you understand? The life you've had. It's not fair. You never deserved to be treated that way. You never deserved to be abused or taken advantage of. Do you know how angry it makes me that any of those bad things happened to you? Because some piece of shit decided to take advantage of a woman who was shattered? I could kill any person that hurt you. I'd love to poke their eyes out with my own two fingers."

Michael made a poking motion with his fingers. Elvira looked at Michael like he was losing his mind.

"You're so wonderfully amazing and beautiful, I had to write it all down for you to see. On top of it all, you saved me. You saved my life. There's no me, without you. It never would have happened. I never would have learned to love myself, or any woman ever again. Because of you, my soul is saved. You brought me to God. If I told you the crazy months I've had. You would have thought I was seeing things."

Michael kissed Elvira and then hugged her tightly. He threw his novel down on the floor and picked up his suitcase.

"You remember that spot in Port Washington, the one I took you?"

Elvira nodded.

"I went there, every single day, to write my novel," he said. "No matter if it rained, if it was cloudy, or sunny. I didn't care. I took the bus and a train there. It was a two-hour commute. Every single time I got off that bus, I prayed I'd see you there. I hoped you'd be sitting on a bench, wearing that hat I bought you, reading a book."

Michael walked towards the door. Elvira picked up Michael's novel and held it in her arms, along with the plane ticket.

"I guess what I'm trying to say is that the next girl I find isn't going to be you. That's why I came to California. That's why I asked you to run away with me. That's why I love you. I never knew I wanted any of this in a woman until I met you.

Even though you drive me absolutely crazy, I love every second of it. I only want you."

Michael slammed the door shut behind him. Elvira didn't move. She didn't cry. She didn't even whimper. Elvira examined the plane ticket. She didn't even think of checking the destination this entire time. Elvira was so caught up by the idea if running away with Michael that she didn't even think to ask where. The plane ticket was one-way to Rome, Italy. Michael wrote on the back of the ticket. It read, "Positano."

Elvira smiled. She remembered what Michael had promised her the first night they made love. She forgot that Michael wrote the ending to his novel first. She tore apart the typewritten pages of Michaels novel, and read the ending herself. Elvira realized the ending to Michael's book, was a fantasy he was trying to live out. A fantasy he promised her, would one day come true. A fantasy they both wished they could have. His book was less of a story, and more of a documentation of their love as they lived. She read all of what happened to him with Jesus, and the salesman. Elvira knew all those experiences were because of her prayers.

Elvira's final examination was tomorrow morning, and the entire rest of her life was ready and waiting to be started. She crawled into her bed, knowing she wasn't going to get much sleep. How could she even think about her test after what Michael told her? After the way he professed his love for her? Elvira never thought there would be a man on this earth who could ever talk that way. Sometimes she thought Michael was from another planet, or even another universe. He was the definition of every girl's dream. Elvira knew he could have whatever girl he wanted, yet he still would always choose her. In less than twenty-four hours, the next decision she was going to make would impact the rest of her life. Her decision would answer the last of Michael's five questions, how much does she love you?

16

CHAPTER

Michael waited at the airport terminal, frequently checking his watch, counting down the seconds until the flight began boarding. He shook his leg nervously. Michael didn't take his eyes off the entrance to the terminal. He stared at every person that walked by. Every time Michael saw a woman with blonde hair, he jumped, only to be met with disappointment soon after. His face was extra pale. Anyone could see the energy was completely drained from his body. Michael was a nervous wreck.

The ticket agent stood behind a desk at the terminal. He picked up the microphone, and announced the plane was about to begin boarding.

"Flight one twenty-two to Rome will begin boarding," the ticket agent said. "Will flyers with a first-class ticket please form a single file line."

A crowd of people lined up at the door of the terminal. One by one, they handed in their tickets and boarded the plane. As the number of passengers in the terminal dwindled, Michael's fears grew. He legitimately started to question whether Elvira was going to show up. As the time flew by, his confidence shrunk.

"Passengers holding tickets from rows twenty to twenty-eight, please begin boarding," the ticket agent said.

Another group of passengers lined up next to the terminal door. Michael checked his ticket. It was his turn to board the plane. He looked around the terminal one last time, holding out hope that Elvira would show up. She wasn't anywhere to be found. Michael decided to get on the plane by himself. If Elvira didn't want to be with him, it was best that he went away for a long time. Michael needed a break from reality for a while. He dragged himself over to the line and waited with the other passengers.

Michael approached the ticket agent, who promptly demanded his passport. Michael reached into his pocket, but the passport wasn't there. He frantically patted his body down, trying to see where he may have misplaced it.

"Just my luck," Michael mumbled.

The ticket agent sighed. "Could you please step aside sir," he asked. "Come back when you find your passport."

Michael searched his bag for his passport, but still couldn't find it. He retraced his steps and went back to his seat at the terminal. Michael checked under the row of seats, and his passport wasn't there. He even put his hands between the crease of the seat, only to find nothing.

"Rows twenty to twenty-eight are now finished boarding," the ticket agent announced.

A woman tapped Michael on the shoulder. She had a friendly face. Her voice was soft-spoken. Michael was extremely high-strung and anxious at this point, but her presence seemed to calm him.

"Is this yours?" the woman asked.

She handed Michael his passport.

"Oh my God," Michael said. "You saved my entire day! Thank you."

The woman smiled and nodded. "No need, to thank me," she said. "Thank God."

The woman walked back into the massive crowd at the airport. Michael smiled. He looked up towards the sky, where heaven is supposed to be.

"You're always looking out for me," he said.

Michael boarded the plane. He smiled at the pilot, who stood attentively at the cabin of the plane. Michael had never been on a plane this large before. The plane's going on trans-atlantic flights were known for their space. The passengers awaited attentively in a line, trying to make their way to the back of the plane. Michael checked his ticket. His row of seats were the very last on the entire plane. At least Michael knew he wasn't going to be sitting next to anyone crazy, Elvira had the other ticket. He'd have an entire eight hours of flight all by himself.

Michael placed his luggage in the small cabin above his seat. He plopped down at the window seat of the plane and gazed out to look at Los Angeles. It was going to be a long time before he came back to America again, especially after this elaborate charade. Michael couldn't see his family and friends anymore. He was tired of it all. Michael didn't want them to lecture him about how he shouldn't have done this.

He took a picture of Elvira out of his wallet. It was a picture of her at the beach. Michael smiled.

"You don't even understand how much I'm going to miss you," Michael mumbled. "There's no me, without you. I always thought it was going to be Michael and Elvira against the world. Not just Michael against the world."

The flight attendant walked down the rows and checked if the passengers were properly seated. Michael fastened his seatbelt. He leaned back in his seat and closed his eyes.

"Everyone please fasten your seat belt and prepare for takeoff," the flight attendant said.

Behind Michael's seat was a small cabin where the stewardess kept the food and beverages. There was also a small bathroom. The stewardess noticed the bathroom was closed. She knocked on the bathroom door.

"Excuse me," the stewardess said. "You'll need to exit the bathroom now."

Elvira exited the bathroom. She walked over to Michael's seat. Elvira watched as Michael tried to sleep. She quietly sat down next to him and waited until he noticed she was there. Elvira saw the picture Michael had of her in his hand. She could tell he was holding it tightly as he slept. Elvira laughed to herself when she saw it was a picture of her in a bathing suit. She tried to keep quiet, but she slowly became impatient. She jumped up in her seat and plopped back down.

Michael grunted. "The seat next to me is taken," he said.

"I don't think so," Elvira said. "The ticket says that my seat is right here."

Michael opened one eye. He slowly turned his head. He was greeted with a smile, unlike any other he's ever seen before. Michael hugged Elvira tightly and then kissed her five times. Elvira giggled at the way Michael covered her in kisses.

"I don't understand," he said. "How?"

"I saw you waiting on line to board," she said. "I waited until you got off the line and went back to your seat. Then I made my way onto the plane when you were talking to some random woman."

Michael's eyes were teary. He started to cry and hid his face. Elvira picked his face up with her two hands. She couldn't handle seeing Michael cry.

With tears in her eyes, Elvira asked, "Why are you crying?"

Michael kissed Elvira. He gently rubbed his fingers on her soft skin.

"Because it's true," he said. "My novel. All of this is real."

Elvira wiped away the tears from Michael's eyes. "It is," she said softly. "It's all true."

Michael slowly ran his hands down Elvira's arm. He rubbed her hands between his.

"There's one more thing," Elvira said.

"What's that?" Michael asked.

Elvira pulled Michael's novel out of her purse. She placed it on his lap.

"Get to reading," she said.

"What?" he replied.

"I only read half of your novel. Whatever you left in my apartment the day we broke up. That's all I know. I put that together with the other half you brought me yesterday. Now, for the first time, we have the entire novel in our hands. I don't want to read it myself. I want you to read it to me."

Michael picked up the novel. He turned over to the first page.

"Right here on the plane?" Michael said.

"I don't care if every passenger on this plane hears you. I've been waiting almost half a year for you to read me this novel."

Michael read the novel aloud to Elvira. The rest of the passengers quietly listened. He paused in the middle of the first paragraph.

"You think we'll make it in a foreign country?" Michael asked.

Elvira laughed. "I already know how this story ends," she said. "I think so."

Michael finished reading his book to Elvira around six hours into the flight. She collapsed and fell asleep on his shoulder soon after he finished. Elvira had a long and exciting day. Michael ran his fingers through her hair as she slept. He gazed out the window of the plane, into the clouds, where heaven is. He looked back down at Elvira, sleeping so quietly on his body.

"Thank you," Michael said. "Thank you, Jesus. Thank you for bringing her back to me. I should have never doubted you."

17

CHAPTER

Michael and Elvira arrived in Rome with no money. All they had were the clothes on their back, and a small dream. They were the definition of the saying, *living on love*. Together, Michael and Elvira didn't have more than a few hundred dollars. They would both have to find some sort of work to hold them over for the time being. Michael managed to contact a cousin of his that lived in the outskirts of Florence. His cousin, Maurizio, owned a farm there. Michael and Elvira were welcomed with open arms by his Italian family.

Elvira had a more difficult time adjusting than Michael because she had to learn the language. Michael spent every day practicing with her. In order to pay their rent, Michael agreed to work on the farm for Maurizio. It was only temporary until they managed to get on their feet. When Elvira learned enough Italian, she got a role as an understudy in a local theatre. Elvira fit right in with the rest of the Italians. Michael was always right when he said her soul was Italian. She was a perfect fit for the easygoing European way of life.

This time was especially tough for Michael. He felt horrible because he wasn't able to treat Elvira the way that he used to. It was hard for him to surprise her without any extra money to spend. There was no wiggle room for dinners, or gifts. Michael tried to do whatever he could with his own two hands.

Michael carefully cut an assortment of cheeses. He went down to the cellar in Maurizio's home, and took a bottle of wine. Michael carried the basket filled with wine and cheese to a towel that laid under the Tuscan moonlight.

Michael stood only a few feet away from Maurizio's home. Every star in the sky was out on this very night. The moon was full. It was the perfect night for a little romance. He looked up into the sky and took a deep breath.

"Elvira!" Michael screamed.

Michael saw the lights of Maurizio's home turn on. Maurizio marched out the door holding a shotgun. Elvira followed him.

"*Bastardi!*" he screamed out.

Michael waved his hands back and forth to let Maurizio see it was him.

"Maurizio! *Sono io,*" Michael cried out. "It's me!" he screamed again.

Maurizio smiled. He put his gun down and walked back inside. Elvira stood on the porch of their temporary home. She slowly walked towards Michael.

"What's all this about?" Elvira asked curiously.

Michael moved closer to Elvira. He held her waist between his hands.

"I know things have been tough lately. Before all of this, everything was different. I feel bad that I haven't been able to do anything special for you."

Elvira gave Michael a confused look.

"Do you mean gifts?" she asked.

"I guess so," Michael replied. "I feel bad about it."

Elvira motioned for Michael to sit down on the blanket. She poured him a glass of wine and sat next to him. Elvira ran her fingers through Michael's hair.

"Michael," Elvira said. "You know I don't care about gifts. I actually don't even like gifts that much."

"What?" Michael replied frantically. "What do you mean? You don't like anything I got you?"

Elvira laughed. "I love the gifts you got me," she replied. "I love the meaning behind them and the reason why you got me them, but I'm able to live without gifts in general."

Michael was still confused.

Elvira continued. "I'm ok with you taking me to a crappy diner for a cup of coffee. I wouldn't even care if we went to White Castle. I don't think there's any in Italy, but you get the idea. All I care about is being here with you talking and laughing together. You're my gift."

This was one of the very special parts of Elvira's personality. When Elvira loved, she was all in. The way she loved was truly special. It was something that drew Michael to her, because he loved the exact same way. In the midst of what seemed to be a hard time, Michael and Elvira still managed to be happy. All they ever needed was each other—everything else was just a bonus.

Elvira pushed Michael to send his manuscript to publishers around Italy. Trusting her judgment, Michael complied. He quickly met with harsh criticism, and months of rejection from multiple publishers. Not one of the bigger publishing companies would take a chance on Michael's book. Michael reached too high. He still was a no-name author.

Michael knew that Elvira couldn't be wrong. He trusted his soulmate. Instead of giving up, he decided to send his manuscript to smaller companies. Within a few weeks, Michael was met with positive responses. One publishing company was so desperate to publish Michael's book, they already had a check signed before Michael walked through the door. Without even thinking twice, Michael took the offer. Within a few more months, his book was published. He was finally an author. It became wildly popular, inspiring millions of people to find true love, and never settle for less.

The first person to see any money from Michael's royalties was his mother. As he always promised, the first thing he did was send his mother money. Whatever his mother ever needed, she could now have. Michael used the rest of the money to explore Italy with Elvira. It was finally time to visit the little town where his novel ended. The town of Positano.

Positano was one of many small villages along Italy's famous Amalfi Coast. The village was filled with little homes, painted in different colors. The homes were all built on the side of a large hill. There were hundreds of steps, leading up and down the hillside. The beaches were legendary and looked as if they were straight from the heavens. It was surrounded by water from the Tyrrhenian Sea. Fisherman stayed out in the sea all hours of the day, trying to make ends meet.

Michael and Elvira rented an apartment that overlooked the ocean. The sun shined in through the drapes. The wind lightly blew the curtains up into the air. Elvira stared out into the sea. Her hair, as short as it was, blew along with the wind. Michael was cooking breakfast in the kitchen. On a big tray, he brought out fresh fruit, pastries, and coffee to a table on the balcony.

Michael walked behind Elvira and placed his hands over her eyes.

"I have a surprise for you," he said.

Elvira smiled.

Michael guided her over to the table then released his hands. He grabbed Elvira's chin with his two fingers and kissed her. Elvira stared at the food that Michael freshly prepared. She got up out of her seat and sat on Michael's lap. She placed her arms around his neck.

"That dream we had for so long," Elvira said. "It looks like it came true."

18

CHAPTER

After years of exploring Italy, Michael and Elvira finally decided to settle down in Florence. They bought a small, beaten up, villa in Tuscany. It was in the center of a valley and a beautiful field of trees. There was a statue of the Virgin Mary holding baby Jesus that stood tall near the entrance of their home, with an assortment of beautiful flowers that Elvira planted around the statue. Michael grew most of their food from a garden in the backyard. He even found the time to start a grapevine, so they could produce their own fresh wine. That was the part of the house they both loved the most. The villa was over one hundred years old and full of history. The two of them renovated the villa together. It took almost sixth months to get their home up and running. The villa was too big for them, and God saw that. He blessed Michael and Elvira with three children. Their names were Christopher, David, and Amanda.

Elvira got her first job as a psychologist in Florence. She learned to speak Italian better than Michael ever could. She brought a new meaning to the word therapist, because most Italians were so put off by the idea. Her own Freudian approach became well-renowned across Italy. She published various books on psychoanalysis and presented them at universities across Italy. She was honored with awards for the advancements she made in the mental health field.

Michael's novel became a best seller in Italy, and eventually rose to the top of the charts in the United States. His novel became a *New York Times* best seller right before they purchased their home. He used the royalties as a down payment. Michael went on to publish not one, but five more novels in his lifetime. When Michael wasn't writing or with his family, he taught American Film and Literature at the University of Florence.

When their first child was born, Michael and Elvira made a promise to each other. That they would learn from the mistakes both their parents made. Parenting can be one of the most challenging jobs of a lifetime. Michael and Elvira made it look easy. They were truly model parents. Elvira was not only a world class psychologist, but a world class mother. She always made time for her children and never deprived them of anything. They never got tired of the endless amount of Buck Seasoning Elvira used in her cooking either. Michael took his sons out to play catch and taught them about sports. He was a little extra protective over his daughter, but what father isn't? Michael was at every sports game, dance recital, and play the children were involved in. Michael and Elvira raised their children in a life of Christian faith, taking them to church every Sunday. Together, they helped their children say prayers before bed from a young age. As the years went by, Christopher, David, and Amanda became outstanding adults. They even went on to have children of their own.

Michael and Elvira retired in their sixties. The day never came when they lost their love for each other. Every kiss was as fresh as their first on the stoop. Every dance held just as much intimacy as the first. Every time they made love, it was always as special as the first. They were blessed with a life full of passion. There was always a date night, or a surprise Michael had for Elvira. They refused to go to bed angry at each other if there was ever a fight. The part they really enjoyed the most was "making up."

If there's one thing life teaches us, it's that everything can change in the blink of an eye. Michael and Elvira were about to face their biggest challenge yet. One day, Elvira suddenly became ill. She couldn't eat any of the food she loved. Her body frame became bony and frail. It appeared that the life was slowly getting sucked out of her.

Michael brought her to a doctor who ran various tests. He informed them that Elvira was diagnosed with a rare form of leukemia. She had only six months to live. When the news was broken, Michael's world froze. He couldn't see or hear anything. For a few moments, the world went black. Elvira cried and hugged Michael for support. She wanted to fight the cancer tooth and nail. She opted to get every treatment available. Neither Michael nor Elvira could understand why this happened to their family. They refused to question their faith in God and held out hope a miracle would occur.

Every day of those sixth months Michael stood by Elvira's side. He drove the nurses crazy on how to properly care for her. Michael held her hair while she threw up, he walked her to and from the bathroom, and he even fed her when she was too weak to eat herself. It killed Michael to watch the love of his life wither away like this. He always stayed strong for her and never shed a tear. He refused to let her hear any negativity. Michael could never let her see, but he was dying inside.

The seventh month came, and it was clear that Elvira wasn't getting any better. The treatments had failed. It was only a matter of time. The hospital room was packed with get well cards and endless bundles of flowers. Elvira was special not only to Michael, but to everyone around her. She saved lives as a therapist and all her clients were eternally grateful. Christopher, David, Amanda, and Michael were all seated at Elvira's bedside. With all the strength she had left in her body, she called Michael's name.

"Michael," she moaned.

Michael was beginning to have health problems of his own. He was losing all the strength in his legs. He found it difficult to stand at all sometimes. When Elvira called him, Michael got up out of his seat and limped towards her. The worst kind of pain in the world couldn't have stopped Michael from coming to his wife's aide. Elvira motioned for him to come closer to her. She kissed him.

"It's time Michael," Elvira said.

Tears streamed down Michael's face. He knew what she was referring to. Elvira was letting him know that she was going to move on from this world soon. Their children cried hysterically. Michael sat on the side of Elvira's bed. He ran his hand along her face. Elvira tried to smile, but she was too weak. Michael couldn't find the words to comfort his dying wife.

"You're just as beautiful as the first day I laid eyes on you," Michael said.

Michael wiped away the tears from his face. He tried to compose himself. He held Elvira's hand and leaned over next to her ear. With his tired, old voice, he sang to her. He sang the old Italian love song, "Anema e Core." His voice was so soft, it almost sounded like a whisper. Michael knew this would be the best way to comfort Elvira in her final moments of life. It was also the best way to profess how much he loved her. As he sang, Elvira closed her eyes. She remembered the life they built together, and she remembered every kiss, love letter, dance, fight, and moment they had together. It took all the life she had left, but Elvira finally smiled.

"I'll see you in heaven," she mumbled.

"What?" Michael replied frantically.

Elvira took her last few breaths. Michael collapsed into her body and cried uncontrollably. The doctor and nurses came in the room. They tried to pull Michael off Elvira, but he wasn't moving. His children finally convinced him to go home and rest. He had barely left the hospital during Elvira's sixth month battle. They were worried about losing not one, but both parents.

A few days after Elvira's wake and funeral, Michael became increasingly ill. It was strange because the doctors couldn't diagnose him. There was nothing physically wrong with Michael. His tests came back negative. The doctor informed Michael's children that in these cases, sometimes it goes beyond science. Later that day, Michael was found slumped over the side of his bed. He died while praying. The cause of death was still not clear, but Michael's children didn't need a doctor to tell them what happened. It was clear that Michael died of a broken heart. He couldn't live another day on this earth away from Elvira.

When Michael died, his soul left his body. He was taken through a bright tunnel. As he traveled through the tunnel, his life flashed before his eyes. Michael watched an entire film reel of his life. There were no bad moments, only happy ones. Michael saw his birth, first day of school, parents, and accomplishments. At the end of the film reel were his memories of Elvira. From the first day they met at the coffee shop, to their first kiss on the stoop, to the end of her life. Michael's journey through the bright tunnel ended. There was a large golden gate in the middle of a vast green field of colorful flowers. The skies didn't have the slightest blemish. Michael looked down at his hands. He noticed that he looked young again. There wasn't any more pain in his legs, he could walk normally.

Michael was greeted by a powerful force at the gate. This being had no shape or any physical form at all. It had a warm and calming voice. It let Michael know that he was in heaven and told him that he could now live in eternal happiness. The gates opened. Standing on the other side of the gate was Elvira, patiently waiting for Michael. Elvira wasn't sick anymore. She was cured of her cancer and her youth was restored. Michael ran to her. They hugged and kissed each other.

Elvira whispered in Michael's ear, "I told you we'd be in heaven together."

ABOUT THE AUTHOR

Photo by Sofia Monge

Anthony Sciarratta was born in Maspeth, New York, to Italian-American parents. Being very nostalgic, Anthony takes great pride in labeling himself an old soul. His love for classic films, music, and literature shows through his work. Anthony wrote *Finding Forever* over a four-month period. *Finding Forever* is authentic to the 1970s, an iconic era in American history. *Finding Forever* was originally self-published through Amazon Kindle Direct Publishing, where Anthony received exposure for his work and managed to build a personal brand. His success story as such a young writer is inspirational to all aspiring young writers and self-published authors.